BATTLE

BATTLE

THE WIZARD AND THE WARRIOR
BOOK THREE

Vivienne Lee Fraser

www.viviennelfraser.com.au

Vivienne Lee Fraser
www.viviennelfraser.com.au

Cataloguing-in-Publication details are available
from the National Library of Australia
www.trove.nla.gov.au
ISBN: 978-0-6482181-5-9

Formatting and cover design by KILA Designs
www.kiladesigns.com.au
Cover images: ©bigstockphoto.com

Illustrations provided by Anna Bazel
www.fiverr.com/annabazyl
Map illustration: ©Jim Simpson

For Heather.
This series would not have been the same without you.

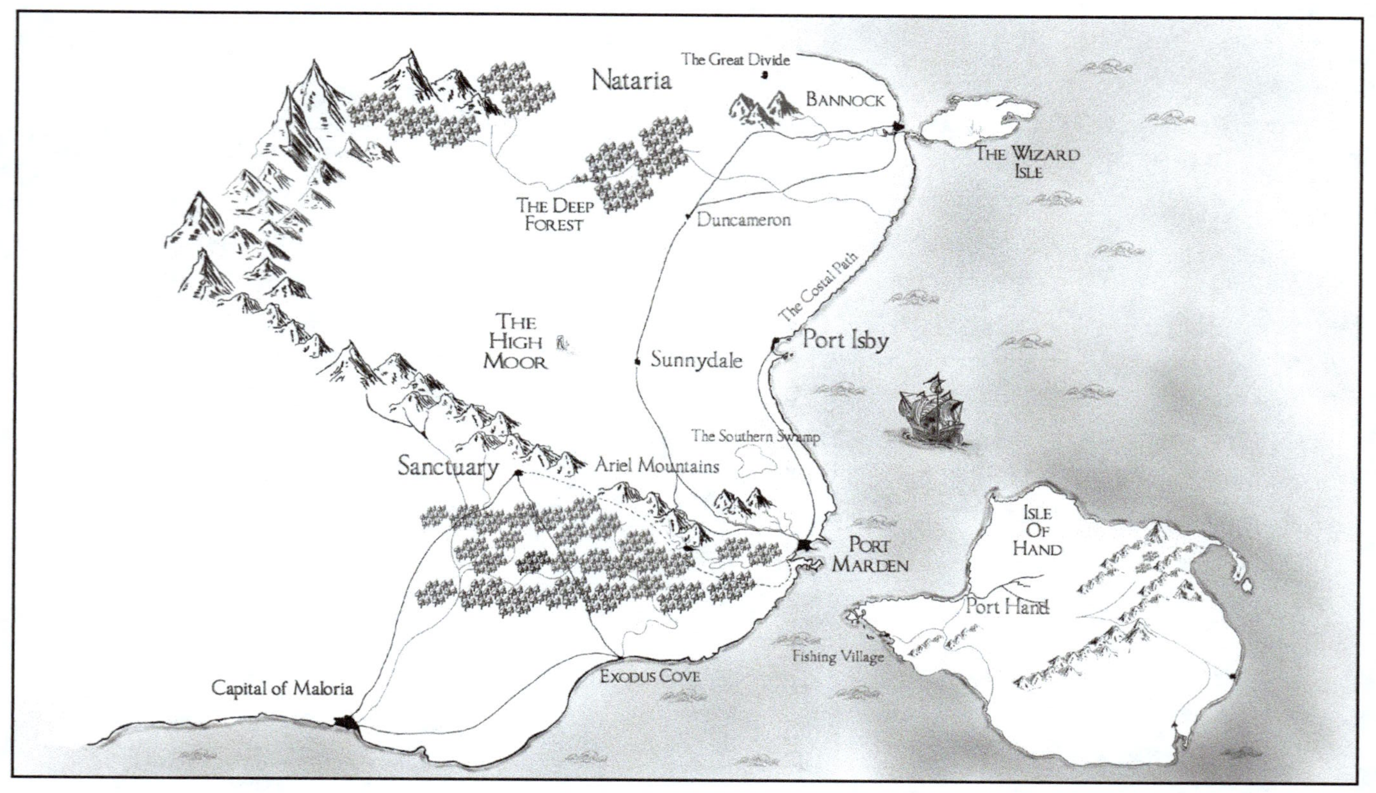

Nataria
The Great Divide
Bannock
The Wizard Isle
The Deep Forest
Duncameron
The Costal Path
The High Moor
Port Isby
Sunnydale
The Southern Swamp
Sanctuary
Ariel Mountains
Isle Of Hand
Port Marden
Port Hand
Fishing Village
Capital of Maloria
Exodus Cove

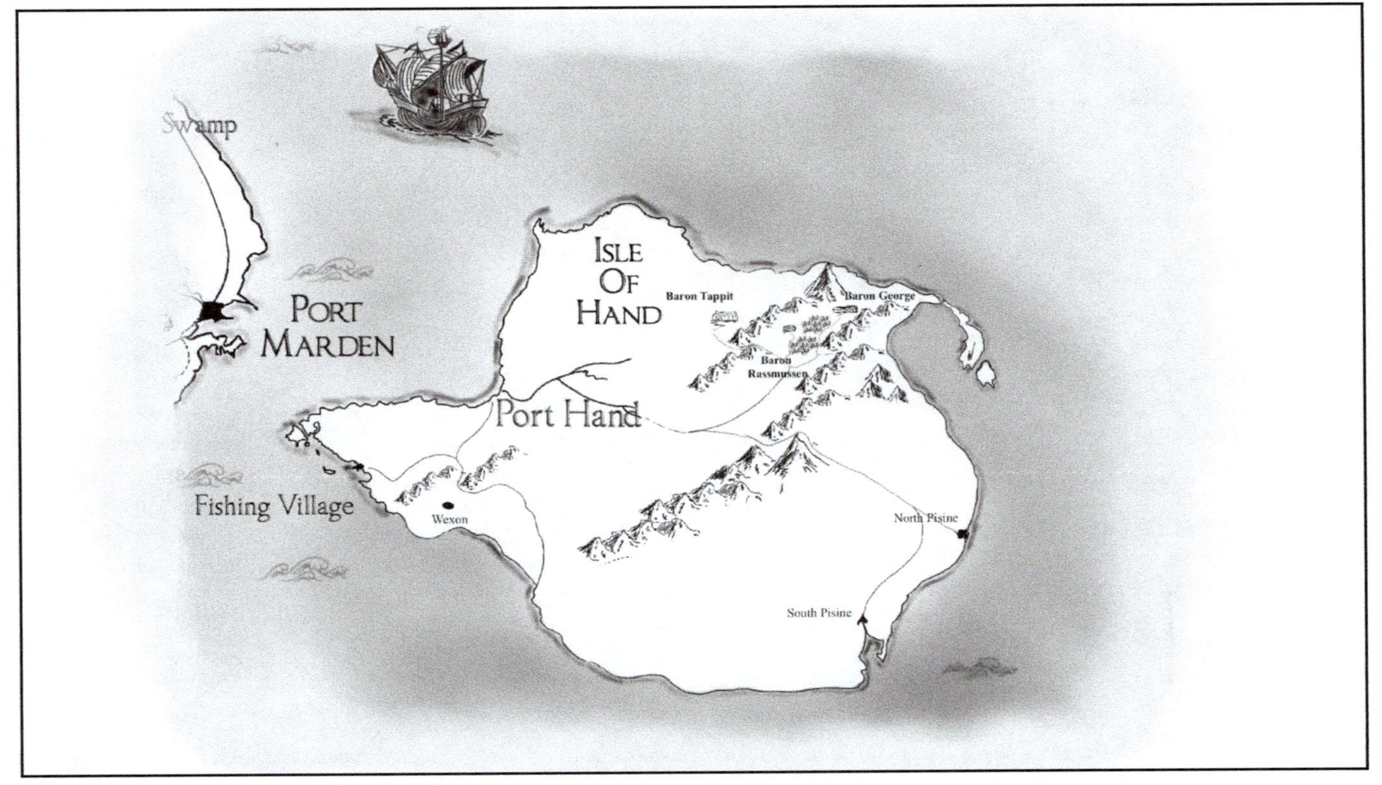

Swamp
Port Marden
Fishing Village
Isle Of Hand
Baron Tappit
Baron George
Baron Rassmussen
Port Hand
Wexon
North Pisine
South Pisine

PROLOGUE

After the decimation and the fall,
When the new power rises
And the Wizard and Warrior meet,
Old and new blood will combine
With the two who are not what they seem.
The key is the Ember Casket, to trap and calm the chaos,
Or send it beyond to save one and all.

The petite woman stumbled out of the cave and fell face first onto hot sand. She struggled to stand, too exhausted to move any further. Shadows sheltered her body from the mid-afternoon sun as her two companions joined her.

'I see there is a new Seer in Sanctuary,' a friendly voice congratulated her.

'What did you learn?' a more demanding voice asked. 'Did you find out how to defeat the god?'

Gentle hands helped her sit, and cupped her fingers around a mug of water. She downed the cold liquid, and only after she quenched her thirst, did she answer.

'Our god can be bound or he can be banished whence he came. There is a scroll in the library at Hand containing the details we need to achieve this.'

'Obviously you must go there and ensure the document is found,' the second voice decided. 'I will make the preparations while you rest and recover from your ordeal.'

Hot sun scorched her again as the man departed. Before she could pull herself to her feet, a light touch on her arm halted her. The grip firmed as her friend assisted her to stand.

'I guess life is going to be a bit different from here on in,' he said as he tucked her hand through the crook of his arm and led her into the cool entrance of the Sanctuary.

1
AN INAUSPICIOUS START

'When this is all over, I do not want to see another boat again. I am wet through, tired and ...'

'... exceedingly grumpy,' Aliah finished for him, and Seamus could not help but laugh.

'Yes, that too. Were we really not able to find somewhere better than the palace on Hand to plan this final battle?'

'Let me think ... No.' Dominic, Liam, Emer and Daniel laughed at Aliah's reply.

'There is nowhere else on the doorstep of our enemy

with an extensive library for us to research how we might defeat him. Well, nowhere with a ready-made guard for our protection, and comfortable beds.' Aliah finished listing off the benefits of his home island as the fishing boat they were travelling in dipped quite heavily in the growing swell.

Seamus' stomach threatened to expel its contents and it took all his concentration to stop that from happening.

During the battle the day before, he had faced a god. The ensuing fight drained almost all the energy from his body. Even after sleeping most of the day, he still was not up to travelling through the night to the Isle of Hand.

'Could we not have travelled in something bigger than a fishing boat?' he continued, as much to take his mind off the churning in his gut as to voice yet another complaint.

'Was yesterday's battle not enough for you?' Emer asked. 'You know the enemy is probably camped on the other side of the island. Did you want to announce our presence to the entire Carsten Army so we can fight them again?' He had hoped Emer at least was on his side, but she was laughingly supporting Aliah.

'No, I guess not,' he admitted, finally running out of things to whinge about.

Liam decided to add his thoughts to the argument. 'Our enemy has a god on their side, so it would be prudent to assume they know what we are up to anyway.'

'Thank you, Liam,' Seamus commended his cousin for coming to his support.

The small fishing boat lurched again, throwing the two boys together, as if the vessel was reacting to Liam's comment. As their fisherman guide righted them, Seamus

BATTLE

was pleased to find the outline of Hand Port appeared in the distance. He hoped they arrived soon, otherwise he would be forced to embarrass himself by throwing up over the side of the boat. A hand slid into his, and he turned to find Emer beside him, concern written on her face.

'Not long now,' she whispered. 'You will feel much better about this after some food and sleep.'

'Food? I am not sure my stomach could take it, but I like your optimism. And I also find it hard to see how I will ever feel better about having to fight a god and rid him from this world.' He forced a weary smile at his joke, appreciating his attempt at humour was pretty weak.

'Hey,' Aliah interrupted. 'You are not alone in this. We are the Wizard and the Warrior, remember? We are in this together.'

'And what are we? Extra baggage?' Dominic playfully shoved Aliah and she grinned.

'If the cap fits ...'

Seamus understood they were trying to lift his mood, but he continued to worry none-the-less. Relaxing was not an option while he attempted to figure out how a warrior princess, a disappearing spy, a shape-shifting girl, two soldiers and a trainee wizard, could hope to get rid of a god who seemed determined to set the people of this world on a chaotic path to war.

The boat dipped alarmingly again and the captain swore. Shouting over the noise of the sea he said, 'I do not like this at all. I have never seen a wind like this in the seas between Port Marden and Hand.'

Seamus looked questioningly at Aliah, who shrugged her shoulders. It was possible the god-enemy might have something to do with the odd weather. Certainly if he got rid of them here, there would be no one to stop him from taking over Aria, followed by the rest of the world.

Having hauled every able-bodied person from Carsten into this war, there was no reason to think he would not do the same with the people of Aria. Seamus and Aliah would fight with everything they had to prevent that from happening.

Hands gripping the seat, knuckles white with the strain, Seamus considered what actions he might take to ensure the fishing boat made it safely to the docks as they passed through the entrance to the harbour.

As though the sea recognised its quarry was almost beyond its grasp, the waves gave one final shudder and Seamus was flung through the air, before disappearing under the ice-cold, churning waves.

Icy wet fingers clutched at him as he started to sink through the midnight black water. Part of him thought how easy it would be to allow himself to carry on to the bottom. He would never have to worry about facing a superior foe with Aliah ...

Wait, Aliah.

Where was she? Forcing himself upwards, he broke the surface spluttering and gasping for air.

Treading water to stay afloat, he turned around and around, trying to find his friend. She could not swim and must be terrified. The fishing boat was on its side, the captain using all his skill to try and right it. Aliah must be in the water.

Swimming around the boat he found her, struggling for breath as Dominic tried to keep her head above the water line. He shouted something and Seamus assumed he was telling Aliah to stop struggling.

When this is over, that girl really needs to learn how to swim, he thought as he turned to check on the others.

Liam and Daniel were also on the opposite side of the boat, gathering belongings from the water. Where was Emer? His stomach lurched again as he frantically scoured the water for her. At a noise from above he raised his eyes, catching sight of an eagle overhead.

I am fine. I had time to change. Take care of yourself and I will meet you on the docks. I want to scan around and check if the weather is the only thing they sent to vex us.

With her words sent directly to his head via mind-speak, Emer flew off. Holding onto the side of the boat, he attempted to help the captain.

'Leave me,' the man bellowed. 'Make for land. If I cannot save her, I will follow behind you.'

Seamus nodded his understanding and as he turned to comply, something bumped into him. He let go of the boat to reach for the object and found it was his travel pack. He grabbed a hold and combed the waves for other salvage. As he searched, his body started to shake uncontrollably, and he realised if he did not head to land soon, cold would overtake him and he would not make it at all.

Leaning his chin on the pack, he set out swimming for the port, heading for the docks. Alternating swimming on his side using his left arm, then his right arm was slow going. At one stage he even considered leaving the pack and making a dash for the shore. The only thing stopping him was the thought of losing his wand, which he was sure was in the bag.

Gifted to him by the gods when they named him the Wizard, it was irreplaceable. Besides, he might need it if he survived today, if only to assist him while he learnt to control his magic.

The distance to the dock was longer than he first thought, and he was not in the best condition to be swimming in the freezing night water. He pushed on. His vision grew fuzzy, and he resisted the urge to close his eyes. Soon his arms and legs were moving automatically and he drifted into a half-sleep that was much more inviting than the freezing water.

'My sword!' Aliah yelled again, certain Dominic had not heard her the other three times.

'I got you the first time. The sword is no use if you drown or die of the creeping cold. Calm down so I can support you and get you to safety.'

Listening to the tone of his voice, she realised if she did not do as he instructed, she would be putting both their lives in danger. She willed herself to relax and let Dominic support her.

'Better. Listen, Liam and Daniel grabbed most of the packs, and I think I saw Seamus swim away with one. Was your sword in your pack?'

Aliah's panic levels rose again. 'No, beside it.'

Without any further conversation, Dominic pulled her towards the half-overturned boat. There in the bottom she spied the scabbard containing the weapon the gods gifted her when she proved herself to be the Warrior of Prophecy.

BATTLE

'Grab a hold of the side.'

Aliah forced her freezing fingers to grip the wood as Dominic leaned forward to free her sword from whatever prevented it from falling into the ocean. As far as she could tell, there was nothing holding the sword in place. Her weapon had magical powers, maybe it waited for her to come to the rescue. She laughed out loud at her fanciful thoughts.

'Hold this,' Dominic said, before rolling her on to her back and starting the slow journey to the dock.

They had not gone far when she felt the cold creeping into her lower limbs, she realised if she did not move, the cold would soon kill her. Yet she was unable swim to keep herself warm. Panic began to swell in the pit of her stomach.

She shouted, 'Dominic, my feet are going numb.'

Her rescuer's initial response was one best suited to a guard's barracks.

'All right, you need to start kicking your legs. No, wait until I finish,' he told her as she writhed in his arms. 'They need to be large, slow kicks. You need to keep your legs straight and not bend your knees. Keep your body as still as possible. When you kick that way, I can still support your head.'

After a couple of attempts, she was kicking evenly and they were moving much more quickly towards the wharf. Her feet were still a little numb, but at least the cold had stopped moving up her body. In what seemed like no time at all, Dominic placed her hand on the wooden strut of a ladder and she was able to climb up onto one of the wharves.

As she stamped her feet to return circulation, she saw Liam and Daniel yelling to Dominic, whose head had just popped above the timber of the jetty. A moment later, he let go and dove back into the water with a resounding splash.

'What is happening?' she asked a worried looking Liam.

'Seamus. He was swimming towards us, then he just stopped. I do not know what is keeping him afloat, it must be something in his pack. He is drifting back out to sea and I cannot attract his attention.'

Aliah peered into the dawn light, and was just able to detect Dominic dragging Seamus towards the dock. Only the fact the younger boy clutched the bag he used to keep himself afloat showed he still clung to life.

Liam pushed her aside and climbed part-way down the ladder to help bring Seamus up. Just as Liam pulled the younger boy's body out of the water, Emer appeared beside her. In human form, the girl carried a pile of blankets.

'When I persuaded the Harbour Master we needed these, I did not realise how much.' Emer offered one to Aliah. 'He has more if we need them. He said to help ourselves as he and his men are going out to assist our captain to right his boat before it crashes into the rocks.'

Aliah took a blanket and wrapped herself up, grateful for the added warmth. Leaving her side, Emer went to assist with Seamus.

'Take his clothes off and wrap him in these blankets,' she ordered the others, who worked fast to oblige. Even with her limited knowledge, Aliah could tell it was not enough. Seamus' mouth was turning blue, and he was so still she could barely see the rise and fall of his chest.

BATTLE

Emer frowned in thought. 'With the creeping sickness you need to be warmed slowly from within. There is no healer to help us, and I do not know what else to do.'

'I might be able to do something,' Aliah volunteered tentatively. 'My sword is working to warm me and refuel my body. I shared energy with Seamus in battle yesterday, and I think I remember how to do it without his guidance. Perhaps I could use the same process to share some of my sword's healing powers.'

Emer looked at her thoughtfully and nodded her head. 'I believe you should try.'

The others moved to give Aliah room. With one hand on her sword, she placed the other one underneath the rough woolen blanket, on Seamus' chest. Turning her thoughts inwards, she searched for the strand of magic coming from her weapon. When she found it, she imagined taking a hold of it and pushing out towards Seamus. The magic leaked through the skin of her hand and then dispersed, as though it did not know where to go.

'It is not working.' Her voice shook with frustration. 'Why not? What is different?' She closed her eyes, blocking out everything else, and went through the steps she and Seamus had taken to share their power when they defeated the King of Carsten. An idea came to her. 'Hurry, find Seamus' wand.'

There was rustling behind her as they searched their belongings. 'I cannot find it,' Liam muttered. 'No, wait, his head is still lying on the pack he carried to shore.'

Gently, Liam placed his cousin's head on the wooden planking, and hurriedly undid the straps. The wand fell out, almost as though it were trying to reach Seamus by itself. Liam grabbed it, unfolded the blanket, placed the wand in Seamus's hand, then replaced his coverings.

Aliah took a deep breath. Finding the magical strand was easier this time, and at the edge of her hand it jumped forward, almost as though it sensed the wand and reached out towards it. The sword gifted to her by the gods warmed them both. Lying down beside her friend, she wrapped her blanket over both of them and concentrated on keeping the energy flowing.

'Come on Seamus, do not leave me now. I cannot do this without you,' she whispered, blinking the tears from her eyes as she snuggled under the covers.

Some part of her was aware Emer organised the others to arrange transport to the palace, but that was her last conscious thought as the sword lulled her to sleep.

'NOOOOOO.' The god's anger reverberated through Gaius' body as he cowered in the safe place he had made for himself in the corner of the invader's mind. 'They escaped again. This vessel is worse than useless.'

Give it back to me if you do not want it, Gaius thought before turning his attention back to the activity outside his self-imposed prison.

'You chose to take a human body so you could act in this world,' Millard explained in patient tones, as if he were explaining a complex idea to a child. 'You took it knowing your powers would be limited to those of the body you occupied. Gaius did not have an aptitude for weather magic when he was alive, you cannot expect him to have one now just because you took over his body. Only your guidance and knowledge allowed his limited skill to raise enough wind to overturn the boat.

'What is more, I explained all this to you when you told me of your plan to kill Aliah and Seamus. I said Gaius' weather magic would not be able to cause a big enough swell to ensure the party travelling to Hand would drown.'

'Your human bodies are too limiting. Perhaps I should get rid of this one like I did the last,' the god growled, and Gaius froze in fear.

During the battle to invade Aria, the divine entity had possessed the body of the King of Carsten. When that brat Aliah and the boy Seamus caused the king to faint, the angry god blew up the king's entire ship, not only destroying the body he inhabited but killing hundreds of innocent men. With their commander gone, the Carsten invasion faltered. Before they could regroup, a magical force had driven them out to sea, beyond the island of Hand.

With his body gone, the god was released back to the only shape he was able to take on this plane of existence, a spirit form. Unhappy with his inability to act without a physical presence, he decided he once again needed a body to use.

The god had forced his way into his and Mallard's heads. Gaius had retreated to the smallest corner possible and imagined himself walled within a box, using a similar technique taught to novice magicians to manage their magical flow. Taking this for submission, the god decided Gaius' body was a better option, and took possession with no thought for the man who already owned it.

Please do not blow up my body, Gaius pleaded to himself.

I would like it back when you have no more use for it.

Millard too seemed to have plans to keep his apprentice's body in one piece. 'Yes, you could do that, but then you would be totally reliant on me to work magic for you. The form you inhabit is strong in different magics, and is still useful in helping us bring you fully into this world.'

Gaius sensed the being who controlled his body retreat into his thoughts, and he wondered if the god knew he was privy to all that went through his mind. Did the divinity even know he still existed?

Although he might have appeared weaker willed, Gaius had a strong desire to live. With little to do, he waited and planed for a future that did not include his body being used by a higher entity.

Once the god established himself and felt comfortable in his new skin, Gaius had allowed a small hole in his box and taught himself to walk around in his own mind without being noticed. So far, the divine being gave no indication he realised the body's original owner was still there. Terrified every waking moment he would be found out, Gaius knew this great risk might bring great reward.

Looking out from his safe place, Gaius quietened his thoughts to lessen his chance of detection, content for the moment to observe and learn and plot. When the god left him to take his true form, Gaius would have leant much and would be a stronger wizard than Millard. He would over-power his old master, then it would be he who ruled Aria.

'Might I make a suggestion?' Millard asked the thoughtful god, who stirred and once again looked outwards at one of Aria's strongest magicians. Gaius wondered if Millard realised the god thought of him as little more than an intelligent animal to do his bidding.

'Instead of trying to find ways to beat the Wizard and Warrior in your current form, formidable though it might be, perhaps we should concentrate on the plan to bring you through to this place. Everything we need is here on the Island of Hand. We can set the army to harry the Arian forces and keep them occupied while we search unhindered for the solution.'

The god turned the idea over in his head, but was yet to be convinced. 'The Wizard and the Warrior still live, and are looking for the solution too. The casket is a double edged sword, it can be used to contain my essence before I return to my natural form, or free me by bringing my body here from where it slumbers.'

'Then we must use all the resources at our disposal and be the first to find its location,' Millard pressed. 'We have the advantage in that we at least know what we are looking for, and we can keep an eye on our friends to ensure they are not ahead of us in the search for the chest.'

Retreating into his own thoughts again, the powerful entity gloated, *When I take my true form in this world no one will be able to stop me from doing what I came here to do.*

'All right, magician, we will do it your way, for the moment. Bring me the man who now calls himself leader of the Carsten invaders, and let us set this plan in motion.'

2
SCROLL, SCROLLS AND MORE SCROLLS

Seamus dropped another scroll on the table, toppling the pile of discarded documents already there, causing the whole lot to tumble to the ground.

'Goddess!' he muttered as he bent down to pick them up, placing them on the shelf cleared yesterday to store the completed works. 'How many more of these are in the area my father told us about?' He directed his question at Liam, who carried another armful of ancient writings from the lower library.

'I estimate we are about half way through once we read these.' Liam dumped his load on the far end of the table, where they joined another twenty or so unread tomes.

Emer groaned and fell across the table, her head cradled in her arms. 'I cannot go on. It has been two days, and there is not even a hint of anything to tell us how to stop a god from taking over Aria.'

'What are you complaining about? At least you get to sleep at night. Seamus' god friends insist on us training together every evening, linking our gifts, fighting and using magic at the same time, providing energy to each other.

'Their gift of sleep recharges my body, but I am mentally exhausted before I start here.' Aliah stood and stretched out her stiff back.

'I thought you said the gods made sure you woke up refreshed after your classes.' Daniel peeked worriedly over the document he had been immersed in.

Aliah continued stretching her back and legs. 'They do. It is hardly their fault the lessons are still running around in my head when I wake up. I come here and I spend all day cramming more information into my tired mind. Sometimes my head feels like a squishy melon about to explode.' She slumped in her chair to add emphasis to her words. 'Besides, even without sleep I look better than you. Are you sure you are not coming down with something?'

'Just a bit of a tummy upset,' Daniel mumbled, ducking back behind his scroll before Aliah could find something else to complain about.

'The problem is …' Seamus began, and stopped mid sentence.

BATTLE

All eyes in the room swung to him. So many people looking to him for leadership was disconcerting. Especially as only two days ago he almost killed himself while escaping the overturned fishing boat. If Aliah had not warmed him, he would have died from the creeping cold, and then where would Aria be?

Since almost drowning, Seamus had been berating himself. When he took air from the King of Carsten, causing his collapse and throwing the invaders into disarray, he used up much of his magical reserves. To make everything worse, he followed up by sending the fleet from Carsten out beyond Hand, over-using his energy, and he collapsed. Not looking after himself then meant he almost died when he was thrown into the water of Hand Harbour.

At his next lesson a taciturn god reluctantly finished healing him, grumbling under his breath as he did so. Once Seamus was back to full strength, the god warned him using magic was like over-exercising; use too much and it drains your body, which adversely affects your health and can even kill you.

The god then continued to lecture Seamus to practice using his magic more, because the more he trained, the less toll it would take on his body when he used it. This became the subject of their class, as their god-instructor drilled them in sharing energy in a way to enable them to both remain strong.

Still, Seamus felt a little foolish. Walter's first session on magic included instructions to think about using it like you would intense physical activity. You would tire quickly unless you trained, and you needed to eat more to replace the lost energy.

In the heat of battle that first very simple guideline slipped his mind. Now everyone turned to him to lead the group, and he was not even able to take care of himself. Shaking off the negative thoughts, he remembered the others were still waiting for him to continue.

'Er, umm, what I was saying is we are not scholars. We have no idea what we are looking for. We scan scrolls for mention of anything religious or magical, and that may not be helpful at all. What we seek may be less obvious than that. We need Walter and Amelia. Emer, do you ...'

The door swung open, interrupting Seamus. Dominic entered, a grin plastered over his face. 'They are here. Walter and Amelia, I mean. A ship just docked, it must be them.'

'Are you sure they are on it? Did someone confirm it or see them?' Aliah frowned at the king's spy.

'Well, no.' Dominic's smile faded. 'But who else would come to Hand with an army of occupation just over the mountains? Come to think of it, who else would your father allow to come here when we are supposed to be in hiding?'

'My father may be the king, but he does not personally oversee the actions of every single subject in the realm,' Aliah countered.

Seamus sighed, sometimes Aliah and Dominics' bickering wearied him. Today it particularly grated on his nerves. Time was running out and they were still no closer to understanding how to stop a god-driven army from overrunning their homeland. They had more important things to focus their energies on than petty squabbles.

'It is them,' Emer said.

'How can you be sure?' Liam asked.

'My father travelled to Port Marden with them. He and some of the other magic users from Sanctuary have volunteered to help repel the Carsten invaders. They arrived last night. Walter and Amelia left with a small, personal guard this morning.'

'When were you going to tell us this?' Seamus' anger burned bright, but it left him as quickly as it came when Emer's face crumpled at his harsh tone.

'We have had so little good news, I thought the surprise of their arrival would cheer us all up. I was just waiting for the right time to announce it,' she said through gritted teeth as her spine stiffened.

Seamus regretted his tone as soon as the words left his lips. He could do nothing right at the moment. He had not meant to snap at Emer, who had been nothing but supportive of him. Part of him had been waiting for Walter and Amelia, perhaps as he hoped they might shoulder some of the burden currently weighing him down. Still, that was no excuse for being rude.

'I am sorry, Emer.' He reached out and touched her shoulder. 'I am such a grump at the moment. Please forgive me.'

Emer's dark eyes bored silently into his own. 'We all understand, Seamus, but you need to learn to control your fears, not take them out on those who are here to help you. You are forgiven … this time.'

Seamus broke contact first and found everyone still

watching him. 'I guess I owe you all apologies as well.' The silence in the room confirmed his fears.

'I am sorry. I am not handling this at all well,' he acknowledged. 'I know you are all here to help me, but in the end, it will come down to whether my magic can defeat this threat to our people.'

'And what am I? Just someone to hang off your arm?' Aliah growled at him. 'I will be there at the end as well. We will all face this together. Remember the prophecy, the gods said we cannot do this alone.'

Taking a deep breath, Seamus attempted to let go of his worry. He knew Aliah's words to be true, but they did not change how he felt. Since he and Aliah fought the god to fend off the attack on Port Marden, the enormity of what they needed to do consumed his every waking moment. His fears crowded out everything else, even his common sense, to the extent he often wondered why he was risking everything to do this.

'I am overwhelmed by everything at the moment,' Seamus admitted. 'I do not see how we can win, and I do not want to lead my friends to their deaths.'

'Silly, you are not leading us.' Aliah walked over to him and placed a hand on his shoulder. 'We are walking beside you to our doom.'

He had to laugh at the absurdity of the six of them facing a powerful other-worldly figure. At least if he ever managed to pluck up the courage to confront their foe, he would do so in good company.

'What shall we do while we wait for Walter and Amelia to arrive?' Liam broke the silence.

'Scrolls.' Seamus laughed as the others groaned.

BATTLE

With Walter leading, Amelia walked the familiar corridors of her childhood home towards the library. Stopping abruptly, she expanded her senses. Something was not quite right.

'Walter, I think someone might be observing the palace. Can you sense anything?'

Walter did not answer straight away, but the air tingled as he sent his magic out to test her theory. The warm glow slowly expanded, then suddenly disappeared.

'You are right. Someone is using scrying to keep an eye on what is going on in the palace,' Walter answered before releasing her arm.

Again she sensed the warmth of his magic, but this time it extended outwards, like a bubble. The sensation of being watched disappeared.

'You are a clever man. How long will that hold for? And will it keep out ...'

'... a god?' he finished for her. 'The scrying was carried out by a human. Well, at least I think it was a person. I imagine magic from the deities looks different from ours. When Seamus returned from his trial his magic felt different, I could not sense it at all. As his abilities are god-given, it is therefore reasonable to assume the magic they use is also different.

'Anyway, I think we should be safe from prying eyes for a little while. We are lucky you are here to sense if things change.' Walter said as he took her hand and placed it back on his arm, continuing to the library.

As she and Walter entered, the room fell quiet. Strong arms enveloped Amelia, hugging her close, wrenching her hand from Walter's arm and nearly pulling her off her feet.

'Seamus.' She hugged him back. 'I take it you are pleased we are here?' His enthusiastic welcome warmed her heart.

'We are. Not only did we miss you, but we could definitely use your help sorting through these scrolls,' Seamus said into her shoulder before letting her go.

Amelia experienced a momentary panic as she lost all sense of where she was in the room. Only for the blink of an eye though, because Walter soon tucked her hand back through his arm.

'Seamus, we are pleased to be here too, and not just because we bring information to share with you all. But first things first, let us find Amelia a chair before we get started.' Walter took control.

A gentle hand on her elbow propelled her forward. The person thoughtfully guided her hand to the back of the chair, enabling her to seat herself.

'Thank you, Emer.' She correctly guessed the daughter of the seer from Sanctuary was her helper. Living with a sightless father, she instinctively knew how best to assist Amelia.

'You are welcome, Seer,' the girl responded.

'No, I do not deserve that title yet,' Amelia said as she sat down. 'My training will not start until after we sort out this mess we have on Hand.'

'Will someone explain what is wrong with my aunt?' Seamus' impatient tones cut through their conversation.

BATTLE

'Amelia has undergone her trial to be a seer, obviously successfully,' Emer said.

'I got that. But why is everyone treating her as though she is breakable?'

'Oh, of course you would not know. If a person is successful at a seer trial, they lose the use of their eyes to increase the power of their inner sight,' the girl informed him.

'What?' Seamus gasped, and a set of large hands enveloped her smaller ones as her nephew asked, 'Amelia, is this what you wanted? To walk through the world unseeing?'

Concern was evident in his voice. She could almost see the frown that must be furrowing his brow. Grasping his hands in hers, she took a deep breath before responding.

'If given a choice, I would not give up my vision for foresight. Then again you did not choose to be the Wizard either. From what the gods told me during my trial, my seer sight will be needed to help in your battle against the rogue god. Like you, I would never refuse to serve our people.'

Seamus' body stiffened, and anger laced his voice as he responded. 'Amelia, the people of Hand expelled you from their island because of your magic. You, of all people, do not owe them anything.'

'Oh, Seamus, I know you do not truly mean that. You too will face exile once this is over, and yet you choose to continue on regardless. Our family and friends should not be left to fend for themselves when we can help. That is why we do this, even though it is not in our best interests.'

'I, for one, am not sure we should be doing anything. I mean, no one asked us if we wanted our lives to be taken over in this way.'

'Seamus, I hope you do not truly mean that. We are who we are, and we help when we can. In time, I will be able to move more freely. The Great Seer, Caraig, told me as my skill in foresight develops, I will be able to sense things in the world again.'

She untangled Seamus' hands from her own and turned to where she knew the others in the room were seated before she continued. 'I am blind, not useless, and I am here to help. So will one of you please tell us what we missed?'

'Are you sure you would not like some refreshments first?' Emer asked. 'I know from my father your journey here was swift, with little time for rest.'

'Thank you, Emer, but I will not be able to relax until I find out what has been happening and how you all are.'

'Amelia, it is nice to know your newfound sight has not changed you one bit. I am so pleased you are back with us.'

Grateful to hear Aliah's voice, Amelia was happy the young woman had taken her at her word and decided to continue as if nothing had changed. As much as Amelia attempted to behave as she had before, she was still a little lost without her sight, and more than a little concerned she would no longer be useful. The princess' support meant more than she could say.

'Seamus and I, with Emer and Dominic's help, managed to stop the Carsten ships reaching the mainland, at least for the moment. It appears the god possessed the body of Carsten's king. When Seamus and I worked magic to cause him to collapse during battle, he had a tantrum and blew the ship up. But I guess you already know that, having journeyed through Port Marden.'

'We heard,' Amelia interrupted. 'Lucky for you we managed to persuade the king and his advisors we are indeed battling a god here. He has reconsidered his stance on having you both face the Wizard's Council for misusing magic once the threat to Aria has been repelled.'

When Amelia and Walter first met with the King's Council, the members had been highly concerned about Seamus and Aliah's potential use of battle magic during the Carsten invasion. Battle magic, defined as magic used against a person, was illegal and punishable by having your magic removed.

When questioned by the king and his advisors, Aliah and Seamus argued they fought a god, not a man. They maintained in this instance, using their magic on whatever form the god took was not only justified, but essential, if they were to defeat him. In principle the council agreed, magic used on a god was legal under the current laws. However, they were unable to believe Aria faced a non-human enemy.

In order to find a solution agreeable to them all, Dominic suggested they wait until after repelling the invasion before making a decision on whether or not Seamus and Aliah had used battle magic. A relieved king agreed.

Together Amelia, Walter and Caraig persuaded the council their foe was indeed a god and, after a long discussion, they decided Aliah and Seamus were justified in their actions against the being leading the invasion fleet.

'Well, that is a relief, not that I believed they would follow through on their threats. Seamus and I have been most careful about how we use our gifts,' Aliah continued. 'The fleet is now off the far side of Hand and has been harrying our ships night and day.'

'I believe the king can manage to deal with them.' Amelia again stopped Aliah mid-flow, trying to move her on to more relevant topics. 'In fact, Caraig travelled with us and remained with the Port Marden garrison to assist your father with keeping the Carstenites from landing. We need to focus on dealing with the larger threat. Do you know where our enemy is now?'

'No.' Seamus was once again all business.

Although he and Amelia only met a few moons ago, when his aunt stumbled on him leaving Port Marden, heading to the Wizard Isle in the hope they would accept him for training, he gained a great fondness for her. Their familial bond strengthened on the journey from Hand to Sanctuary when Seamus and Aliah travelled there to find out if they were the Wizard and Warrior from prophecy. Amelia had gone to support them, and also partly because she wanted to meet the legendary Great Seer.

Having grown close, she did not want her loss of sight to affect their budding relationship.

'We believe the wizards from the Wizard Isles who took part in the invasion conspiracy are now with the forces from Carsten.'

'What makes you say that?' Walter sat forward in his chair, eager to hear the answer.

'We saw Millard and Gaius leave with the departing Carsten fleet, and while we were in Port Marden, a number

BATTLE

of wizards absconded and could not be found. We assume they joined Gaius and Millard, and are on the other side of the island with the Carsten army,' Seamus advised them.

'I heard my old friend Millard finally displayed his true colours and came out openly in support of the Carsten invasion,' Walter said dryly.

'Yes, their plot to remove the royal family and rule Aria themselves was uncovered in advance of the Carsten fleet turning up on our shores. Thanks in part to the information Seamus and Aliah journeyed from Port Marden to Bannock to bring to the King, and thanks also to you, Walter.' Daniel now added to the conversation. 'As luck would have it, support amongst their fellow wizards was not as high as they believed, and the Wizard Congress expelled them all.'

The guard seemed pleased at the removal of a threat to their nation. Not least because his father, previously Captain of the King's Guard, was now the King's Chief Advisor, the role having been left vacant by Millard's departure.

'Although I am pleased the plot was exposed, now the invader's magical strength has been added to by wizards who are happy to break the age old laws against battle magic,' Walter said. 'I cannot help wondering if I might have stopped Millard and Gaius had I been with you. That would have been a blow to our enemy. Instead, they are back with their god, and we have no idea where to find them.'

Not wanting to indulge Walter's fear about having made the wrong decision when letting the others travel back to Port Marden without him, Amelia moved the conversation in a different direction.

'Seamus, have you found anything of interest here?'

Groans of exasperation filled the room, and Amelia suppressed a smile as Seamus grumbled, 'Nothing. So many scrolls, so little information.'

Amelia shifted in her chair and patted Walter's hand. 'Now, Walter, I understand why you wanted to travel here with the others, and what you gave up to remain behind with me. Surely now you realise our discoveries while remaining in Sanctuary more than make up for that.' Turning around so she faced the table, Amelia grinned. 'We found some very interesting information, which I am sure you are all waiting to hear. But first, perhaps you would give us an idea of what scrolls you have read and how you approached your task.'

From his safe place, Gaius learnt he could once again use his own eyes if he left his thoughts quiet, and was satisfied with observing the world rather than controlling and commenting on what he saw. At the moment, he looked through his eyes, watching events unfold in the palace on Hand through Millard's bronze mirror.

His body fidgeted as the god inhabiting him became more agitated, his anger barely kept in check. The mirror went dark and he lost control, giving a roar that shook the ground. Gaius momentarily lost the link to his eyes.

'What is this? Why can we no longer see what they are doing? I thought you said your strongest far-sight wizard set the scrying spell.'

BATTLE

'He did, and he is very good at what he does. Something must have changed in Port Hand. There is a new power there, one able to block our vision. I will task our best wizards with finding out what happened and who caused this. If that fails, we can contact our eyes and ears in the ducal palace to find out what the Wizard and Warrior are doing. It is a momentary set back, that is all.'

Millard steered him away from the other wizards, who were clearly unsettled around their old friend whose body now housed a god.

'There is some positive news. One of the wizards back in Carsten located a scroll that might help us find what we seek. I am just heading out to their ship now so we can link with him to find out the details.'

'I will come with you.'

'Perhaps you should stay here. You tend to make everyone nervous, and that affects their ability to work.'

The god stopped and stared at Millard, contemplating the thin, greying man who always appeared to be looking down his nose at people, even those taller than himself. He wondered at the power this nondescript being held over others of his kind.

'They do right to fear me. However, mind speak is difficult over long distances, even for one as strong as I. In this instance I will listen to your advice. Mark me though, there are only two people in this world I wish to know of the chest's location: me and you. You, because you need to bring me the item, and me, because I do not completely trust you.'

The god stared directly at Millard, ensuring the wizard heard his next words. 'If the others have found it, you know what you have to do.'

'I am not sure killing them is necessary.' Millard blanched at the thought. 'We may need all the magical help we can get in this battle.'

The Gold Wizard had always shown a distaste towards killing people. Well, at least with his own hands. To Gaius' surprise, the god laughed, the sound coming from deep within his belly.

'Your own twisted mind provided that particular solution, wizard. It may surprise you to know, I appreciate too many deaths unsettle those who serve my goals. A little mind wiping will suffice in this instance. Wait, I perceive this is not a skill you possess. Perhaps I had best join you after all.'

The god strode off towards the transport boats dotting the shoreline, and Millard had no choice but to follow.

3
OLD FRIENDS RETURN

While Seamus outlined their approach to working through the scrolls in Hand's oldest library, Aliah took the opportunity to observe Amelia. Although she met the other woman only recently, she respected her as a strong, independent soul. Now, her dark hair was peppered with a little more grey, and her once brown eyes were more opaque. Tension around those eyes told Aliah maintaining the facade she was still in control was not completely effortless.

Of course she had lost her sight, and so many of her

movements showed a hesitancy not previously there, although she did seem to be able to easily identify who spoke. Her questions were insightful, and kept them all focused on the subject at hand when they drifted off onto more interesting topics.

What concerned Aliah was the way she kept hold of Walter's hand throughout the entire conversation, as though he anchored her to the world. As if she sensed someone watching her, Amelia's head lifted and she turned her sightless gaze in Aliah's direction.

Do not worry so, Aliah. Although I miss seeing things, in its place I am developing other gifts. In time I will not need to rely on Walter quite so much, but I am thankful he is with me now.

How did you read my thoughts?

I did not, well not exactly. I have found I am more aware of other people's feelings than before, which is perhaps a byproduct of losing my sight. I sensed your unease, and it was easy enough to guess the reason why because on the way here Caraig, Walter and I spent time discussing how the changes to me would affect you all. We knew you in particular would be concerned about how all of this affected me mentally. And Seamus, he will worry I am not physically able to help now until I am used to being without my sight.

I am a little disappointed, I think. I really thought you could read minds. Aliah caught herself before her laughter bubbled up and out.

Amelia's own amusement at the comment coloured her thoughts. *Thank the Goddess, no. I do not think I would be able to work with you all if I could do that. With my heightened senses your tension and angst are tangible, and that is more than enough for me to guess the rest. I want you to understand that while I regret losing some of my independence, it is only for a short time, and the closeness I now have with Walter more than makes up for that loss. All the years I lived alone, I forgot the warmth and comfort of a like minded companion can provide.*

Why, Amelia, you are not going soft on us and falling in love are you? Aliah joked, and was met with a silence she did not expect. *Oh, Amelia, how thoughtless of me to be so brash.*

Amelia paused before she responded, trying to gather her jumbled thoughts. *With everything going on I had not considered my feelings for Walter in that way. You bringing up the idea merely threw me off balance.*

Do not mind me. Whatever you and Walter feel for each other, it is no one else's business but your own, Aliah reassured her friend.

'Excuse me, Amelia? Aliah? Have we bored you both to sleep?' Seamus' impatient voice caused her to lose eye contact with Amelia as she turned to face him. 'Did you hear any of what we said?'

Amelia saved her from answering. 'I am sorry, Seamus, I became lost in my own thoughts. Your approach was thorough, but quite broad. With the information we brought with us, I fear you may have wasted much time as you could have targeted your search a little better.'

Seamus' face turned beetroot as he worked up to an explosion. Aliah held her breath, waiting for the outburst. Instead, Seamus walked away from the table and left the library, the only sign of his anger was the door slamming behind him. The room was quiet. Before the silence became awkward, Emer spoke for them all.

'Responsibility has been weighing Seamus down. In his head, he understands we all share the burden of fighting this god, but his heart is yet to accept this,' she told the new arrivals.

'Duty always lay heavily on the shoulders of my family,' Amelia said. 'Let him walk off his frustration. In the meantime, perhaps we might organise some refreshments. I believe a break away from the library would do you all some good. Aliah, would you be so kind as to ask the cook to send up some food to your rooms, and we can all meet up there?'

The request surprised Aliah. Although as a princess she held a higher status than the others, she worked hard to be treated like everyone else. Even so, it was unusual for anyone to ask her to fetch and carry for them.

As Amelia asked her politely, and she owed this woman a debt of gratitude for her help in leaving Port Marden, and for seeing her ready for the journey north to warn her father of the coming invasion, she did as she was bid. Closing the door gently behind her, she turned and was sure she glimpsed self-satisfied smirks on Amelia and Walters' faces.

Although she had only been back in the palace a few days, she had made sure to learn the way to the kitchens early on. With so few servants left on the island, the group ate their meals at the large table usually used by serving staff. Closer to the kitchen, the smell of roast lamb filled the air. She hoped it was being prepared for their evening meal as the delicious scent had her stomach rumbling already. Aliah opened the door to her destination only to be nearly bowled off her feet by a whirlwind with red hair. Her jaw dropped in shock.

'Aliah, you are safe. Walter said you were, but I would not believe it until I saw you with my own eyes.'

Aliah returned the hug of the younger boy who a moon or so ago led Walter, Seamus and herself out of Duncameron through the sewers below the streets. Pauley had been forced to share Aliah's horse all the way to Bannock to avoid capture. They parted ways abruptly, leaving him at the markets with the farmer who had smuggled them in to town, while they went to report news of the pending invasion to her father.

She always regretted not being able to say a proper farewell to the boy, and only found out Pauley had made it safely home from his adventures a couple of days ago. He then left a short time later when some mutual friends came south to help fight against the Carsten invasion.

'Pauley, it is good to see you too. What are you doing here?' Aliah untangled herself and found the man everyone called Boss sitting at the table with a mug of steaming tea in front of him.

'Princess, it is a relief to find you alive and well. Pauley, let the girl catch her breath. Go and fetch her a tea.'

Pauley paused briefly. Thinking better of disobeying the older man, he disappeared into the kitchen to find her something to drink. Aliah took a seat at the table.

'Boss, you are the last person I expected to meet here.'

The man in front of her smiled a slow smile and took a sip of his tea, and Aliah wondered if Amelia sending her for refreshments was as spontaneous an action as it first appeared.

'When I ran in to Walter in Port Marden and he mentioned he needed a guard, I volunteered. Better than manning the gates at the port.'

'And Pauley?'

Boss barked out a laugh.

'That lad pretty much does what he wants. His parents were against him coming with us when we left for the war, but we found him stowed away. Much like someone else here.'

Boss referred to his finding Aliah in his wagon in Duncameron, having secretly journeyed with them from Sunnydale. When they found her, instead of handing her over to the authorities, they introduced her to Walter. They also helped her get back to Bannock when they learnt of her mission to tell the king about the invasion from Carsten.

'When he heard about my journey, knowing you were here as well, let me just say we found him when it was too far for him to swim back to Port. Very determined is that young boy.'

'As Walter is safe here with the garrison left behind to defend the palace, he no longer requires your services.' Aliah probed a little more.

'He is indeed safer here, but Amelia asked us to stay. She said there is still work for us to do.' Boss frowned into his tea. 'Odd, it felt almost like a prediction.'

'Maybe it was,' Aliah agreed.

Pauley returned with a fresh mug of tea for her. Handing it over, he slipped into the chair beside Boss.

'Amelia is a seer,' he informed her proudly.

'I know, Pauley, but not everything she says is a foretelling,' Aliah said as she took a sip from the mug.

'She did say we needed to stay because our part was not yet complete. That means we have important work to do to help you.' Pauley puffed out his chest, proud of the responsibility.

'Or it may merely mean Walter wants another pair of hands he can trust.' Boss added wryly.

'Pauley, I need you to do something for me, if you do not mind?' Aliah solemnly asked the boy, who beamed at the possibility of helping her. 'I need cook to gather some refreshments for my friends so I can take them upstairs. Do you think you might help her do that for me?'

'I certainly can,' Pauley affirmed. 'I used to help in the inn kitchen at meal times. Leave it to me.' He scampered back into the kitchen.

'I think you have found an admirer,' Boss chuckled.

Ignoring the remark, Aliah said, 'He is a good boy. Am I right in thinking Amelia sent me down here specifically to meet with you?'

'She did,' boss nodded as that slow smile returned to his face.

'Do you know why?'

'Mostly because she thought you would want some time with us before we meet the others, but also because she thinks we are to be a part of whatever is going on. She is telling the others about us now, and I think she wanted to make sure you and Seamus are happy about ...'

'... about what?'

Aliah turned in surprise at the voice from the hallway.

'Seamus, good to see you again boy, or should I call you My Lord?'

Aliah had the pleasure of seeing her friend smile for the first time in days.

'Boss, you need never call me anything other than Seamus. You gave me work and you protected me from that wizard, even though it placed you and your family in danger. It is good to see you.'

A couple of moon-turns ago Seamus drove a wagon from Sunnydale to Duncameron for Boss Allum, unaware Aliah had stowed away in the back of one of them.

On that journey he first encountered one of the rogue wizards from the Wizard Council looking for Aliah. After he threatened Seamus, Boss arranged for Pauley to take him to Walter. After teaching Seamus to control his magic, the wizard then escorted him to the sewers, where they met up with Aliah, and they all escaped to Banrock.

Pauley returned carrying a tray loaded with savouries and cakes, dishes clattering together as he placed them on the table.

'Cook will not let me carry the drinks,' he complained as he raised his head and caught sight of Seamus. A smile replaced the annoyed look on his face. 'Seamus, hello. I am about to go and ask cook to give me the tea to bring at least this far.' With that he disappeared back into the kitchen.

'And there is a little bit of hero worship there too I see.' Boss laughed. 'Ever since Amelia told us you two are now our Wizard and Warrior, Pauley had been busting his gut to meet with the you two again. He finds it amusing when you first met, he assumed you were the ones from the legend. He says you denied it, but he knew all along.

'Anyway, Amelia wanted me to make sure you two were happy about Pauley and I joining your group before introducing us to the others.'

Seamus' smile left his face. 'I am not sure we can ask any more people to put themselves in danger.'

Aliah did not need magic to appreciate the more people who joined their endeavour, the heavier the responsibility on Seamus to keep them all safe.

'Seamus, Amelia thinks it is important they stay, otherwise she would not have asked them to be here.'

For a moment she thought he was still going to refuse, but instead he shook his head and settled into the seat beside her.

'I do not know whether more people lessen the danger, or it means more people I care for are placed in harm's way. Unfortunately what I think does not really matter in this instance. Amelia is right. Boss and Pauley need to be here, for the moment at least.'

Aliah placed her hand on Seamus' arm in a gesture of solidarity.

'While we are here in the palace, we are all relatively safe, and there is nothing suggesting they are meant to carry on with us when we leave. If they do, we can worry about that later.'

'Well, I would not count on our being too safe here.' Boss Allum folded his arms in front of his chest and refused to say anything else, no matter how much they cajoled, merely repeating, 'I promised Walter and Amelia I would share that information with everyone at once.'

Seamus held the door for Aliah and Pauley as they carried trays into the sitting room of the guest suite he and Aliah once again occupied. Without his parents in the palace, the family quarters seemed empty, so he joined the others in the guest wing.

Having arrived before them, the company were comfortably settled into the chairs around the fireplace. The chairs from the table by the window were squeezed in between the more comfortable ones. Pauley flopped down on the floor, back against the wall, as the others seated themselves.

Seamus waited until everyone loaded plates and helped themselves to tea before he introduced the newcomers. Formalities out of the way, Seamus started.

'Boss, you said you learnt something we all needed to hear?'

Before Boss answered, there was a knock at the door. Dominic opened it and found the duke's steward, Robin, outside. He had no option but to step aside as the man pushed passed him and entered the room.

'Excuse me, Your Highness, Seamus, but I wanted to ensure you had everything you need. Do you want someone to tidy away the scrolls in the library if they are no longer required?'

Seamus frowned, he ordered the library off limits when they first arrived. No one was to enter, not even for cleaning. He even went to the trouble of placing a guard outside the door when they were not in there so no prying eyes could work out what they searched for.

He shook his head, deciding he was jumping at shadows. Robin arrived at the castle as a young boy and had worked closely with his father since then. The duke trusted him, that was enough for Seamus.

'Thank you, Robin. We have everything we need here, and our work continues in the library, so my orders to leave things as they are still stand.'

'As you wish.' The man lingered by the door, seemingly reluctant to leave.

'Is there something else?' Seamus asked.

'Well.' Robin looked sheepish. 'From time to time I research things for your father, and I wondered if you might not find what you are looking for sooner if I assisted you.'

Seamus relaxed, the man was only trying to be his normal, over-helpful self.

'Thank you, Robin, that is very thoughtful of you, but we are fine. Perhaps, though, you could ready some guest quarters for our new arrivals. They will all be staying a few days.'

'Consider it done.' He bowed and walked backwards out of the room.

Dominic watched him retreat down the corridor before shutting the door behind. 'We may need to watch him,' he said as he retook his seat.

'He is perhaps a little over-zealous,' Seamus reassured them. 'My father trusts him, so we should too. Boss, you were going to tell us some important news.'

'I am not sure how important it is for you, given I know very little of what you are doing here.' Boss sat up straighter in his chair as everyone directed their attention to him.

'I recently received a report from the underground, from one of the wizards currently with the Carstenites on the other side of the island.'

'Wait a minute,' Dominic and Daniel said at the same time. Daniel nodded for Dominic to continue.

'You mean to say you placed a spy in the Carsten camp? How did you manage that? Not even the king's Spymaster was able to get someone close enough to the traitors for them to be taken into the inner circle.'

As one of Aria's most accomplished spies, Dominic was aware of the difficulties involved in inserting someone into a foreign enemy's camp. Also, his daily briefings from Port Marden had not mentioned any information sources close to the Carsten leaders.

'Many of you know my group closely watched some wizards on the isle, having realised for some time they were plotting against Aria and the king. That was one of the reasons we assisted Aliah and Seamus to get a message to King Terion about their activities.

'Earlier on our concerns led us to place a man with the traitors, and he has been feeding information to us since. This was way before the wizards were cast from the isle. As part of the inner-circle of conspirators, he left with the others when the king expelled the traitor, Millard. He has been risking his life for his country since then,' Boss responded.

'Have I met him?' Walter asked. The older wizard had been exiled from the Wizard Isle when he stumbled on the conspiracy Boss spoke of, and there was a real possibility the man on the inside worked with Walter in the past.

BATTLE

'You have,' Boss confirmed. 'I was unable to tell you this before because I needed to ensure his safety, but in fact he was one of your students. I remember you sharing your disappointment when he began spending time with Millard.

'You always thought his change of heart odd, as he had previously despised the man and his methods. His brother served with me for years, and when the wizard voiced his fears about what Millard and his friends were up to, he was able to persuade his brother to spy for us.'

'So you are telling me …' Walter started, before Boss rushed in.

'I do not like to say his name out loud, anyone might be listening. If we have spies in their camp, we must assume there are spies in ours.'

Seamus sat upright and stared pointedly at Dominic, who shrugged his shoulders.

'We are aware of at least one person here who is passing messages on to our enemy. We made sure the information they have access to is misleading. However, it is only smart to conclude where there is one, there may be others. I am keeping an eye out, and so is Daniel.'

Seamus was silent for a moment, unable to understand why someone on Hand would want to help the invading force. It made him uneasy, but he could do little about it. What he could do something about was the fact no one had discussed this with him.

'You did not think to talk about this with Aliah and me? Or does she know already?' He glared at Dominic, but it was Daniel who answered him.

'No, Seamus, we have not talked to her about this.

Emer, Liam, Dominic and I have been making sure the two of you are safe and secure, and able to concentrate on what you need to do.

'Of course if that situation changes we will include you in future plans.'

Seamus did not know what annoyed him more, Daniel's calm manner as he offered his explanation, or the fact he was right. The king had placed the guardsman in charge of the group's security so he and Aliah would not be worried by such details, then requested the others work with Daniel to keep them from harm.

Although he raged inside, he knew there was no point in pursuing this any further, they had more important things to discuss. Taking a deep breath, he pushed his frustrations down, and carried on.

'So, Boss, what news did your spy send?'

'I am sure this first bit of information will come as no surprise to you,' Boss started. 'But the wizard, Millard, is with the Carsten Army.'

'We saw him escape Aria with one of their landing forces, so we guessed that was where he would go.' Seamus spoke for them all. 'We are also aware if he is there, he is ensuring our enemy succeeds so his own plans to rule Aria come fruition.'

'I see you have his measure then,' Boss continued. 'However, I am sure this next piece of news is going to sound unbelievable. My informant told me we are not just fighting an invading army. He believes some magical force inhabited they body of our enemy's king, controlling his actions. The report stated whoever controlled the king blew up the Carsten command ship.'

BATTLE

Boss held up his hand, expecting objections to this bizarre news. 'Before you tell me this is all madness, hear me out. This wizard believes the magical entity now resides inside that slimy wizard, Gaius. The one who followed us to Duncameron, Seamus.'

No one spoke for a moment after Boss finished. Then, as if on some secret queue, most of the room burst out laughing. The perplexed look on Boss' face soon turned to anger at not being taken seriously. Before he did something he would regret later, Aliah pulled herself together and shushed the rest of them.

'Oh, Boss, we are not laughing at you. In fact, we believe you. We know the king was indeed possessed when he died, although it was not by a magical entity, as such, but by one of the gods.'

Now it was Boss' turn to let out a full belly laugh of his own. 'You are teasing me. A god? They are things the churches make up to keep us all in line.'

'I wish that were so. It may surprise you, but only last night I talked to a god. Seamus has spoken directly to them all, except the one who is trying to take over the world. The gods of old tried us and named us the Wizard and the Warrior.'

Pauley stared at Aliah, a look of wonder on his face. He was still young enough to believe in magic and fairy tales. Boss was another matter. The ex-guard had seen much in his life, and was a skeptic by nature. He took some convincing.

Eventually Walter, whom he had trusted for years, managed to persuade him they were not joking. They were actually preparing to face a god and stop him from turning their world into a battlefield for his own amusement.

'Our laughter was partially from relief,' Aliah explained. 'We all dreaded revealing who our real enemy was to anyone outside our group. Most people find it difficult to believe.'

'The god will be hard enough to face, but it will be harder if we cannot find him. Now we know he resides in another human body we will at least know what he looks like. And we also confirmed he is back with the invading army, which is helpful as well,' Seamus continued.

Although he was giving them the benefit of the doubt, Boss still appeared a little unsure of himself as he asked, 'So what does it mean, you being the Wizard, and Aliah being the Warrior? How does that help us in all of this?'

Everyone turned to Seamus, waiting for him to answer, but he said nothing. It was not only that he was still learning about being the Wizard, nor even that he was not sure he wanted to be the Wizard at all, it was deciding what to tell Boss.

He trusted the man, but learning there could be a spy in their midst made him a little more cautious. Looking at Walter for guidance, the older man shifted his weight in his chair then stood and moved to stand in front of the fire.

'I have known you for a long time, Boss, and I have trusted you with my life. You fought for Aria as a guard for years, and after your service you set up a network to fight against a danger you saw coming but few others believed in.

'Your loyalty is to your network, and that is as it should be. The people here, well, our loyalty is to each other, to see the Wizard and Warriors' task through to the bitter end.

'If we share our secrets with you, we need to know you will put us first until the god is vanquished. No one will think any less of you if you decide this is not the fight you signed up for. But if you stay, we must have your full commitment.'

Boss thoughtfully tapped his fingers on his leg, then spoke slowly, as if he were still thinking things through. 'Before I make my decision, I need to ask you a question. Do you personally believe the plot we fought to foil, to stop the wizards from ruling Aria, was a smaller part of this bigger threat?'

'I do, Boss. That is why I am here now.'

The room was silent, as if everyone was holding their breath.

'I cannot speak for all of my network, but I personally will stay and support you all for as long as you need me.'

Walter glanced back to Seamus. 'If he is with us then he deserves to know everything.'

Nodding his agreement, Seamus waited until Walter had retaken his seat before starting off. 'Your daughter found out about my magical abilities when I travelled with you. They turn out to be quite unique. I am being trained to use them so I will be ready when we face the god. Aliah has been given skills to balance mine so we have a chance when we eventually battle our foe. At the moment we are researching ways to fight him.' Seamus stopped short.

There was little more he could tell Boss about what they would do with those powers because they still had not found the scroll telling them how to defeat their enemy.

Amelia started to rise, but before she did, Emer stood and moved to stand in front of the fire.

'If you are to join with us, I think it best you know Seamus and Aliah are not in this alone. Nor are they the only ones with unique skills. Dominic?' Emer looked to the spy, who blushed, but did not move. 'If we are to be a team we all need to know what the others can do.'

Again Dominic did not move, but simply faded away. For a moment he disappeared, then he was back.

'Goddess, I have never seen anything like it.' The words escaped from Walter's mouth before he turned and whispered to Amelia.

'I heard tales of the old ones from the north who could melt into the shadows, but I always thought it a myth,' Amelia said after hearing Walter's explanation.

'Wait, there is more, is there not Emer?' Dominic smirked.

With everyone's attention on her, Emer changed into her wolf form, then back to human. The amazement he felt when Emer first showed Seamus her skill appeared on Boss, Pauley and Walters' faces. Walter leaned over and spoke to Amelia, her mouth forming an 'o' of surprise.

Liam gave a nervous laugh. 'With two wizards, a magical warrior, a seer, a shape shifter and an invisible man, I consider it somewhat of an honour to be one of the non-gifted people in the room. I cannot help thinking though, surely we cannot fail with so much talent on our side.'

'You, Daniel, Boss and Pauley are as important in all of this as we are. You all have unique skills even if you do not possess magical abilities,' Seamus told them.

'Umm.' Pauley shifted uncomfortably on the floor. 'Umm, me mam says I have a gift, so I guess I should tell you.' He waited for Boss to give his permission before proceeding. 'I can see in dark rooms or places where there are no lights. I can also find my way around streets and places I have never been to before. It was my skill that guided you through the sewers.'

It was Seamus' turn to be surprised. He thought the boy's ability to lead them out of the sewers under Duncameron came from studying the paths.

'I had no idea,' Walter said. 'Your parents kept that secret well hidden.'

'They did not want Pauley to go to The Wizard Isle for training, so they kept quiet about it. Only a few of us know,' Boss informed them.

'How is it Dominic, Emer and Pauley have these gifts, yet I cannot sense magic in them, nor can I sense anything when they use their skills?' Seamus asked his old teacher.

'I am not sure,' Walter answered. 'Just as I cannot explain why I could sense your magic once, but when you do something magical now, I sense something is happening but it does not feel the same. But these are perhaps questions for another day.'

Seamus nodded in agreement, and continued, 'Pauley, thank you for sharing with us. Who knows when your skills might become useful? As for those without magical gifts, your skills are equally as important. We need strong arms to defend us against non-gifted enemies. This is more than my opinion. Since we gathered here today I have a feeling of ... well, the best way to describe it is rightness.'

Amelia nodded her head. 'I believe all those we need to complete our quest are here. Now, moving on, Walter and I brought back with us another piece of the puzzle; we found what we need to do to defeat the god.'

Gaius spent most of the afternoon in his safe space as the restless god rifled through his memories, searching for information to help him find the casket he needed. It was called the Casket of Ember and, so far, he had not uncovered anything useful. On the other hand, Gaius found out about the casket, its importance to the god, and a little something about the being who now lived in his body.

He now knew that having his brothers and sisters refuse to help him escape to the world of humans, he needed to take matters into his own hands. He designed a wooden box, about the size of a small travel pack, for the express purpose of storing enough magical energy to transport himself to this world without their help. Forged in a river of embers to increase its strength, and filled with magic from their home world, the casket was discovered and confiscated by his family.

In a fit of anger, the god drew a large amount of magical energy and attempted to escape his siblings. Although taking in so much power had almost killed him, the magic had not been enough to bring him all the way through. He ended up trapped between two worlds.

While he recovered his strength, his siblings expended a great deal of energy and sent the casket to this world for safe keeping. They believed it to be secure and, if by some chance, the god ever managed to break through there, it might be used to assist the people against the god's havoc.

Knowing he might eventually try to reach his original destination, they planned and prepared for the coming of a wizard and guardian warrior to balance his power in the world of humans. If they could get to the casket, they would have the means to send their brother home.

For millennia, a lack of magical energy imprisoned the errant god on the in-between-world. Frustrated, he lashed out. Causing a volcano in a far land to erupt, destroying villages and killing many.

The event caused chaos, giving him an energy surge, just enough to enable him to move his spirit to this world. Chancing on the leader of the people of Carsten, he pushed the weak willed man aside, then took control of his body and the country he ruled.

Now everything hinged on the casket. It was an object of great power, but could equally be used for or against him. Its construction meant it could imprison his spirit and prevent him from acting in this world again.

However, the casket still contained the power he harnessed a millennia ago. Destroying it would release a burst of magical energy, enough to allow his body to be brought through to this plane of existence if he incited the right spells while releasing the power.

Until the god began sifting through the memories Gaius allowed him access to, he had never heard of a magical chest. Nor had he been aware the old gods still kept an eye on their world.

In the distant past the country now called Aria worshipped many gods, but in recent years, The Goddess held sway on the continent. Although she was a popular figure, no one used her actual name in worship as they did in the past. In fact, as far as Gaius knew, no one even remembered what it was.

When he stumbled on memories of the forgotten gods, his oppressor was initially angry he and his brethren were now so little thought of. Then his mood changed and he laughed out loud.

These heathens have forgotten everything about my family. The fact they are no longer known by name means their power here has diminished, which in turn means they have little more influence than I do. I am unlikely to find anything else from this source of information, as the wizard who had this body before is unfamiliar with the old ways. I need to find worshippers of the old religions. Where is Millard?

Gaius shrunk further back into his safe place, away from the invader's mind. Going through what he learnt, he started planning what he might do should he manage to gain control of the magical artefact first.

4
HOW TO KILL A GOD

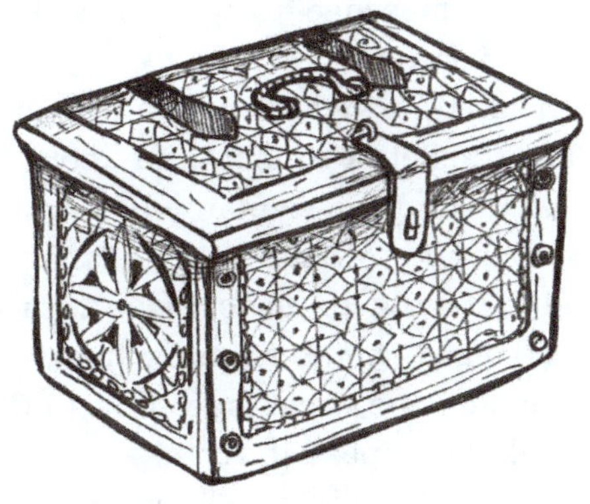

Amelia turned towards the fire. Enjoying the heat on her face, she also appreciated the break from the assault on her senses. With so many people in the room and so much going on, the constant input was over-whelming. She thought about how best to approach the knowledge she needed to share before she started speaking.

'I spent a large part of my trial talking with the gods, and sharing revelations around the prophecy of the Wizard and the Warrior. The gods are careful not to upset the balance of powers governing our world, but at the same time, they are unable to stand by and let one of their own roam free causing havoc. To allow him freedom to do as he pleased would cause such disharmony we might never recover.

'Many years ago, a special relic was sent to Aria, and the reason we currently face invasion is because the god wants to retrieve it. When I shared my vision with Caraig, he remembered a scroll from the Sanctuary library. Its contents had been deemed so obscure no one had been able to interpret its message. Caraig allowed us to study it in light of my vision.

'When translated, it told of the making of a magical item called The Casket of Ember, and about the people here in Aria who the gods appointed to protect it. The chest, which we think is about two handspans wide and about one and half handspans across, was brought here to use against the god should he make his way here. The primary function of this chest is to contain the essence of the god should he appear in Aria.'

She did not need her sight to know how restless her news made everyone. Sensing the array of questions flowing through their minds, Amelia held up her hand for silence before they escaped their lips. 'Please, let me tell you everything first, and I will answer all your questions later.'

No one spoke, and although the room stilled, she had no way of knowing what was happening until Walter gently touched her arm, signalling for her to continue. Facing the others, she found she had a strong sense of those she shared a close bond with: Liam, Seamus and Aliah. The others appeared as background noise to her newly honed senses.

However, if she stilled her mind, she found vibrations through which the others transmitted their worries and their fears. Although this was all new and interesting, it was distracting her from her task.

She continued. 'Obviously we need to find the casket as this is our best and easiest way to control the enemy we must defeat. We will talk more on how we might do that in a moment. Before moving on, we need to consider something Walter found in a related scroll.'

Sitting forward in his seat, Walter continued, almost as though they rehearsed their presentation beforehand. 'The ancient relic is a source of unimaginable power as it is strong enough to contain the essence of a god. We must also remember the god himself is searching for it. The scroll I read hinted the chest is a double edged sword. If the god manages to retrieve it first, he might be able to use it to his advantage.'

'How?' The voice sounded like Daniel.

'Well, as best I can make out, he might be able use the power to draw his physical form into this world.'

Gasps escaped.

'He did warn us he was coming,' Aliah said. 'Why else are we focusing on stopping him from getting here before that happens?'

'I know he did, but I hoped the boast he made when we fought him was an empty threat, meant to scare us off.' Seamus shared his thoughts out loud. 'It never occurred to me what would bring him here would also be what we would need to control him. In my mind I had it all planned; we find a magical object to help us, then face him, and hopefully defeat him.'

'I thought that too. Now we will have to plan carefully, and gather everything we need to vanquish him in either form before we retrieve our final weapon. While doing this we also need to ensure he does not get to the magical object before us.'

'Wait, there is more,' Amelia interrupted. 'Imprisoning him in the casket is the easiest way for us to prevent the god from tearing our world apart, but I also found another, more difficult, way to deal with him.

'As best as I can understand, the god is not truly here. Nor is he on the same plane as the other gods themselves, but rather stuck somewhere in between. In my vision, when the god ran away from his siblings, he used a huge amount of magical energy to pull himself from his home towards our world. Unfortunately he did not gather enough, and he was unable to complete his journey.

'Now, he either needs to come here, or return to the world where his body lies. If we could find a way to send him back home, the gods might then be able to restore the balance in their world and ours.'

The room filled with unasked questions, but no one wanted to speak first.

Boss broke the silence, summing up the situation in true military fashion. 'It seems the obvious course of action is to contain the god in the ember casket, but the best solution is for him to return home.'

Walter agreed. 'Yes, except at the moment the only option available is sending him back, unless we can find the casket, that is.'

'And where do we start looking?' Aliah asked.

'All the scroll said is the casket has been looked after

by an ancient, secret order. I got a glimpse of one of their ceremonies during my vision, but I was not shown who they were or where they might be located.'

'How ancient would this order be, Amelia?' Seamus asked.

'Quite old, I would guess.'

'Hold on, wait here,' Seamus said, and she heard the click of the door closing.

Shutting the door behind himself, Seamus turned and almost fell over Robin.

'What are you doing lurking in the corridor?' Seamus gasped in surprise.

'Lurking, sir? I never lurk.' Robin managed to look both superior and a little guilty. 'I came to see if you required more refreshments.'

Seamus frowned. 'I thought we agreed my friends and I would serve ourselves as most of the palace staff left for Port Marden with my father and mother.'

The man in front of him shifted uneasily. Small in stature, dark haired and with darting dark eyes, Robin often appeared shifty. Seamus remembered being told off by his mother when he told her his father's chancellor was the image of a sneak thief in one of his story books. He quickly brushed the thought away as Robin answered him.

'We did, Sir, but I noticed you were all hard at work so I took it upon myself to make sure you were being looked after.'

He should be grateful, but Seamus was annoyed. Robin

ignored orders coming from both his duke's son and the king's heir. Seamus always felt uneasy in the man's presence, but deciding it was not the time to dwell on personal animosities, he attempted to smooth things over.

'Thank you for thinking of us, Robin. As we explained when we arrived, we are more than capable of looking after ourselves.' Seamus went to pass the chamberlain, but found himself blocked.

'I am not sure your father would approve of the Heir of the Realm looking after herself. He would expect me to see to her comfort.'

Keeping a firm grip on his rising temper, Seamus ground out a terse response. 'I think, as the eldest son of the duke, the hospitality is mine to extend. At this moment I can assure you Princess Aliahanna is more than happy with the level of comfort we are providing. If anything changes, I will inform you.'

He swept past Robin and continued down the corridor, fists clenching as he imagined wiping the smug smile from the man's face. By the time he reached the stairway to the lower floor, he realised Robin had remained outside the guest room door.

'Robin, I am sure what the princess would most like at the moment is privacy.' His voice rang through the corridor. He hoped the others would hear his warning and realise someone might be listening.

This time he waited until Robin passed him and was half-way down stairs before he continued through the entrance hall, past the state rooms, and down the narrow corridor to the old part of the palace housing the library. Looking round the room, he confirmed someone had tidied up since they had left, just as suspected from things Robin had said. *Goddess, how will I find that scroll now?*

When he had been listening to Amelia talk about the secret sect who might be looking after the chest, something niggled at the back of his mind. One of the documents he read yesterday contained an account of a group on Hand similar to the one Amelia described, a report to the then king from one of his men. Initially he discounted the document because it did not speak directly of magic, or gods, and was old. Now, he was having second thoughts.

Scanning the documents, he resisted the urge to delve into the scrolls and tried to identify when he had read it. Early the previous morning perhaps? He picked up a scroll. No, he had read it this morning. He chose another; late yesterday. He moved again. No, those were from the first day. Picking up a few scrolls in between, he soon found the one he searched for. Rolling it back up, he returned to the guest room.

On the stairs he met Emer carrying a tray with fresh tea and some cups. His automatic response was to offer to carry it for her, but he stopped himself. Like Aliah, Emer would see the gesture not as good manners, but as a comment on her ability to carry out a simple task. Instead he walked ahead of her, opening the door to ease her way.

Waiting until she placed the tray down, he held up his find and announced, 'I read something I think will help.'

'What?' Walter asked, an excited twinkle in his eye.

'Early yesterday, I read this report from one of my ancestor's Guard Captain. He tells of a vassal on the southern coast who set up a monastery in tribute to one of the minor gods, the God of the Sea. Two things stood out when I read it. The first being the rise of religious houses worshipping the Goddess around the same time. Many of the monasteries and churches for the other gods were being abandoned, or converting to her.

'The second was the secrecy surrounding the order. Neither the guard nor his men had been admitted to the area dedicated to the monastery. In fact, they were turned away by force of arms.' Seamus laid out the scroll on the table, and all but Amelia, Pauley and Boss gathered round to read it.

'This is pretty flimsy to base our next moves on,' Daniel said, and Dominic nodded his agreement.

'Except,' Liam interrupted. 'The current Baron Wexler, like most of his forefathers, refused his place in the Ducal Court, preferring to stay close to home. Few people visit him, and he is almost a recluse.

'There have also been rumours about the monastery he has on his lands. There are enough men there to make up two guard units, or more, and those who have been seen in the village are said to carry themselves more like soldiers than monks.'

'My father sent emissaries inviting Lord Wexler to court to attend councils, but most of them were turned back at the gates to his lands. The only one who was let through was allowed to stay the night because he arrived in the midst of a horrendous storm. He dined with the staff and, as soon as the storm cleared the next morning, he was sent on his way.

'When he reported back, he told my father he had not even met with the baron, and the staff he ate with barely spoke to him,' Seamus added. 'I think there is a very good possibility this may be what we are looking for.'

'Amelia, what do you think?' Walter asked.

'I have had no vision about this, if that is what you want to know. But if it is my opinion you want, then my seeing led me to believe we needed to be on Hand, there are things for us to do here. It would therefore be reasonable to assume what we are looking for must be here.

'I also agree with Liam and Seamus about the Wexler's. For generations they have held themselves apart from others on this island. Add that to the rumours the lands they gifted to the monastery included some ancient caves and dwellings believed to be magical.

'The long held belief is that particular parcel of land was given to the order because the Wexler's wanted to rid their lands of the taint of magic. It is just as likely the land was used because its magic was needed to protect something of importance. I cannot think of a better place on the island to start our search.'

'I am not totally convinced, but at least if we follow this lead then we will be doing something other than reading in a library. So, shall we prepare to leave in the morning?' Aliah asked.

'Wait a moment,' Daniel interrupted. 'Let us not get ahead of ourselves. Firstly, we need to find out a little more about what is happening with the soldiers camped on the other side of the island before we leave the safety of the palace.

'Those ships off our coast contain rather a lot of men, and they must be running low on supplies. As they have not yet made landfall on the mainland, they must now be thinking about taking control of this island. Hand provides the perfect foothold to launch their next attack, while also giving them access to food and water.'

'I did not think of that.' Aliah frowned.

'Nor did I. I really must discuss this possibility with the captain of the guard to ensure we are prepared to defend the island, and provide refuge to those left behind should they need it,' Seamus added.

Daniel placed a hand on the younger boy's shoulder. 'Seamus, that is why I am here. Your only job is to learn how to vanquish a god.'

'But I cannot leave the people of Hand at the mercies of an invading force.' Seamus seemed to shrink as the weight of this new problem settled on his shoulders.

'There is little we can do about it tonight.' Emer moved to stand beside Seamus, as if by physically being near him, she was able to shoulder some of his burden. 'I suggest tomorrow I take a flight over the island so we know exactly what is happening. After, we can make plans to take care of the people of Hand, and to find what we need to do to beat this rogue deity.'

As always, Seamus was calmed by Emer's pragmatic approach. Every time he found himself caught up in the enormity of the task they faced, it was she who came up with something practical to do to move forward.

'I agree, further planning can wait until tomorrow. We have come a long way today, perhaps it is time to take a break and enjoy the dinner cook prepared for us.' Seamus stood and stretched.

'Just so long as we do not spend tomorrow in the library, I can agree to that,' Aliah said.

BATTLE

'I for one vote we go and find what cook has prepared for us, I am sure I smelled lamb before. I mean we cannot be expected to fight a God on and empty stomach, can we?' Liam's own stomach rumbled, emphasising his point.

Laughing, Dominic opened the door. 'Lead the way, Squire Liam, I think we could all do with some of cook's fine fare, especially if we are soon to be dining on travel rations again.'

A gentle touch on her shoulder awoke Aliah.

'Warrior, it is time for training.'

Seamus, already dressed, stood waiting by the door. He turned and led the male god out of Aliah's room so she had some privacy to throw on some outdoor clothes.

Since she had been included in the night time training sessions, Aliah had taken to sleeping in trousers and a shirt. All she had to do was pull on some boots and a warm jacket and she was ready to join the others.

Moments later, they were all down in the back courtyard. The space was enclosed by the palace on one side, the garrison quarters on another, the stables opposite, and a high wall adjacent to the stables closed the square. Sheltered from the elements and prying eyes, it was the perfect place for their nightly lessons.

Aliah began limbering up, then she and Seamus went through the forms of unarmed combat they were developing. Based loosely on sword forms, running through the attack and defence positions helped focus their minds for the coming lesson. Before they completed the attack forms,

Seamus stopped and turned to the watching god.

'Before we begin tonight, I have some questions for you. May I ask them?'

'You know I cannot give you information about the forthcoming battle.'

'Yes, but I understand you are still able to provide me with some general information.'

'I am not sure what you mean by that question,' the god said, regarding Seamus quizzically.

'Can you tell me things about the gods as a group? Or your world as opposed to the world where we live?'

'I do not believe answering such questions will affect the balance. So yes, you may ask.'

Seamus winked at Aliah, and she wondered what he was up to.

'We found a scroll suggesting we must find the Casket of Ember.'

'I am unable to talk to you about that.'

'I do not want to talk about it either. While I was reading the scroll, it occurred to me we call you all gods, yet here in Aria we worship only one of you, and we simply call her Goddess. When meeting with you all together, I met four female and three male gods, and the one we are looking to banish would make four males.

'You told me each of you have different abilities, and I think this has something to do with the balance you speak of. Balance in numbers, balance of the sexes and balance in powers.'

Intrigued, Aliah stopped her warm up to listen.

'So, here is my question: were you once worshiped as individuals by the people of this world who knew and used those names?'

After thinking for a moment, the god answered. 'Yes, in the past people used our names to pay homage to us and the individual gifts we bestow on the earth.'

'And when we worshiped all of you, there was balance and unity in our world, and yours?'

'That is correct.'

'Is there a power in knowing your names, or using your names?' Aliah chipped in.

'I am not sure you would call it power in the way you understand the word. Using a god's name calls their attention, creating a direct, mutually beneficial link between a worshipper and their chosen god.'

'That is almost as I thought. If one god was worshipped more than another then there would be disharmony?' Aliah continued.

The god considered this for a moment before responding. 'That depends. When we are all worshipped equally, there is complete balance, but we are also paired. For instance, you worship the Goddess here, in the southern realms they worship her male opposite, so the world stays in balance.'

Aliah was pleased she figured the direction Seamus' enquiries were heading. Though his next question caught her by surprise, and made her realise how much thought Seamus had been putting into defeating their foe.

'So, if I know the god's name, and I use enough force behind my command, he will have his focus drawn to me. In effect, binding him to me in some way?'

'I guess that is one way of looking at it.'

If the last question had been a surprise, the next totally confused her.

'This un-named god is not on your plane of existence, and he is not on ours, is there a place where he actually exists?'

The god thought for a moment. 'Yes and no. My brother is between worlds. He is alone with some stray souls also trapped there. It is not a place where life grows, so magic is sparse, and his existence is limited.'

'As I understand it, he wants to move here for some reason and you want him back, thus restoring the balance on both worlds. What stops you from just getting him yourselves? No, wait, you cannot because you would be pitted against each other, causing destruction on a level we can only imagine.

'May I ask another question? Can we deal with him while he is where he is now, or must we wait until he is here?'

'Of course you can fight him if he reunites with his body, and in some ways this would be the best course of action for all as he would be returned to us in one piece. However, there are also ways to defeat him before he fully manifests.'

Aliah's jaw dropped. She could not believe the gods thought they should let their brother fully enter their world before confronting him because that was best for them. Angry, she forced her next words out through gritted teeth. 'If you wanted us to fight him in person you could have warned us earlier, or at least trained us specifically for that eventuality?'

'We are not able to tell you the best way to fight our brother as that would have the same effect as fighting him ourselves. However, we can confirm whether or not you are on the right path as that is within the balance.'

Blindsided by the notion they might truly have to face the god in his physical form, Aliah lashed out in anger.

'Damn your balance. You gods had a fight amongst yourselves and one of your number decided to take off on his own and wreak havoc on our world. You failed to stop him, and now you are expecting us to clean up your mess. Yet you say you cannot give us even the most basic of information to help. If he is not playing by the rules, why should you?'

'Because that would make them as bad as the god they are trying to stop. If they break the rules to capture him, then what is to stop them breaking the rules for other things?' Seamus answered for the god.

Aliah paused, unsure why her friend was standing up for them. As his words sunk in, she grinned. 'A good point, two wrongs do not make it right.'

'But still frustrating?' Seamus raised a quizzical eyebrow.

She laughed out loud. 'Very. Have you finished your questions, or is there something else we need to ask about?'

Seamus sucked thoughtfully on his bottom lip. 'I do have more things to ask about, but I need to think a little on what we learnt tonight, move the pieces around and see how it changes things.'

'Do you want to share?'

'Yes, soon, but not yet.'

'Do not leave it too long. Now, I need some physical activity to work off this frustration.'

Side by side they started at the beginning of their forms to refocus for the night's training.

5
WE NEED A PLAN

Amelia awoke in darkness, shaking, her body drenched in sweat. The door opened and she tensed under the bedclothes.

'Amelia, are you all right? You shouted out again. Are you having another bad dream?'

She relaxed as the welcome voice of Walter filled the blackness. 'Thank you, Walter, I am fine now.'

'Do you want to talk?'

She felt the weight of the bed shift as he sat beside her, then took her hand in his. 'No, really, I am fine.' The mattress moved as he made to stand. Changing her mind, she gripped him tightly. 'No, please do not go. I think maybe we should talk. You might be able to help me understand what is going on inside my head.'

Waiting until he settled back down, she continued. 'The last two nights the same dream haunted me, and I cannot let it go, not even during the day. I am unsure whether my dream is a seeing, or just my imagination creating nightmares.'

Amelia hated relying on someone else, but losing her ability to see, on top of the changes in her gift had shaken her usual confidence. Over the last few days she had begun to wonder if her loss of sight was not to improve her foreseeing, but to teach her a lesson on not being so aloof and arrogant. The need to rely on others simply to move around was teaching her a large dose of humility. An unfortunate side effect was she now questioned other decisions, and even her visions.

'I am not sure I can be of much help. I never studied foretelling and prophecy in any great detail. Caraig would be of more assistance, perhaps we can ask Emer to help us contact him.' Walter's voice sounded uncharacteristically uncertain.

'Caraig has other more pressing duties, like helping to prevent the Carsten army gaining a foothold on the mainland. Besides, all I require is a good old dose of common sense, and you have that in abundance.'

'If you say so.' Walter chuckled. 'Let me get a chair from the other room so I can make myself comfortable.'

Walter and she occupied the suite of rooms across from Seamus and Aliah in the guest wing of the palace.

BATTLE

Although the rooms were not as spacious or ornate, the layout mirrored the suite across the hall in that it contained two bedrooms joined by a common lounge.

Normally Amelia would have preferred a single room to herself, but in the few days since being named seer and her sight being taken, she found having someone close by helped her relax. It may just have been that the sounds of someone else moving filled the silence, but she was self-aware enough to know she also appreciated having help at hand should the darkness overwhelm her.

When they first arrived, Emer offered to share with her. Even though she was busy with other duties, she thought herself best qualified to help Amelia as her own father had not been able to see for most of her life. Travelling from Sanctuary to Hand, Amelia had grown used to Walter's strength, and his ability to assist without suggesting she was unable to do things herself, so she turned the girl down.

Walter returned and placed a chair by the bed. She waited a few moments while he made himself comfortable before speaking.

'Remember the night before last, in Port Marden, you woke me from a horrendous dream?'

'You sounded in such torment, everyone within earshot worried for your safety.' Walter took her hand, which she found reassuring.

'That dream was similar to the one I had tonight. I was somewhere dark and confined and I think physically I could get out, but I was trapped none-the-less. An overwhelming sense of dread filled me every time I thought about leaving. I believe perhaps something dangerous

73

waited there for me.

'Every now and then, I caught a glimpse of things on the outside, and as I watched I gathered information. Perhaps to plan an escape, or for something else. Or maybe I was preparing to fight my captors—no, maybe not that.

'My captor frightened me. In fact, I have never been so scared of anything in my life. He had the power to extinguish my very existence, and he would do it without a second thought.

'Yesterday and tonight's nightmares were similar, only it is growing more intense.' Amelia finished speaking. Walter said nothing. 'What do you think?' she asked, unable to bare the silence any longer.

'Before I answer, I would like to hear what you think.'

She took a moment to gather her jumbled thoughts and calm her nerves before answering. 'After the first night I thought such a vivid and disturbing nightmare might be a reaction to losing my sight. Without being able to see, I do feel somewhat trapped. Although I am sometimes able to make out shadows and shapes, I am saddened to think I will no longer experience the beautiful colours of the world around me. My improved foresight is no where near compensation for losing so much, but it would be a stretch to say I am terrified by the experience.

'Then tonight's dream differed slightly. I was able to glimpse some of my surroundings, and the land was not familiar, which I thought to be strange. Also, I could swear I saw guards in Carsten livery sitting around a fire. I am now wondering if I am having a different type of foreseeing.'

With no immediate response from Walter, the silence

in the room made her uneasy. 'Walter?'

'Sorry, I am thinking, trying to remember something I read once when I was teaching on The Wizard Isles.'

Amelia attempted to quieten her unease, taking calming breaths while she waited for Walter to continue.

'I am not sure what I am going to share is one hundred percent accurate, and I am not in a position to double check my facts. Some time ago, I had a student with the gift of foresight. While teaching him I did some research as he developed some strange abilities. Not only was he able to predict the future, he also experienced what I can only describe as extreme empathy.

'My research into the subject found some of those gifted with foresight are also able to pick up other people's emotional turmoil. Sometimes it assists them in seeing into the future, other times it merely alerts them to someone's distress. Is it possible you are sensing what is happening to someone on the other side of the island?'

'It is definitely possible, except I was not trapped in a cave or prison, or anything else so mundane. If you are pressing for a more accurate description, I would describe myself as being mentally or emotionally trapped.'

'There is more than one way to be held prisoner. Perhaps some of the people over there are being forced to work with the army, or are too scared to leave. Perhaps the person whose emotions you have linked with came into contact with our god friend in Gaius' body. Their reaction to meeting a god might generate enough fear for you to make a connection.'

Amelia considered his words before responding, struggling to capture the essence of her experience to see if

Walter might be right. 'If I am honest, the fear was completely overwhelming, almost paralysing, I do not believe an encounter of that type would generate the crushing fear in my dream. Any other ideas?'

As another frustrating gap in the conversation lengthened, Amelia realised how much she once relied on visual clues to tell her what a person was doing. Had Walter's attention drifted from the conversation? Was he thinking, or had he fallen asleep?

As she waited, she tried to use her other senses to find out what was going on. If she closed her eyes—she did not know why she still did that when she needed to concentrate, but she did—she envisioned someone shuffling through scrolls or books.

'Walter, are you trying to remember something else you read?'

'Yes,' his tone was quizzical. 'Why do you ask?'

Amelia laughed at her discovery and explained it to Walter. This was one way her other senses were developing to help her make up for not being able to see. It appeared once she tuned into a person's thought waves, it was much easier to read their actions, or inactions in this instance.

'That confirms my suspicions. Your abilities definitely lean towards the empathetic side. I think that makes it all the more likely you picked up someone else's feelings while you slept and your mind was more receptive. The question we need to answer now is who might be having intense enough feelings for you to tune into them from so far away?

'Mmm, someone who is trapped? Someone in mortal fear for their life?' he mused.

BATTLE

The image of a lamp being lit and illuminating a room flooded into Amelia's mind. 'Walter, you have worked out who it might be.'

'I believe I may have. Think Amelia. Who do we know of who would consider themselves psychologically trapped, scared to make themselves known in their own body?'

'Oh. Oh, Walter, you clever man. Of course. If a god took over my body I might feel just like I did in the dream. We should tell the others. This might be useful to know.'

'Amelia, it is not yet dawn. Perhaps waking everyone up now is not such a good idea. Shall I go and get us some tea while we wait?'

'Yes please,' Amelia said, and she waited for Walter to leave so she could ready herself for the day.

Sitting by the fire, Aliah sipped her tea and let her mind wander back over Seamus' conversation with the god the night before. The depth of the questions Seamus asked surprised her, and annoyed her as well. They were a team. They should be working together. So why did he not discuss his ideas with her first?

As her tea cooled, her anger bubbled. Seamus had been taking the lead in almost everything since they passed their trials. It was almost as though fighting the god was his personal crusade, and she had been relegated to supporter and ego booster.

The more she dwelled on it, the angrier she became. How dare he slot her into the traditional role of a woman, being supportive rather than active? Besides, Emer already filled that role, he did not need her hanging round cheering him on as well.

Oh, she stopped herself. That was unfair. Emer was not only a guard by profession, but she had taken on the dangerous role of scouting for the group. Aliah was ashamed she used the girl's growing fondness for Seamus against her, even if only in her mind.

Gazing into the flames of the fire, she went back through the past few days and considered her actions. Soon her anger was as cold as her tea. It struck her Seamus was not responsible for her background role, she had relegated herself to supporter.

When she failed to leave the trial area by the allotted time, the gods took her away. She was only here because Seamus came and rescued her. From that moment she had been proving to herself, and to the others, that she deserved the title of Warrior. While she concentrated on showing her worthiness, she had forgotten who she was, and what she could contribute outside of the gifts the gods bestowed on her.

This ends now.

Having given herself a wakeup call, she decided it was Seamus' turn. Thinking they had much to discuss before they met with the others, she walked over to his room. She knocked and flung open the door in one movement, only to gasp in embarrassment and walk straight back out.

'Well, that is a sight I can never un-see,' she said when Seamus entered the room a few moments later, clothed and ready to face the day. Her attempt at lightening the situation failed dismally.

'It is traditional to knock and wait to be invited into

someone's sleeping quarters, especially when they are from the opposite sex,' Seamus commented dryly as he poured himself some tea, still unable to look her in the face. 'Perhaps if you did, you would not walk in on people when they are not fully dressed.'

Or not clothed at all. 'Sorry.'

Blushing with embarrassment, the one word apology was all she was able to manage.

'So, what have you made your mind up about?' he asked as he sat down in the chair opposite.

'How do you know I have decided anything?' she countered, playing for time as she attempted to compose herself.

'You always get impatient when you make a decision, as though you think you will change your mind if you do not immediately act on it.'

Aliah sighed. She disliked it when people guessed her thoughts. Then again, if she and Seamus were to work closely together, maybe it was not such a bad thing. Still, it would not do their relationship any good if he learnt he could read her so easily.

'Well, you are wrong. I only wanted to talk about what happened last night, and agree how we move forward from here so we can present a united front.'

'Thank the Goddess.' Seamus' response was unexpected, and momentarily stopped her in her tracks.

'What do you mean by that?'

The temper she calmed earlier flared again. Seamus looked like an animal caught in a trap as he lowered his eyes and flicked an imaginary fleck of something off his trousers.

'I am not sure I should say, given your tone.'

'No, tell me what is on your mind,' Aliah insisted, sitting forward on the edge of her chair.

Working really hard, she managed to push her anger down so she could focus on what Seamus had to say, and not react straight away.

'All right.' Seamus sounded skeptical but ploughed on in spite of his fears. 'Recently you seemed more interested in your warrior training than actually thinking about how we are going to defeat our enemy. You have pretty much left all the planning to me.'

'I have not.' The words escaped from Aliah's lips before she could stop them. 'Sorry, maybe you are right. It is just hard to listen to someone else say that.'

Seamus took a deep breath. 'At the risk of you snapping my head off again ... over the last couple of six-days you have been working on being more like a leader, and part of that is allowing people to work to their strengths and you taking more of a behind the scenes role but ...'

Seamus stopped and looked at her, as if deciding whether or not it was safe for him to continue. She forced herself to calmly meet his gaze, hiding the hurt his words caused. It was one thing telling yourself off, but someone else doing it, however much the criticism was justified, was difficult to take.

'Well, I do not think you were chosen as the Warrior for your measured thinking and ability to let others take the lead. I think we need your spark and, dare I say it, the way you sometimes just act on instinct. No one can predict when you might do that, and I believe it is a weapon we will need when we face our final battle.'

BATTLE

'Oh.' No one had ever praised her impetuous actions before.

'It is bad enough I must dither and think things through until I understand it from every angle. If you are doing that too or, even worse, not making any decisions at all, then I am worried we will not be able to act decisively when the time comes.' Seamus sunk back into the chair, as if a great weight had been lifted from his shoulders.

'Oh,' Aliah said again. It was more of a placeholder while she organised her thoughts, than her actual response. 'So you think I have not been pulling my weight?' It sounded like an accusation, although she did not mean it to.

'Well … I would not have put it so bluntly.'

'Sorry, Seamus, I did not mean to say that out loud, or to attack you. In fact, I was sitting here thinking something very similar before I came and got you. I admit I concentrated so much on proving myself the Warrior and a leader, I forgot so much of warfare is not about the battle, but about the preparation and planning. A good leader should concentrate on both. And a good partner should be more supportive.'

Seamus sat forward to speak.

'No, please wait a minute, I need to get this all out. While we are being honest, I must confess I am a little intimidated by your foresight. If you are already certain about what we should do, what more can I contribute?'

Now everything was out in the open, relief surged through Aliah and she felt a renewed sense of vigour.

In contrast, Seamus' earlier energy seemed to leave his body, and he slumped even further in the chair.

Only then did Aliah realise the mistake she and the others had been making. They always stated they were working as a team, but in reality, they had been relying on Seamus to move them in the right direction. So rather than supporting him, their actions increased the pressure.

'Seamus, how reliable is your gift at predicting our best course of action?'

Seamus stared at the floor.

'When I know something for certain it is as though a piece of a puzzle has finally fallen into place. I can almost hear the click. Like yesterday when I sensed all the people we needed to defeat the god were here.

'Almost everything else is far less reliable. For instance, when we talked about how to stop the Carsten invasion I believed we needed to remove the king or the battle would continue until many died. What I did not know was how to do that, or whether or not we would succeed.'

'So ...' Aliah strung the word out while she sifted through the information in her head. 'How much are you certain of? Are you sure of what we need to do to defeat the god? And by sure, I mean what do you know for a certainty from your gifts?'

Seamus raised his head, displaying the worry in his eyes. 'Just what I told you, all the people we need are gathered here.'

'What about retrieving the casket?'

'That is an odd one. I cannot tell if it is important for us to find it, or if it is enough that we stop the god from getting his hands on it.'

'So, the casket and anything else is speculation? Even

the questions you asked last night?'

'Yes. Everything has been spinning around in my head since we arrived. Yesterday was helpful in that some ideas began to form. Until then, it was like looking at thousands of puzzle pieces, not knowing which ones were important, and which were not. Last night helped clarify the relevant pieces, and I feel a little more confident of the direction we should be looking in.'

'Not to mention having it confirmed from on high we might not get to fight the god until he is here in Aria.'

Seamus smiled a wry smile. 'Yes, that was a bit of a worry. Still, better to find out now than later. I have been forming a plan to fight him in person, but I view it more as a worst case scenario option.'

'Well, at least we agree on that. He is scary enough when he speaks into our minds, I shudder to think what it would be like facing him at his most powerful.

'So. What does this plan look like so far?' Aliah asked.

Seamus found the imaginary piece of lint on his trousers again.

'Seamus?'

'It does not look like much really. I believe we need to isolate him so we are not distracted when we face him. Which means the other's role must be to protect us while we deal with the god.

'We need the casket, although I am not sure whether we need the power it contains or the casket itself, and we need to send him back to his home.'

'Mm, not really a detailed plan, is it?'

'I guess not,' Seamus admitted. 'I have been focusing more on ways to control him, or be rid of him before he gains his full strength. I believe we have a better chance of success if we face him when he has not gained enough energy to be fully here.'

'Have you considered he might be weakened by reuniting with his, like you were after the battle the other day?'

Seamus' head jerked up. Clearly this had not occurred to him. 'No. So if he does make it here, we need to attack him quickly, before he recovers. That means we cannot let him get too far away from Hand.'

'So, you sure you want to fight him before he has his body? He has Gaius' power at the moment and he is quite a strong wizard.' Aliah just wanted to be certain Seamus had thought everything through.

'Yes, I am. Gaius' power is from here and we know how it works, as well as its limitations. I would rather face his magic than the power I sensed in the gods.'

Aliah sighed with relief. 'Me too. You also asked about the god's name last night. I appreciate you think it might be able to be used against him, but have you figured out who he is, or are you still working that out?'

'I am not certain of his name, but I think there is something in the library that might help me figure it out. If I find it, I do not want to say it out loud, or write it down, in case his attention is drawn to us before we are ready. The element of surprise might come in useful.'

Aliah thought for a while, and weighed her need to know against the usefulness of knowing now. Realising there were more important things to discuss before the others arrived, she decided to let it go.

'Back to our main problem,' she started, not sure how Seamus would take the next bit. 'You need to stop taking so much on yourself, and perhaps tell us if you are worried about something. If we had all understood your gift a little better, we would not have relied on you to set our course quite so much. You would have felt less pressure, and would have behaved less like a spoilt brat.'

'Oh.' Lost for words, Seamus traced his finger thoughtfully over his lips. 'So while you should have been acting like more of a leader, I should have been acting less like a dictator?'

Aliah laughed out loud. 'That is one way of looking at it, but I am serious. You need to accept a little more help.'

'All right, you made your point. We should have more talks like this,' Seamus said dryly.

Not sure whether or not he was being sarcastic, Aliah decided to take him at face value. 'Yes, we should, because if we cannot be open with each other, how can we even consider taking on a god together?'

'I am not sure we should,' Seamus responded.

Aliah laughed, but when Seamus did not join in, she stopped dead. He was serious.

'Seamus, what do you mean?' Aliah said the words slowly, suddenly fearful of where this conversation was leading, but deep down knowing it was important she understood what was going on in Seamus' head.

'Aliah, we can plan all we want, research all we want, and train all we want, but I have to say I have serious doubts about whether we can actually take on this god and win.' The words were wooden, and Seamus would not raise his eyes to meet hers.

'Well, it is a bit late for this,' Aliah responded, a shiver of fear running through her. How could they save Aria if

Seamus was not fully committed? 'If you were not prepared to do this, we should never have gone to Sanctuary to be tested.'

Slowly Seamus raised his head and reluctantly met her gaze. 'I will follow through what we started, Aliah, because there is no one else to do it. But our last fight with the god showed me how woefully unprepared we are, and I cannot help thinking maybe there is someone out there better able to win this battle than me.'

'Than us, Seamus. Than *us*.'

'Us then. But this is not some training exercise, Aliah. This is perhaps the biggest battle in the history of our land, and our chances of success are not good.'

'Well, Seamus, we will not be letting you stand before the troops to rally them for battle, will we?'

When Seamus' head dropped again, Aliah realised her attempt to inject some humour into the situation had fallen flat. This called for a more heartfelt approach. Moving from her chair, and crouching so Seamus could see her face, she tried again.

'Seamus, if you think we do not all know the odds are against us in this fight, then you are wrong. Just because we do not dwell on it does not mean we forget the stakes are high, for us as well as for Aria.' Holding his gaze so he would know the truth of her words, she saw the moment they sunk in.

'So, we can sit here and wallow in our worry, or we can get out there and do the best we can with what we have—which is quite a lot by the way.' She stood up and looked down at the top of his head. 'I know what I choose to do.'

BATTLE

Seamus finished dressing quickly and slipped out of the suite he shared with Aliah. There was something he wanted to do before he met with everyone else.

Walking briskly to the library, he experienced a confidence he had not felt in days. This he was good at. Searching through scrolls, finding information, putting together a plan. If this was all the Wizard was expected to do then he was fine.

It was not though. At some stage he was expected to battle a god and win. This was the bit he was not so sure about. He still felt sick at the thought of what he had done to turn back the Carsten ships from Port Marden.

His actions caused a whole ship of people to be blown up. Oh, Aliah could talk all she wanted about not being responsible for how people responded to something they did, and part of him believed that. Still, the guilt weighed heavy.

Then he had pushed those ships out to sea. It had seemed a good idea at the time, but he had not considered whether or not he was able to move the fleet without killing the thousands of souls on those vessels.

It was those decisions that needed to be made in the heat of battle that scared him. He had not trained to be a guard or a soldier. He had been educated to be a duke, someone who had time to think through all the options and consult with others before making a decision.

Mentally shaking himself, he remembered Aliah's words. *"We can sit here and wallow in our worry, or we can get out there and do the best we can with what we have."*

She was always so confident, or at least she appeared so on the outside. Maybe that was her secret, if you act as though you can do something, perhaps you eventually believe you actually can. There and then he decided he would hide his fears and do his best. And then maybe he too would come to believe in their eventual success.

Nodding a greeting to the guard on duty, he opened the door to the library and slipped inside. Searching through the documents they had read through, he found what he was looking for; a scroll of the creation myth.

Yesterday he had cast it aside, today he was not so sure. Now he knew names were important when dealing with gods, he thought he should learn more about them. Opening the scroll, he skipped the first stanzas about how the creator of all built the physical worlds, looking for the bit where he created his children to tend his creation. Then he stopped.

Wait a moment, yesterday Amelia had said they could send the god back to his own world. This might actually be important as it appeared many a truth had been hidden in myths and legends.

"In the void of before The Great Creator used all that was around to build a home, populating it with plants and animals. The Creator was happy. With nothing left to do, he again entered the void and built a new world, and then another, and another, until he used up all that was around him.

Returning home, the Creator was too tired to continue tending to the numerous worlds he had made so, in one final burst of creativity, he birthed children to help tend to his creations."

Before reading on, Seamus stopped to consider how this information might help. It confirmed the idea there were a number of worlds out there other than their own, one of which was the home world of the gods. He read on.

The next section told him the Creator birthed four boys and four girls, something he already knew. Running quickly through the females: Zoia, Goddess of Life; Xira, Goddess of Land; Armonia, Goddess of Harmony; Polema, Goddess of War; he moved onto the male gods.

In opposition to the females, the male gods represented death, water, chaos and peace. Logically he thought it unlikely Erinos, the God of Peace, would start a war. Given the Wexler monastery was dedicated to the oceans, the God of Water could likely be ruled out as well.

Death? Or chaos? It could be either. He would need to do some more digging. Rolling up the scroll, he had just returned it to the shelf when the door opened behind him and the others began wandering in.

Everyone except for Boss sat around the table in the library. Given the recent discussions about someone in the household spying on them, the retired soldier elected to stand guard to ensure their privacy. So far Robin had been the only one to venture down the corridor, and only then to ask if they needed any refreshments. When Boss explained they would be happy to go to the kitchens themselves, he left. Pauley slipped in behind him, declaring he was too young to spend the day sitting around in a library.

After Amelia told them of her dream the night before, there had been a brief discussion. Prompted by Aliah, Seamus then told them what he found during their nightly training session, after which they sat quietly, waiting for Emer to return.

I can sense your impatience, Seamus, but I am truly flying as fast as I can. I can see my bedroom window and will be with you soon.

I am not impatient, Seamus sent.

Hah.

All right, a little, but I was worried as well.

I have done this before. No one saw me. Patience now.

Emer's presence left his mind and Seamus turned his attention back to the map of Hand in front of him. The Isle of Hand was divided by a mountain range; giving the island the fertile ground around Hand Harbour, a high plateau where most of the island's cattle and sheep grazed, and the coastal flats on the other side of the island which was the primary source of seafood for the locals.

Without the mountains, it would take two days to ride coast to coast. With them, it usually took three or more, depending on how well you knew your way through twisting alpine paths.

The mountains were bisected by four passes, two from this side of the island; the Low Pass which led from Port Hand to the village of Wexon, and the High Pass which was more northerly and led to the village of High Hand. The other two passes connected the fishing villages of North Piscine and South Piscine with the rest of the island.

BATTLE

Lord Wexler's lands were almost directly due south of Port Hand, on the southern end of the high plateau. Close by as the crow flies, the mountain range added time, making the journey take the best part of a day. Not far from the manor was the small village of Wexon, which serviced the farms in the region. The land given to the Brotherhood of the Elm was closer to the coast, between the village and Baron Wexler's holdings.

Aware the Carsten fleet waited off the North West Coast, and were likely using North Piscine as their base, they would not be able to confirm any further details until Emer returned. Almost as though his thoughts had called her to him, the door opened, admitting the shapeshifting girl.

All eyes turned expectantly to Emer as her report on enemy activity would largely dictate their next moves. Gathering round the map, they all watched while Emer described her fly over the enemy position.

'Given they have now been anchored off the coast of Hand for a full six-day, it was surprising how many soldiers are still living onboard ships. Row boats were moving between them and the land, dropping soldiers, then coming back in. From the sky it looked as though they are giving groups shore leave, rather than disembarking the entire army.

'Some of the ships sailed off towards Port Marden, I assume for their daily attack. Apart from that, activity on the other vessels was limited to a few watchmen.

'The leadership is in North Piscine as we expected, but the village is not fortified in any way. They removed people from their homes and commandeered fishing boats to transport soldiers, but little else. It is almost as though they are not planning to stay. There are patrols around the village, and it did look as though a garrison was building a camp near the High Pass.'

Having completed her report Emer stepped back and waited for questions.

'Are there any other signs of what they might be doing militarily?' Daniel asked.

'Apart from the gathering of soldiers near the High Pass, as best as I can tell, they seem to be waiting.'

'For what?' Liam pondered out loud, and started pacing around the map as though looking at it from a different angle might give him some new ideas.

'What about the people from North Piscine?' Seamus asked, frowning.

'There were some heading through the High Pass towards High Hand. Still others were making their way towards the Lower Pass. A tent town has sprung up on the outskirts of South Piscine. Also, I saw people packing things into fishing boats there, I believe some may be preparing to leave.'

'Surely they would not brave the treacherous waters around the southern coast? They would be risking their lives at this time of year,' Seamus worried.

'I think we should be more concerned about the men on those warships. There are a lot of them, and their provisions must be nearly gone after such a long sea voyage. There is little in the way of food on the coastal flats, meaning soon they will have no option but to head to the High Plateau. I believe the garrison is securing access to the main route to the rest of Hand. From there, they will be able to raid the farms on the High Plateau.'

BATTLE

Seamus looked at his cousin in surprise.

'What? Do you think all I do around here is fetch and carry for your father? I listen and learn as well,' Liam scolded.

'I think you are right, Liam,' Daniel chipped in. 'I would do the same thing in their position. Manage the passes and you control all the farm land on the island. Once they are secure, you can move your army around at will.'

'I thought you preferred to be just a soldier,' Aliah joked with Daniel, who ignored her, turning back to the duke's squire.

'Liam, how many of the barons left with your uncle to join the fight from Port Marden?'

'None,' the squire answered. 'They all remained with at least half of their guards just in case the invaders tried to use Hand as a base to invade the mainland.'

'So, as I understand it, we need to make sure the Carstenites stay on the coastal side of the North and South Passes otherwise we will lose the island's entire source of food, and most of its defence force. Not only will their presence on the plateau place us in danger, but we will not be able to search for the casket as easily if they control the island. If they are setting up a base camp then they intend to move in the next few days.'

'That is exactly what I thought,' Liam said, and the two turned to the rest of the group who had been silently watching in wonder as the two military minds worked their own special magic.

'So my plan is ...' Daniel started.

'Hold on there,' Aliah interrupted. 'We need to consider

everything together. Seamus' information from last night, Amelia's dream of Gaius, all we learnt yesterday, and of course Emer's report. We have to fit in a lot of things over the next few days.'

'Or we need to split up to cover them all,' Dominic suggested.

The frown on Aliah's face told them she was trying hard not to contradict the spy, causing Seamus to smile in pleasure at the old Aliah's return.

'We can certainly consider that option,' Aliah finally forced out. 'Although I had assumed we would stay together from here on in. After all, both Seamus and Amelia said we were all together for a reason.'

Before the two began an argument, Seamus decided it was time to speak up. 'As I explained before, Aliah, I know it is right we are here now, but I cannot tell you if we are all meant to stay together until our confrontation with the god. Do you have any ideas Amelia?'

His aunt frowned, then shook her head. 'If only foreseeing provided all the answers … in truth, I am unable to tell one way or the other.'

'In the absence of any "feelings" to the contrary we can consider all our options. As I see it, we need to motivate the barons left on the island to defend the passes. We also need to make sure we read all the documents we can about the Wexlers and the Brotherhood of the Elm before we approach them. Having done our research, we have to retrieve the casket and use it to imprison the god's essence.' Seamus finished summarising and waited for ideas. He did not have to wait long.

'If we must split up, then I think we should leave

Walter and Amelia here to research, Liam and Daniel should go and talk to the barons, and you and I should go and speak with Baron Wexler and retrieve the chest.' Aliah outlined her plan and as soon as she finished a massive argument erupted.

Seamus dropped his arms to the table and placed his head on top. This was not one of the times when his foresight would help him dictate a path, and he had no idea of how to begin to moderate the strong personalities voicing their opinions around him.

6
WE HAVE A PLAN

How could one comment cause so much dissent? Unable to hear herself think over the raised voices, let alone call everyone to order for a reasoned discussion, Aliah placed her hands over her ears. Dominic touched her arm to get her attention.

'You need to manage this.' He leaned in close to speak, so close his warm breath brushed against her cheek.

She closed her eyes, wishing the scene away. Dominic was right, someone needed to take control and keep everyone focused on the task at hand, and it may as well be her.

'Quiet,' she yelled, and to her surprise, the room fell silent. Seamus even took his head off his arms and reengaged.

'Maybe I picked the wrong people for the wrong jobs, but the idea itself is sound. Let us talk this through rationally, each having our say and listening to the others.'

Now she appreciated how the tutors in Bannock felt when faced with a bunch of unruly children. When she returned home, she owed them an apology.

'Firstly, let us talk about the research we need to do. Does anyone doubt Walter is the best scholar among us?'

She took their silence as agreement and was about to move on to her next point when Seamus raised his hand. She nodded for him to speak.

'While I agree Walter is the better scholar, I might need to use the knowledge he finds out, and so might you.'

'Yes, I would guess so, but surely he can keep us updated on anything he learns.'

'What if there is a problem and he cannot pass something critical to our success on to us? Something that might be the difference between winning and ... well, you know.'

'That is a good point.' Aliah twirled her plait before answering. 'Am I right in thinking it is only one day to Wexon from here?'

Seamus nodded.

'And at least two days if you were coming via the northern routes?'

'More like three and a bit,' he said.

'All right, we can stay behind for two days and gather as much information as we can, then head to Wexon.'

Seamus agreed and she was relieved to have passed

her first hurdle.

'Right. Amelia needs to stay with Walter to help with interpreting anything he finds.' There was no further dissent.

'As I said before, Liam and Daniel can go talk to the barons and ask them to move their guards to the passes.'

Up until then she had been doing so well, but an eruption of voices followed her last comment as they all tried to shout over each other.

Aliah held up her hand and raised her voice so she could be heard above the noise. 'One at a time, please. Daniel, you go first.'

'I am an Arian Guard. What makes you think the barons will listen to me?'

'Why do you think I am sending Liam with you?'

Liam burst out laughing. 'You think they will listen to me, the son of a minor noble, squire to the duke? Sending me is an insult.'

Aliah frowned. 'I had not thought of that. As Seamus' cousin I always assumed you were as high born as him, especially as no one in the family treats you differently.'

'My father is Duchess Elise's brother. As nephew to a baron he is a minor noble, who manages the duchy business out of Port Marden. While we do not make distinctions of rank within our family, other nobles certainly do.'

'How annoying!' Aliah tugged on her plait again. Liam and Daniel were tasked with keeping them safe while they learnt how to battle the god, and now it seemed like they would not be able to do their job because they were not suitably high enough in rank. 'We cannot send Seamus ...'

'They would not listen to Seamus either,' Liam interrupted. 'The island is small, and by now everyone will have heard about Seamus' magic. They would not allow him in their homes, not even if he carried the Ducal Seal, and not even as the King's Ambassador.'

'But they would let you in, Aliah.' Daniel realised where Liam was heading, and provided the solution.

Silence. No one else spoke. Seamus sat there with a wry smile on his face as though he was enjoying this, and the rest of the group were looking expectantly at her.

'You cannot be serious. It is common knowledge Arians are not well liked on the island, and I know nothing about Hand Protocol. I might single handedly set Hand-Arian relations back centuries without even realising I was doing it.'

'Take Robin with you,' Seamus suggested, his eyes twinkling with amusement. 'He has been desperate to help, and this would give him something practical to do.'

'But I will need to be with you when we face the god.'

How would she and Seamus train if they were not together? And what would happen if the god attacked either of them while there were apart?

'Half a day to Baron Tappit, on this side of the High Pass. One day to Baron George on the other side, and a little over half a day to Baron Rassmussen near the Northern Pass. If you stay overnight with Rassmussen, that gives you time to meet with Seamus near the South Pass after we have searched through the scrolls,' Amelia informed them.

The older woman had been silent since she told them all about her adventure into Gaius' mind the previous night, but it appeared she continued to listen to the discussion.

'But what about our training?' Aliah looked to Seamus for support.

He chewed his lip. 'Last night we were repeating the same exercises together. We can check with our trainer tonight, but maybe there is no more they are able to teach us. Or perhaps we can practice on our own.' He did not look convinced or happy about the thought of them being parted.

Aliah frowned back. 'But what if it is not enough?'

Seamus shrugged. 'I do not know, Aliah. We can only ask.'

'What if something happens while we are apart?' She was unable to shake the feeling it was a bad idea for them to split up.

'I will be here with Seamus, and I can fly to where ever you are in a very short time.' Emer told them.

Although she looked uncomfortable, with all her arguments countered Aliah had nowhere else to go. Tossing her plait over her shoulder she said, 'Right, Daniel, Dominic and I leave tomorrow with Robin to tackle the barons, unless our nocturnal trainer vetoes our plan. We meet with Seamus, Emer, Walter, Amelia and Liam at the South Pass at around midday in four days.

'In the meantime, they spend two days gathering all the information they can, travel to Wexon to get the casket and wait for us near the pass. Emer will carry messages between the groups as needed. Simple.'

'I think you should take Boss and Pauley with you, as you might need the extra protection in case the Carsten soldiers send out some scouting parties,' Seamus offered.

'What about you? You might need support as well.'

'With two magicians and two soldiers in our party I think we will be fine.'

About to argue, Aliah stopped herself. Boss would be a welcome set of hands on this journey, and she always enjoyed Pauley's company. Although part of her wished to command the boy to stay behind, safe in the palace, experience taught her he would just follow them anyway.

Before turning back to the group to sort out the finer details of their travel arrangements, she wondered what Pauley was doing now. With no one to keep an eye on him, he would no doubt be up to all sorts of mischief.

Keeping to the shadows, the young boy crept around the stables and stopped at the end of the block. Risking a quick peek, he pulled his head back as the man he followed turned to check he was alone. Counting to ten, Pauley attempted another look.

Robin had moved to the shelter of a large oak tree and stared down at something in his hands, glancing furtively over his shoulder every few seconds to ensure no one crept up behind him.

Unfortunately the Chamberlain's body was between Pauley and the object, hiding it from view. When the older man turned again to check his surroundings, the boy managed a fleeting glimpse.

His eyes must be playing tricks because it appeared the object in Robin's hands was a common tin mirror.

BATTLE

Surely all this creeping around and hiding was not to provide him with opportunities to gaze adoringly at himself.

Having assured once again he was alone, Robin fixed his attention on the mirror. Sensing this might be his only opportunity to find out more, Pauley slipped from the edge of the stables, running swiftly to a tree. If he timed it right, and was quiet enough, he should be able to loop round through the underbrush until he was in line with Robin. From there he would be able to get a better view of what the man was up to.

As he prepared to move to the next tree, a loud crack pierced the crisp morning air. In his haste he had stepped on a rotting branch.

Ducking back behind the tree, he held his breath and closed his eyes. Shutting out the world would not help him hide, but it helped calm his nerves. This time he counted to fifty before risking a quick look. He was rewarded with a view of Robin's back as he disappeared behind the other side of the stables, returning to the palace.

'Goddess,' Pauley cursed as he left his hiding place, almost able to see his mother's frown as he spoke the curse. He felt justified though. Robin was up to something, and if he had been a little more careful, he would have found out what it was. Well, he would find out eventually, just not today.

For a moment he considered whether or not he should tell Boss about his concerns. The older man was far more experienced in this type of thing, and he might be able to give him some ideas on what to do next.

Shaking his head, he decided to wait a little. He had

no evidence Robin was doing anything wrong, just a gut feeling and a description of some unusual activity which might be easily explained away. He would keep an eye on him. No doubt there would be another chance to catch the creep out.

Although the evening air was cool, Seamus and Aliah removed their jackets in preparation for the training session. Normally they waited for the god to call for them, but tonight they had much they needed to cover, and so decided to wait for their tutor in the courtyard. Rushing through his warm-up, Seamus went over different ways to ask for what he wanted in his head.

'Seamus, slow down. In such a confined space we need to move together if we are not to get in each other's way.' Aliah interrupted his thoughts.

'Oh, all right.'

Seamus stopped, watched until he knew where Aliah was in the sequence of moves they used to loosen up, then joined her. Once back into the rhythm, his mind again focused on his problem.

We need to be able to work as one over long distances. That would not work. What if the gods did not want them to be apart in the first place, he would be handing them an opportunity to forbid it. *Do we need to be together …*

His arm hit something solid and Seamus looked up to find Aliah rubbing her own arm and glaring accusingly at him.

'Seamus, be careful.' Aliah's voice was grumpy.

BATTLE

Shaking his head, he asked, 'What?'

'You just flung out your arm and punched me. Keep your mind on what you are doing, can you?'

'Sorry, I was just ...'

'Tonight we will work on linking without touching. This will require you to work together in harmony.' The god with the face of the Arian Goddess appeared in front of them, a ghost of a smile hovering around her lips. Either she had been watching them warm up and was amused, or there was another reason for her smile.

'Were you reading my mind?' Seamus demanded.

'Seamus, we are gods. If we want to find out what is happening anywhere with anyone we only need to think on it. We learnt of your plans and, although we do not approve, we can think of no better way for you to proceed. So we will assist in this small way.'

Aliah's laugh cut through the night air as Seamus blushed. Sometimes he felt so in charge of everything, other times things like this occurred, reminding him control was merely an illusion.

'Right, let us start. Seamus stand where you are. Aliah take two steps back. Excellent. Now, this works exactly the same as when you are touching. Seamus, you first. Reach down into your body, find your magic, then push it out slowly towards Aliah until you can feel her.'

Seamus took a deep breath, closed his eyes and began the process Walter taught him some time ago to touch his magic. As he slowly pushed his magical essence out towards Aliah, he hit a wall.

'You can sense this is different already. When you touch a person, you breach the natural barrier surrounding their body, so linking minds is easier.

'Try again, and at the same time, Aliah, you need to gently reach out and find Seamus' essence then guide it to you.'

Seamus reached out again and soon touched Aliah's barrier. A moment later there was a tentative pull of what he could only describe as "Aliahness". He grabbed for her and she disappeared. He opened his eyes to a frowning goddess.

'Patience, young man. Combining magical essences is not like a handshake between soldiers, more like a kiss between lovers.'

Seamus grimaced at the image the goddess created, and tried again. This time he was gentler. Instead of grasping for Aliah, he imagined passing a knife through butter and managed to link minds with his warrior.

The goddess had them repeat the exercise to ensure Seamus' technique was perfect. Then she asked Aliah to take a step back, and then another. At each point Seamus managed to connect minds with her, until they were five steps apart. By then his energy was flagging, and he could no longer join with her.

The goddess bid them rest, and when they restarted, it was Aliah's turn.

'We know you managed to share energy with Seamus once before, but it was clumsy, as have been all your attempts since. You need to learn how to make the connection faultlessly with Seamus while touching, before you can move to making the link when you are apart.'

Aliah scowled, but she did not voice her objections. Instead her face became a mask of concentration as she attempted to do as she was bid.

Seamus' skin tingled as Aliah reached out, tentatively at first, then her "Aliahness" surged through, and they were connected.

'Now, do it without the sword.'

'What? Are you crazy?' Aliah turned on the goddess. 'I can only do this because I have the sword.'

'That is where you are wrong. You only connect with the sword because you have the ability to link with magic. It is not an active magical talent, but it is an important one.'

'Like Boss' daughter,' Seamus said under his breath.

'Sorry?' Aliah looked confused.

'Boss' daughter, Megan, could not perform magic, but she sensed when others used it, or had magical abilities.'

'You are correct, Seamus. There are many people with passive magical talents. They are generally no use to them except in the presence of other magic. Now, Aliah, put your sword down and try again. Reach inside yourself until you find the essence that is you, bring it up along your arm and push it towards Seamus.'

Aliah concentrated, trying again and again to connect. Each time she tried, she grew more irritated, until her frustrations finally bubbled over.

'I cannot do it.'

'Yes, you can.' The goddess was not moved by Aliah's anger.

'Remember it took me a while to do this, and I had been training to use my magic for some time.' Seamus' attempt at support fell flat as Aliah glared at him.

'Try again,' the goddess ordered, not prepared to give in to Aliah's show of temper.

Seamus was pleased she said that because he was sure if the words had come from his mouth, Aliah would have snapped his head off. Not that she would not do the same to a god, it was just a little less likely. For a moment, he thought she was actually going to refuse, then she sighed with resignation and closed her eyes.

This time Seamus could feel a slight warmth on his skin.

'Nearly there,' he said in encouragement, and the warmth disappeared.

Aliah uttered a curse more suited to a soldier's barracks than a princess and shot him a look full of daggers, before taking a deep breath and trying again. This time the warmth was a little stronger, and Seamus sent a little of his energy to greet it. As if sensing him, Aliah crashed through the barrier and joined him. Her face lit up with a fleeting look of triumph, before it was replaced with dismay as her presence abruptly disappeared.

'I am barely able to link with Seamus when I am touching him, and he cannot connect with me if he is further than four steps away.' Defeat sounded in her words as her shoulders slumped.

'And you leave tomorrow.' Seamus understood why she was so upset.

'Did you not hear me before? You have the ability to link to anything magical. Your sword, other people with magic …' The goddess stopped as if waiting for Aliah to catch up with her line of thought.

'I know I cannot practice with my sword so that means I need to find someone to work with?'

She looked to the goddess to see if she was correct.

BATTLE

'And ...'

A frown appeared between Aliah's brows. Seamus himself could not see where this was leading. 'But Walter is staying with Seamus. I cannot practice with him.'

'Dominic.' The name fell out of Seamus' mouth before the thought was fully formed in his brain. 'Dominic's ability to blend in with his surroundings is a form of magic.'

Aliah's frown deepened. 'You are suggesting I train with him?'

The goddess looked at Aliah, head tilted to the side. 'I see, no, that would not work. The young boy who travels with you. You could train with him.'

Having considered the options, Aliah slowly nodded her head. 'Yes, that would be acceptable.'

'And you, Seamus, should train with Walter. Now be aware, you do not need to make a full connection with these people, you just need to practice making the link.

'There are rules to this. You must first get their permission, and you must promise not to share with others anything you find while linked. You also need to be aware your connection will not be as strong with your training partners as it is between the two of you. Your magics complement each other, like two halves of a whole, and nothing will ever be as strong as your bond together.

'Although your training is not as complete as we would like, we will not come to you both again unbidden. It is moving close to the time when you will confront our brother, and we cannot be seen to be helping you in your confrontation with him in any direct way. Seamus, if you have any questions on how to use your magic in general, we can still help you, but that is about all.

'I can see little of your path ahead from here, and what I see leads to sadness. Then again, all possible paths from this point lead to sorrow. All that is left is for me to wish you god speed and good luck.'

The goddess blinked out of sight and, suddenly exhausted, Seamus bent over, placing his hands on his knees, drawing in deep breaths, attempting to control his panic.

'Sadness,' he whispered. 'Our way ahead is paved with sadness. Maybe we should not do this?' He looked up to see Aliah shaking her head.

'She said we might find sorrow down which ever path we take. She also said there is not a better option. We went over this time and time again. We should proceed as planned.'

Seamus' body sagged a little with relief, and the heaviness in his heart eased. It was great to have the Aliah of old back to share the burden.

'She forgot to send us to sleep,' Aliah gasped.

Realising she was right, and that they would not wake rested tomorrow, Seamus groaned. 'Of all the nights for one of them to forget, it had to be the night before a busy few days. Best we try and get what little sleep we can then.' He sighed as he picked up Aliah's sword and handed it to her.

As they headed back inside the palace, they glimpsed movement in the shadows. Stopping, Aliah drew her sword and it glowed at her command, dispelling some of the darkness around them. Going first, Aliah checked the courtyard and found nothing there.

BATTLE

'We must be tired,' she said as she sheathed her sword and carried on inside.

Glancing behind him as he entered the doorway, Seamus caught another movement out of the corner of his eye. Unease flowed through him as he closed the door and rammed the bolt home behind them, and it did not leave until they were safely back in their quarters.

Darkness pressed in on her as the sweat on her brow began to cool, making her shiver. Sitting up, she took deep breaths, trying to calm her frantically beating heart. While she was no closer to finding out what danger her dream foretold, she now knew what she had to do.

'Amelia?' Walter's voice came from the doorway. 'Are you all right?'

'Did I scream out again?' A frown creased her brow, this was happening far too often. Her decision to leave Sanctuary to support Seamus and Aliah meant she postponed her training as a seer. Perhaps once she returned, she would be better able to control her visions.

'No,' Walter reassured her. 'I was reading by the fire when I heard you muttering.'

'It was another dream,' Amelia told him.

'A foretelling?'

Amelia closed her eyes. 'Yes and no. I sensed great danger, but that is nothing new given the circumstances we find ourselves in. There was nothing specific, but ... now I am awake, I realise something is telling me my path is not to stay here with you and Seamus, I must travel to visit the barons with Aliah.'

She did not need her eyes to sense the growing tension in the room.

'Amelia, are you sure that is wise?'

Walter's voice was filled with concern. Of course he would not come straight out and say he thought her travelling without him to guide her was foolish. He understood her well enough to appreciate it would play to her stubborn streak, and she would go regardless of what he thought.

No, he would share his worry with her, the very same worries she herself had, and his concern would make her pause and think. If only she had known how difficult it was to make a decision when you cared for someone, she might have let her heart remain in the box she had kept it in for most of her adult life.

Taking a deep breath, she opened her eyes and turned to face Walter. 'No, I am not sure it is wise. I am also not sure how I will cope without you there to guide me. What I am sure of is this is what I am meant to do.'

Walter was beside her in a heartbeat, clasping her hand in his. 'Then I will come with you and help with whatever it is you need.'

Unable to help the grin that appeared on her face any more than she was able to stop the blush from rising up her neck, Amelia gripped Walter's fingers. Goddess! She was behaving like a girl with her first crush. Amazed at how tempted she was to take Walter up on his offer, she knew she should not. Letting go of Walter's hand, she told him so.

'Seamus needs you. He needs your guidance and your

support, and your wealth of magical knowledge. Although he is putting on a good show, he is scared and worried, and he needs someone to be there for him; someone he respects. Also, I do not believe anyone else will be able to find the answers you will in those last few scrolls.'

The bed sagged as Walter sat down, still holding her hand. 'I know, but I will worry less if I am there to protect you should something happen before you are comfortable and confident with the changes in your life.'

'Pauley will be there. I will ask him to act as my guide. It will do the boy good to have something to do rather than running free. Goodness only knows what mischief he caused the castle staff these last few days.' Amelia laughed out loud as a thought occurred to her. 'The boy who can see in darkness will lead the woman who cannot see in the light.'

Appreciating the irony, Walter's laughter joined her's, easing the tension between them. Then he was suddenly silent.

'Amelia, there are things I would like to talk of before you leave,' Walter started, and she squeezed his hand before she interrupted him.

'Walter, we can talk of these things later, when this is over.'

'But there is a chance ...'

'Yes, and if that does happen, we will not be any better off for having had this conversation. We are no spring chickens, and I think our feelings for each other are quite clear. Let us leave it at that for now. If we have a future after this is all over, we can talk then.'

Silence hung in the room, and not for the first time

since she lost her vision Amelia wished for it back. If only for a moment to see Walter's thoughts written on his face. The bed shifted and lips lightly touched her cheek.

'We will have this conversation, I promise you that.' Walter's breath warmed her face as he spoke. Then he was all action. 'Right, I had best find what I can pull together for your travels, if anyone is up to help me. And you had best get some rest as you will not sleep in a bed as welcoming as this for a while.'

And that is how he managed to wriggle his way through defences it took me years to build, she thought as she snuggled back down under the blankets.

7
DIPLOMACY DIES

As Daniel led their horses over Aliah sighed, her breath creating a mist in the chilly just-before-dawn air. Missing her god-given sleep the night before meant she woke up tired and grumpy. The hard ride in front of them to reach Baron Tappit's holding before midday filled her with dread.

'I have a thought. If the baron's stayed behind with enough guards to block the passes and prevent the Carsten Army from taking over Hand, why are we riding like mad things to get them to do what they should already be doing?' she asked Daniel as he drew up beside her.

'I see someone woke up on the wrong side of the bed this morning,' he started in a cheery voice that did absolutely nothing to lighten her mood. Taking one look at her face, he was all business as he continued, 'We are doing this because we do not want them to protect their own areas, we want them to work together to contain the army in one place. Not only so we can do what we need to, but also because it is the best way to protect Hand and Aria.'

'Humph,' Aliah grunted, taking the lead rein from Daniel.

As she readied herself to mount, she was distracted by the sight of Boss leading out another three horses. Looking around the courtyard she found Robin checking the saddle on his horse. Dominic was holding the bridle of a bay gelding as he talked to Seamus, no doubt giving some last minute instructions. She frowned. A horse for Pauley, one for Boss and one for ...

Before the question formed, Pauley emerged from the palace leading Amelia. They were followed out by Walter carrying a travel pack. She relaxed. Walter would be a great asset to their group, although she thought it strange he elected to leave Seamus to finish going through the scrolls, let alone trust him to face Baron Wexler with only Liam and Emer. Still, it would be useful to have a wizard with them.

She mounted her horse, glancing over to see Amelia settling herself into a saddle. Her surprise must have been written over her face because a chuckling Dominic walked over, leading his gelding.

BATTLE

'It appears loss of sight does not stop a person from riding,' he said as he pulled himself into his own saddle.

'Amelia is coming with us.'

Aliah realised she was stating the obvious, but she could not help herself.

'It would appear so. She had a dream last night, and in is sure her path lies in the same direction as ours.'

'Is that wise, given how fast and hard we need to move to have any chance of achieving this mission and meeting up with Seamus?'

She knew Amelia would be more than a little annoyed her ability to keep up was being questioned based solely on her loss of sight, but Aliah's concerns were real. They could not slow down for Amelia, nor could they simply leave her somewhere if she started lagging behind. As if he sensed her discomfort, Dominic's answer was uncharacteristically tactful.

'I asked the same thing, but Walter arranged everything early this morning. Amelia is a confident horsewoman. The mount is her own, and is used to her commands. Boss is happy to keep a lead rein so the horse does not wander off, and Pauley will act as Amelia's guide when she dismounts. Everything is organised to ensure she will not place our mission at risk.'

Aliah considered the information and, although the plan had more holes than a leaky bucket, she would not be the one to forbid Amelia from doing something just because she no longer had her sight. Shrugging her shoulders, she turned her horse.

'Besides,' Dominic added. 'With Amelia in our group, Emer will be freed up to help Seamus and Walter.'

'Oh? How come?'

'She and Amelia can mind speak more easily than I can over long distances, so it is likely she will not need to fly to us at all unless there is an emergency.'

'Well, I guess that is something. All right, are we ready to leave?' she asked, her voice carrying in the morning air.

'Daniel has the maps and, should you manage to get lost, Robin will guide you to safety,' Seamus was saying as they joined the others.

'All right, then let us proceed,' Aliah instructed with more confidence than she was actually feeling.

Seamus nodded wearily, telling her he was just as unsure about splitting the group as she was. Daniel and Robin took the lead, with Boss, Pauley and Amelia falling in behind. Aliah moved her horse beside Dominic at the rear and followed them through the gate.

Turning in her saddle, Aliah caught sight of Walter and Seamus heading inside. No doubt they were eager to cram as much time as they could in the library before they left on their own journey in a couple of days.

Realising she had fallen a little behind, she nudged her horse to catch the others up. Daniel was setting a quick pace. As they rode, Aliah studied Amelia, relieved to find she seemed surer of herself on horseback than she had been walking. If the look on her face was anything to go by, she enjoyed the sense of independence riding was giving her. A rare experience since losing her sight.

Pauley. She groaned. If Pauley was busy helping Amelia, he would not be able to help her practice her magical connections.

'Is everything all right?' Dominic asked, and she

realised she must have groaned out loud.

Without stopping to think, she found herself telling Dominic her problem. 'I was supposed to be practicing making a magical connection with Pauley while we travelled. I am not very good at it, and I need all the practice I can get before Seamus and I face this god.'

It was hard for Aliah to admit she was less than perfect at the best of times, so she was surprised she had been so open with Dominic. Bracing herself for a sarcastic comment, Aliah almost missed his response.

'I can practice with you.'

'What? Really? I knew you could talk with Emer, but I thought that was all led by her.'

'Yes, I have done this before. Wizards and other spies connected with me when I went places they could not go.' Aliah stared at the boy. Would he ever cease amazing her?

'Did you not find it a little, umm, invasive?' she asked, remembering her initial worry about practicing with Dominic last night.

When she joined with Seamus, the moment they connected his emotions swamped her. With him, they had shared so much already it made little difference to how they treated each other. Pauley would have been too young to be bothered with such things, but what if it happened with Dominic? Surely he would be able to pick up on the jumble of emotions threatening to overwhelm her whenever they were together.

'No.' Dominic appeared blissfully ignorant of her concerns. 'I was taught to erect a barrier in my mind so wizards used my eyes only. If I had not, the noise from having another mind inside of mine would have been quite distracting, and might have placed me in danger. I assume one of the first things you were taught was erecting a barrier?'

Aliah considered his words for a moment. 'No, I think Seamus and I are supposed to be able to blend and act as one, a barrier would be counter-productive.'

Dominic fell silent for a moment. 'I am not comfortable letting you link minds with me without having a barrier in place,' he finally admitted. He paused before continuing. 'If you promise to practice making a connection and not the blending, I think my barrier should be sufficient to maintain both of our privacy.'

'You do?' Relief washed through Aliah. 'I know it is asking a lot, but I appreciate it.'

'I am at your service.' Dominic's mocking tone returned. 'Now we are dropping a little behind. If we do not want to lose the others, we had best catch them up.'

Without realising it, their pace slowed during their conversation, and Aliah raised her eyes to find their companions about to drop out of sight as they crested a hill. Urging her horse forward, she and Dominic rode to catch them.

As the afternoon sun began to wane, Aliah glimpsed the outline of a large country house in the distance. It had taken far longer than anticipated to reach their destination. A fallen tree forced them to detour via a more coastal track, extending their journey, which not only lost them valuable time, but also made them tired and cranky.

BATTLE

Groaning with relief at the sight of Baron Tappit's house in the distance, she regretted not spending more time on a horse the last few moons. Every movement of her mount sent a jolt of agony through the tender flesh of her rear end.

A candle mark later, the sun was blocked completely as they rode up the tree lined driveway to the baron's manor. Aliah's daydream of a cool bath was rudely interrupted as a group of armed men challenged them, their stern faces not showing the smallest glimmer of welcome.

'Halt. Identify yourselves!' their leader ordered, sword at the ready should he not like the answer.

Robin eased his horse forward. 'I am Robin Gadfell, Chancellor of the Duchy, and I am here with some very important guests who wish to speak with Baron Tappit about the defence of Hand.'

The chancellor stood tall in his saddle, his voice haughty and full of entitlement, but the man in front of them appeared unimpressed by his show.

'We are not receiving guests at the moment. These are dangerous times. We look to our own safety, the rest of Hand can take care of itself.'

Unmoving, the guards continued to block their path. Appreciating they were at a disadvantage should it come to a fight, Aliah urged her mount forward.

'I am Princess Aliahanna, and I am here on behalf of your king and your duke, I suggest you allow us by, unless you want to answer directly to either of them.'

Behind her Daniel muttered, 'Always use a sledge-hammer to crack a nut, that is our Aliah.'

Aliah bit back a smile as she faced down the guard

captain. Now was not the time to let her imperious manner slip.

'With all due respect ... er ... Princess?'

Aliah gritted her teeth. Any statement starting that way was highly unlikely to be respectful at all.

'Our duke ran to the safety of the mainland, joining the king in a well guarded town. I do not fear his retribution at this time.'

Clenching the reigns until her knuckles showed white, Aliah's self-control was near breaking. Robin moved forward to take charge again before she said something they would be unable to repair, ending their mission before it had even begun.

'Duke Damon went to Port Marden to co-ordinate our forces with those of Aria, and to lead our guard in battle. He left his son and heir, Seamus, to organise defences here. At present he is detained organising the forces left at the palace. We have been sent to rally the rest of the island. With me are King Terion's own daughter and heir, Princess Aliahanna, Guard Captain Daniel, the son of Aria's military commander, and Lord Dominic, the son of one of the northern dukes, sent to aid us. Please do not embarrass our people and your lord by being so discourteous to those sent to assist us in these trying times.'

Ignoring Dominic's scowl at being recognised and presented using his actual position, Aliah lent some force to Robin's introduction.

'We are here to help, and just wish a word with the baron.' Aliah simpered, hating the fact she could not appear as strong as a man and still be taken seriously, but knowing she had to play the game if she wanted to get anywhere.

'You have proof …' the leader started.

'Guard Daniel has a letter signed by Duke Damon himself giving us authority to do what we need to protect Aria and Hand.'

The guard's gaze slipped from Robin to Daniel.

'I will present it only to the baron.'

The guard confirmed the letter's existence, but Daniel was not going to show it to someone of so low a rank.

Although he appeared to want to question them further, the imperious set to Aliah's face must have convinced him against continued questioning of the princess.

'… umm … if you are happy to surrender your weapons, you may continue on to the manor.'

Pondering her options, especially with regards to her own sword, Aliah responded. 'As you just admitted, danger is close by and I would be foolish to agree to my party being unable to defend themselves. You have my word we will not draw arms against your people, and that will have to be enough.' Her direct stare challenged the captain to disagree.

For a brief moment, he looked as though he might object, but changed his mind as Daniel and Dominic drew alongside Aliah. Admitting defeat, the man turned to the guard closest to him.

'Escort them to the house and see their mounts are cared for. I will go and warn the baron of their arrival.'

Aliah watched him depart before riding past the weary gaze of Baron Tappit's guards. As she drew level, Aliah was sure she heard one of the guards mutter, 'At least they did not send that wizard spawn of a son.' Anger rose in her stomach but, given the hostility of the situation, she chose to ignore the comment and carried on up to the manor house

Although her blood boiled at their treatment, she schooled her face to calm serenity. She did not want word of her unease to find its way back to the baron, least he use it to his advantage. Only the set of her jaw alerted those who knew her to the fact her control was near to breaking.

Drawing up at the front of the manor, Aliah waited for one of the grooms to take her horse's bridle before dismounting. Brushing dust from her riding clothes, she glanced up the stairs to take a quick peek at her host, only to find the door remained closed, and he was no where in sight.

'If you would allow me, Your Highness?'

Stifling a frustrated groan, Aliah admitted it would not do for a princess to request permission to enter a mere baron's home. Not only would it be a breach of protocol, it would also place her on the back foot when she came to bargain with the man for troops. She agreed to Robin's suggestion he seek admittance for them.

The door creaked open just as he reached the top step, saving Robin the indignity of knocking, and allowing a tall, gaunt man to emerge. With his nose pointed skywards, he could not have looked more haughty if he tried. Her immediate thought that the baron had seen sense and come out to meet them was crushed as the man spoke.

'If you will follow me, Baron Tappit will meet with you in his study.'

For a mere baron not to greet a princess in person

and welcome her into his home, was extremely bad manners. Robin turned to take direction from Aliah. Biting back her instinct to march herself into the manor and demand Baron Tappit tell her what he thought he was playing at, Aliah straightened her back and led her party indoors, as though the idea to enter without waiting for the baron had been her own.

The baron's minion followed the group in, closing the door with a loud thud behind them.

'This way,' he instructed.

Aliah did not move. She had met the baron half-way, and that was as far as she was prepared to go. She would not attend him in his study like a supplicant. He would have to come to her as he should have done in the first place. Now she was physically inside the man's home, he no longer had the option of ignoring their presence on his lands.

'Please, the baron awaits you. If you will just follow me.' The man indicated the way with a sweep of his hand. His voice wavered a little as he realised he had lost his advantage and did not quite know what to do next.

'And I await the baron here. You can tell the baron Princess Aliahanna, his future Queen, awaits him in the hall. If he wishes to still have a study in this manor after I take the crown, he had better make haste and get himself out here.' Aliah raised her chin and showed she could beat the best of them at being stubborn and haughty.

Wringing his hands in front of him, the man appeared uncertain of his next move. Aliah glared at him, but before she could say anything else and ruin the moment, Robin stepped forward.

'I suggest you do as the lady asks, we would not want to insult the princess anymore than we already have, would we?'

Scuttling away, the man shot a nervous glance back over his shoulder before opening a door to the right and disappearing. Even though the door was made of the stoutest wood, they all heard the baron's voice as he berated his servant for not carrying out his orders.

Waiting for the tirade to finish, Aliah glanced around the entrance hall. Ornately furnished, with thick carpet and heavy dark wooden furniture, displayed around a grand staircase that swept upwards to a second level, it announced loud and clear the Tappits were moneyed and not afraid to show it. The display was obviously intended to intimidate visitors, but the ostentatious decor only served to annoy Aliah more.

A few moments later the door opened, and the servant returned. 'My Lord, Baron Tappit,' he announced as he moved aside to admit a rotund man in his mid-twenties, his face and bald head flushed with barely concealed anger. The waxed moustache sitting atop his sneering lip did nothing to dispel the image of a child playing in the world of grown ups. He stopped just in front of the party and waited. Ever the diplomat, Robin stepped forward.

'Your Royal Highness, Princess Aliahanna, may I present Baron Micheal of Tappit.'

Aliah inclined her head in what she hoped was a regal manner, and held out her hand for the baron to press his lips to it in a gesture of fealty. The baron's obvious reluctance as he followed protocol made up a little for the clammy coldness she endured as his lips met her flesh.

The minimum of formalities complete, Aliah wasted no time getting to the point. 'Baron we are here to request a complement of your men to assist in defending Hand. Is there somewhere a little more comfortable we can talk?'

'You must understand, Princess Aliahanna, Baron Tappit is a second son. His brother died in an unfortunate riding accident, thrusting him into a role he had no desire, and no training for.'

Robin explained this in the privacy of the manner's guest suite. Baron Tappit reluctantly made the rooms available to them, but only after he realised his unexpected visitors were not leaving his manor that night, whether he offered hospitality or not.

Aliah stopped her pacing while she considered the chamberlain's words, then responded tersely, 'That does not excuse his rudeness. All children in noble households are brought up to respect common courtesy. Nor does it excuse his stupidity. His advisor immediately saw the sense in our plan, yet he could not be persuaded to it.'

'The problem is,' Dominic interrupted. 'He is so scared of making the wrong move, he cannot make any move at all.'

Aliah stopped to stare out the window, enjoying the colours of the sun as it set behind the trees surrounding the manor. Unable to comprehend anyone's inability to take action when necessary, none-the-less she agreed with Dominic. The man was clearly paralysed with fear.

'I think you should be happy he agreed to provide men should Baron George send word he will be joining with us.' Dominic's face joined her reflection in the glass as he moved behind her. 'Sometimes you just have to be happy with what you have, and move on.'

Sighing, she moved away from the window and took a seat beside the fire. 'You are right, Dominic, and we only got that concession due to some quick talking. Thank you, Robin, we could not have done this without you.'

'I was just doing my job, looking out for Hand's best interests.' Robin bowed. 'Now, if you will excuse me, I will go and make sure the others are settled into their rooms and see if I can arrange for some food to be brought up.' Robin bowed again as he left.

'I am not unhappy the baron's hospitality did not extend to a formal evening meal,' Aliah said as she stretched catlike, absorbing the heat from the blaze. 'If I had to spend another moment with that spoilt child I swear I would have strangled him.'

Dominic's laughter erupted, filling the room. 'I am pretty sure he felt the same way about you. It seems our baron is not used to having strong women boss him around.'

The room fell into silence and Aliah mulled over whether or not now was the right time to ask Dominic something that had been on her mind for a while. Taking the plunge, she asked, 'Dominic, why do you not like Robin?'

The boy tensed at her question. 'Umm ... it is not that I dislike him, more that I do not trust him.'

'Why?'

'It is hard to place my finger on. All the times I attended the court on Hand I could never get a sense of who he was as a person. His only interest is serving Hand. Everyone else I meet in this line of work has a life outside of their official duties—except him.'

'That is hardly a reason for you to bristle every time he is in the same room.' Aliah turned so she could better read his reactions.

'Not normally, no. But you should note I said he serves Hand, not Duke Damon. I have long since believed Robin works towards his own vision of what Hand should be. While this aligns with Duke Damon he is a valuable asset, but what happens if the duke wants something for Hand Robin disagrees with?'

Head cocked to the side, Aliah considered Dominic's words. 'And you think something happened?'

Dominic shrugged. 'I am not sure, but Robin is acting strangely of late, and he has turned up in places I would not expect him to be. Coupled with the fact he always seems to be hanging around closed doors, well, let us just say I am concerned.'

Aliah turned back to the flames. 'And you would like to use your special talents to check up on him?'

'Mmm, yes. But I do not think you should be left alone in this house. You shamed the baron today, and I do not completely trust him either.'

'I do not think he would do us any physical harm, not least because that would require him to decide to take action. Still, you could send Daniel in to keep me company, and you go and do what you need to do.'

The door latch clicked as Dominic let himself out, and Aliah relaxed back in her chair, letting the warmth of the flames lick her tired muscles. She must have dozed, because the next thing she knew a hand on her arm caused her to tense. With her sword on the bed on the other side of the room, she ran through possible means of escape.

'You are lucky I am not an assassin.'

Her eyes flew open to find Daniel standing over her, his face grey and dotted with beads of sweat.

'With the way you look at the moment you assaulting me would be beyond you, you would be lucky to best a new-born kitten. What is a matter? '

Her friend slumped into a chair. 'I ate something off at dinner. I am sure I will be better by morning.'

'No, I do not believe you will.' Aliah's brow creased with concern. 'Come on, we will go and get Amelia to take a look at you.'

Aliah stood and grabbed Daniel's arm, half-dragging him next door to the healer's room.

'Here you go. This is a little stronger than the tonic I made you in Sanctuary, so it should last a little longer.' Amelia handed two bottles of liquid over to Daniel. 'One finger width twice a day.'

'Thank you, Amelia.' Daniel took the medicine. 'I do not know what I would do without this, or you for that matter.'

'Humph. Perhaps if I were not here to make your tonic the others would notice you were ill, and you would be forced to tell them the truth.'

The guard shifted from foot to foot, uncomfortable

under Amelia's gaze, which was no less cutting for her lack of sight.

'I am fine with them thinking I have had a few stomach aches from eating different food and the like.'

'They will soon start to notice those tummy upsets are becoming more frequent. Anyway, this is as strong as I can make it without people noticing the side effects. Any stronger and you will start to appear drunk or confused to others. Are you sure it is not time to tell them?'

When no response was forthcoming, Amelia tried another tactic. 'You could return to the palace, say you need to oversee defences there. You could rest up, allow your body time to heal and gather some energy to fight this.'

'Amelia, I told you what I want. I need to support Aliah through whatever this is, and do my duty for Aria. You promised ...'

'I know exactly what I promised, young man, and even if I had not promised I would not say a word to anyone. It is a healer's oath.' Amelia's voice was tart, but she softened it before continuing. 'That does not stop you from saying something to them though. They are already starting to notice something is amiss. Perhaps it is time.'

'Soon, Amelia, soon. I must return to Aliah now, but I do not want to leave you alone. Where is Pauley?'

'Off doing the things young boys do, I suspect.' Amelia chuckled. 'Boss is in the corridor outside looking out for both Aliah and myself. If you are going to be with our princess, you can send him in to stay with me until Pauley returns.'

The air cooled as the young guard opened the door,

and moments later she heard the familiar footsteps of Boss as he entered her room.

'Where is Pauley, he said he was just nipping out for some air?' Boss's stern voice announced his entrance.

'You know exactly where he is, Boss Allum. I know what you and he have been cooking up. So there is no need to put on a show for me.'

'Oh, he told you about his concerns?' Having closed the door Boss still felt the need to whisper his question.

'Not in so many words,' Amelia responded. 'My hearing is much improved since I lost my sight, and I overheard snippets of your conversation on the journey today. So take a seat and perhaps you can fill me in on the details as we wait for our young friend's return.'

Keeping to the shadows, Dominic followed the elusive Robin through the manor's back corridor. Before opening the door to the courtyard, the older man turned around to check behind him. Satisfied he was alone, he slipped outside.

Unable to leave the house without being noticed, Dominic slid through another open door into what appeared to be the servant's dining room. Through the window, he could make out Robin standing nearby, staring intently at something in his hand while his lips moved.

Someone had left the window partially open, so the spy crouched to get his ear as close to the gap as he could, hoping some of what his quarry said would drift through.

'I cannot do that, not without people suspecting ...' Robin paused, as though listening to someone, but all

BATTLE

Dominic heard was an almost undetectable hum. 'Can you guarantee ... all right, if you put it like that. I will need to wait until we are closer though. I will contact you again in a day's time.' More low humming, then. 'About my ... Goddess!, you always break off before I get to ask.' Robin shook whatever he held in his hand, and stomped in frustration. He placed the object in a pocket on the inside of his coat and glanced around to make sure he was still alone before heading back into the house.

As Duke Damon's closest advisor drew close to the door, Dominic thought he saw a movement in the shadows by the hedge. Deciding he had all he would get tonight from the chancellor, he allowed Robin to pass by and continued to watch the greenery by the house.

The sun soon finished its descent and as the courtyard fell into darkness, Dominic's keen eyes spotted a slight movement, followed by soft footsteps heading towards the back door. A faint snick told him the door had been opened, and a fainter thud informed him the new object of his interest had entered the manor.

Waiting behind the door, he timed his attack perfectly, and soon held the intruder by the collar, his other hand over his mouth as he dragged the boy into the room, pushing the door closed behind them with his foot. In the light from the dying fire, Dominic lifted his captive close to get a good look at him, then nearly dropped him to the floor.

'Pauley, what on earth are you doing?'

The boy shrugged as Dominic realised he could not speak with a hand still firmly placed over his mouth. Lowering the boy to the ground, Pauley adjusted his clothing before answering.

'I guess I am doing the same as you, trying to figure out what that slimy eel Robin is up to?'

Dominic wanted to laugh at the young boy's daring, but his first thought was one of worry. 'Do you realise you could get hurt if you are found out? Robin may not be much of a fighter, but I think you would be hard pressed to fend him off if he decided to do you some harm.'

Pauley squared his shoulders and stared disdainfully at Dominic. 'He would not be able to get close enough to touch me. More dangerous men than him have tried to catch me and failed.'

Initially Pauley's bravado took Dominic by surprise, then he laughed and took a closer look at the boy. He had guts, and he could see well in the dark, but did he know what he was looking for?

'So, tell me what you found out?' Dominic gestured to the table, and he and the boy sat.

'Well, Robin has this mirror type thing he keeps in his coat pocket. Every day or so he finds somewhere quiet and talks to someone through it.'

'Do you know who he speaks to?'

'No,' he shook his head emphatically. 'I can make out what he is saying, but all I hear from the mirror is a buzzing sound. I am pretty sure you must be holding on to it to pick up what the other person is saying.'

Dominic stroked his chin. He knew what he thought, but he wanted to see how the boy had pieced this together. 'What do you think he is doing?'

'I am sure he is not talking to the duke.' Pauley started cautiously.

'Because?'

'Because if he was, he would not mind others seeing what he is up to.'

Dominic nodded for the boy to continue, impressed with what he had heard so far. More confident now, Pauley told Dominic what he had seen, and what worried him so much.

'He is reporting everything we are doing to the person on the other end of the mirror. It worries me because last night, he told them Aliah was leaving the palace to visit the barons. Even though I do not know who he is talking to, I cannot imagine anything good will come from the information he passed on.'

'You have done well, Pauley.'

Dominic did not give his praise easily. This boy had found out more than he had and, although he did not like placing the boy in danger, he had not been much older than Pauley when he was sent on his first assignment. People often over-looked the young, thinking they could not possibly comprehend what was going on around them.

'I also believe you are correct. Robin does not mean us well. Although my special talent helps me follow him, he is aware of what I do for the king. That is why I think perhaps it is better if you continue to spy on him, and report back to both myself and Boss Allum.'

'How did you ...'

'Come now, Pauley, I would not be such a great spy if I was unable to work out you are too smart to be doing this alone. It is then not such a great leap to work out Boss Allum knows about this too.'

Smiling, Dominic was pleased he had at least managed

to show the boy he had some skills of his own. Truth be told, he was a little put out Pauley managed to discover more than him about Robin's comings and goings, and he had not noticed him doing it.

Making up his mind, the spy decided he would talk to the king about Pauley's future employment in his next dispatch. His monarch was always on the look out for people to act as eyes and ears, and for Pauley, this would be a great opportunity to rise up in the world.

'So, I think I might try to get a look at his mirror.'

'Pauley, I do not think that is such a good idea. In fact, you should not try it under any circumstances.' Dominic was shocked back into focusing on the boy in front of him. 'You would run the risk of whoever Robin is talking to finding out you know about them. Not only would that place you in great danger, but it would blow your cover. At the moment no one knows what you are up to and you are relatively safe, but if they learnt what you were doing ...'

He let the boy draw his own conclusions as he searched his face for compliance, but the stubborn set to his mouth told Dominic he had not convinced Pauley of the danger. It was time to try something different.

'Please, Pauley, I am asking you as a favour to me. I do not want to be the one to tell Aliah something dreadful has happened to you. At the moment it is enough we know we need to watch Robin, and I believe from hearing his side of the conversations we will be forewarned of any danger to us.'

Pleading and using Aliah had the desired effect. 'All right. I will not go looking for the mirror; for the moment.'

'That is all I can ask. Now you had best get back to Amelia. She will be wondering where you are.'

The boy pulled the door behind him, leaving Dominic staring into the fire, assessing the new information in light of what he already knew. Robin was definitely working for someone, but what was he getting in return? If they could find that out, they might be able to work out who his other master was.

Knocking on the door to Aliah's room, he waited for her command to enter, then let himself in. He had been surprised no one was guarding her door, but understood why when he saw Daniel seated opposite the princess drinking tea.

'Good, with both of you here I need only say this once.' Dominic sat on the edge of the bed and relayed everything he learnt that evening.

As he recounted his tale, Aliah stood and started pacing the room. 'I do not understand this at all. Robin was so helpful today. Baron Tappit only made the small concession he did because of Robin's intervention. He has Hand's best interests at heart. I do not believe he is doing this for money.' She tugged at her plait.

'He was working for the good of Hand when he negotiated with the baron,' Dominic pointed out. 'I am thinking maybe it is not Hand he is betraying, but us—we Arians.'

Aliah stopped and gazed into the flames, pondering Dominic's comment.

'You may be right. Duke Damon is no fool. I am sure

if Robin had been up to something before now, he would have been found out. I wonder what he has against us?'

'What if it is not that he has something against us, but rather that someone had something against him?'

Daniel had been so quiet, Dominic had almost forgotten he was still in the room.

As Aliah turned round to face her friend, her plait swung back over her shoulder. 'What do you mean, Daniel?'

'Well, you both are assuming Robin is in this for some sort of personal gain, or because he dislikes Arians. But you have not considered the alternatives. What if someone is blackmailing him, or worse still, holding one of his family members for ransom. There are many reasons why someone would betray their countrymen.'

'We need to find out. I cannot bare to think of the man being held to ransom.' Aliah looked at Dominic.

'Hold on a moment there, we have no idea what Robin's motivation is, and with an invasion and a god to fight, do you not think there is enough for us to worry about?'

'But would it not help us if we helped Robin? If we could find out what is going on, perhaps we can do something about it. Then he would be able to stop spying, and we would have one less thing to worry about.'

Aliah's plan was logical, and Dominic hated to squash her idea, but it was in her best interests that he did so, and quickly before the idea took root.

'We know he is up to something and we are keeping an eye on him. Our resources are stretched as it is. We cannot risk failure against our errant god to try and save one man, and that is if he even needs saving. My advice would be to continue with our current plan.'

'I agree with Dominic,' Daniel said. 'We have no idea who he is working for and why. To make any sort of move we would need more information, and we do not have the time or resources to focus on that task as well as everything else. So if we are all happy, I shall be off to bed and leave the first watch tonight to you, Dominic.'

Assuming Aliah's agreement, Daniel rose from his seat, picked up some bottles from the side table, and let himself out of the room.

Before Aliah realised she had not agreed to anything, Dominic distracted her by asking, 'What is wrong with Daniel?'

'Mmm ... umm ... he has some sort of stomach upset. Amelia made him a tonic.' Wearily massaging her brow, Aliah dragged her thoughts back into the room.

'He has had a lot of stomach problems lately,' Dominic commented, and Aliah was suddenly alert.

'Do you know something?'

Startled by her intensity, Dominic stuttered. 'Umm ... no ... I was just saying ... Hold on, do you think there is something more to it than traveller's tummy?'

'I am not sure,' Aliah sank into the nearest chair, despondency overtaking her.

'You should ask him.'

'I did. I also asked Amelia.'

'I bet that was a fun conversation,' he chuckled.

'They were both very tight-lipped.' Aliah was unable to see the funny side. 'And that makes me all the more worried.'

Dominic moved over to the now vacant chair by the

fire. 'When he is ready, he will tell you. Until then, you just need to keep an eye on him.'

When Aliah did not respond, Dominic decided she needed a change of focus, something to divert her from her worries.

'Are you ready to try linking minds?'

The look on her face would have been comical, if it had not shown him how worried she was about this aspect of her warrior training. 'What? Now?'

'There is no time like the present. Get your sword and we can start.'

Aliah looked as though she wanted to argue, but stood and went and retrieved her sword from where it rested on the bed. Sitting back down she stared at Dominic, waiting for him to begin.

'Right. I think the first thing we should do is figure out if we can make a link.' When Aliah nodded, he continued. 'What do you do when you make a link with Seamus?'

'I place my hand on the sword, and I touch him. Then I push my mind out towards him.'

'Then that is what we will start with. Go ahead.'

Dominic held out his hand and Aliah took a hold of it. With her face a mask of concentration, he observed her until a whisper of a touch stroked his senses. Letting down his natural barrier a little, Aliah tentatively entered his thoughts.

Hello.

The link broke.

'Why did you do that?' Aliah snapped.

'I was letting you know you had succeeded.'

'Oh.' Bewildered, she admitted, 'I did not even know

I had joined with you. When Seamus and I link minds, I can pick up his thoughts right away.'

'You are both new to this. When you are a little more practiced you can let someone into your mind and share only what you choose to. If you imagine your mind as being a house, you can let someone into an entry hall, then choose which rooms you allow them access to.'

'Oh. How come you are so good at this?'

Dominic could not tell if she truly wanted to know, or was just putting off any further lessons.

'My spymaster was able to mind link, it was one of the reasons he was so skilled at his job. When he found I had a talent for it, he taught me as well. It made reporting easier as he could see everything I experienced on a mission as if he were there.'

'Oh.'

'Shall we try again?'

'If we must.'

This time when Dominic felt the gentle brush of Aliah's mind, he let her inside the part of him in the room at this moment, sealing off all other feelings and memories.

'I did it?'

'Yes, you did.' Her pleasure rushed through him, almost overwhelming him.

'All right, now do it again.'

The connection came more easily this time. She was ready to try this without touching.

Excellent. Now let go of my arm, Dominic instructed.

Are you sure?

Yes.

Again her presence faded, then returned. Not as strong

as before, but she was still there.

Now walk to the door. Slowly. Making sure each step you take the link is maintained.

He studied her as she did as he asked, feeling her struggling to maintain contact. About half-way across the room she disappeared from his head.

'Goddess!'

'No, that was very good. Let us do it again.'

They repeated the process until Aliah was able to keep the link up all the way to the door.

'Well done. Now try linking to me without touching the sword.'

'I do not think I can.'

'It should be easy, given the last two times you linked with me you did not touch it at all.' Aliah's eyes widened in surprise. 'Now, see if you can do it consciously.'

Aliah took his hand and closed her eyes, concentrating. Frowning, she let go of his hand.

'I cannot do it!'

'Yes, you can. Try again.'

He felt her tentative brush against his mind, then she was gone. Her head dropped down and she stared at the floor.

I cannot do it, no matter what he says. He is so infuriating.

Not so much infuriating, as right.

'What?'

'See, you did it without touching me. Try again.'

You know you are a right royal pain in the …

Princess Aliahanna, that is no way for a lady to speak.

Aliah's blue eyes sparkled with pleasure as she looked at him. 'Do I try walking away and keeping the link again?'

BATTLE

Dominic shook his head. 'We are both tired, and I cannot send you into a healing sleep. It is a long ride tomorrow, so I think it best we finish for now. Besides, I am meant to be guarding the corridor.'

Aliah stood and stretched, and the stretch turned into a yawn. 'I guess you are right.'

Dominic rose to leave, but was stopped by Aliah's hand on his arm.

'Thank you. I feel so much more confident after tonight. You are a way better teacher than the gods.'

Hiding his embarrassment the only way he knew how, Dominic made light of the situation. 'So, you are saying I am godlike? Or I am more than godlike?'

'Ahhh...boys. Go.'

Dominic departed before Aliah decided to throw something at him, the warm glow growing in the pit of his stomach giving him a surprising sense of happiness.

8
A GLIMMER OF LIGHT

The palace was quiet, almost too quiet. Seamus' footsteps echoed as he made his way to the library. Sighing, he opened the door and steeled himself for another day going through dusty scrolls. He found Walter already at work, in fact the magician was so engrossed he did not notice Seamus enter the room, grab an armful of scrolls, and dump them on the table. Even noisily pulling the wooden chair out and slumping down onto it could not pull Walter from his study.

Unfurling the scroll closest to him, Seamus let out a

groan, predicting today would be much like yesterday. After the others left, he, Walter, Liam and Emer went straight to the library. Around lunchtime, Liam suggested an afternoon of outdoor training, and Emer leapt at the chance of leaving the dusty documents for a while. Seamus watched them go, longing to join them.

Although sword training did not really interest him, the release of physical exercise appealed to him more than an afternoon of study. However, his sense of duty forced him to stay with Walter, and he had left the library later that day as frustrated with their progress as when he entered.

Now they only had the remaining day to go through the last few documents to try and find something to give them a little edge over the god they were to fight. Frustrated, he called on the gods for an additional training session, hoping to salvage at least something from the day.

While he waited, he managed to work off some steam. His intention was to work with the god to contact Aliah. Although he wanted to find out how her mission was going, he also wanted to see if they were able to communicate over long distance. The god's response to his request further added to his frustrations.

'No.'

'Because we might be overheard?'

'No.'

'Why can I not try a mind-link with her?'

'Because the Warrior is busy with her own training. I do not want to interrupt her and her instructor.'

'She is working with a god tonight as well?'

'I did not say that.'

BATTLE

Once again, the god's inability to answer a question directly annoyed Seamus.

'So what are you saying? Or is this one of the times when you are unable to say anything? Will contacting her upset the balance or something?'

The god looked at him in confusion. 'I answered your questions.'

Seamus replayed their conversation in his mind and he realised the god had, in fact, given the information he asked for, and not one shred more. Thinking for a moment about the essence of what he wanted to find out, he reframed his question.

'Who is Aliah training with and what is she learning?'

'She is training with the one you call Dominic. He is teaching her mind-linking.'

Seamus could not hold back his snort of laughter. He would love to be a fly on the wall in that training session.

'Is there anything else, young Wizard?'

Seamus paused before answering, not quite sure how to word what was on his mind. 'I am worried. Aliah is so far away, and I think we should be working together to plan how to deal with your brother. I believe I should be with her, or at least talking with her.'

'You know as well as I there is nothing to indicate whether you and Aliah being together or apart leading up to your confrontation will change the outcome.'

'I know, but I would feel better if we were together.' Even as he said the words out loud, Seamus heard how childish they sounded, but it was how he felt.

'You will know when the time for your warrior to rejoin you has arrived, until then, you should concentrate on the tasks assigned to you.'

The god's words were practical, but did nothing to calm his fears. Still, he knew there was nothing he could do about anything there and then.

His lesson that night was to practice his magic with and without his wand. If taken by surprise, he might not have time to draw it, the god explained, but if their enemy managed to bring his own body here, Seamus would need the wand's power to increase and focus his magic.

When he could barely stand, the god led him to his room, wished him luck, then gifted him a deep sleep before leaving. This morning he had awoken refreshed, if not completely enthused about another day leafing through dusty documents.

At breakfast, Liam and Emer offered to organise the horses and food needed for their journey. Liam had even said he would sort out Seamus' pack for him—anything to get out of more reading. Reluctantly he left them to their preparations and headed to the library alone, still not unable to shake his unease about Aliah not being by his side.

A little while later, he was seated and began scanning his first scroll, a lengthy tome on breeding cattle, that he quickly assessed as useless. Before starting on the next text, he made sure he rolled the first one up and re-tied it, putting it to the side so he did not end up reading it again.

He learnt that lesson yesterday when he thought the library contained duplicates of some scrolls, then realised for a candle mark or so he had been picking his reading material from the completed pile. When he complained,

BATTLE

Walter treated him to a long and detailed explanation of why being orderly and methodical was the linchpin of any scholarly endeavour. Today he was not just attempting to avoid duplicating his efforts, he also wanted to avoid another lecture.

As he unrolled the second scroll, his heart leapt into his mouth. This document contained a drawing of a casket, similar to the one Amelia described to them the other day. Not wanting to get his hopes up, he sped through the first two paragraphs of the document. It was a letter from a previous Baron Wexler to a captain of the Ducal Guard, the same captain who produced the report he shared with everyone when Amelia told them of the casket's existence.

The first paragraph explained Baron Wexler appreciated the duke's concern about a new brotherhood devoted to the god of the ocean, especially one with a military arm. He wanted to reassure everyone his new brotherhood would not be used against anyone in Hand. It would only be used to protect an important religious artefact.

The second paragraph was quite apologetic in tone, and while reading it Seamus thought the baron sounded like he could not quite believe what he was writing. Apparently he had been visited in the dead of night by a god, who gave him a casket. He instructed the baron that he and his descendants now had the sacred task of guarding the chest, ensuring its delivery to the Wizard and Warrior sometime in the future. Until then, the very existence of the casket was to be kept secret.

When the captain and his men arrived at the Wexler estate, the baron was flummoxed. He did not want to commit treason, but nor could he tell anyone about the casket. So he refused entry to the duke's men. This act left him uneasy so he prayed on the matter and received divine guidance.

The god informed him the Wizard and Warrior would come to the duke's library in Hand for answers on their quest, so writing a document explaining everything to the captain would serve two purposes; to reassure the duke Lord Wexler was no threat, and provide valuable information to the Wizard and the Warrior in the future. To this end, once he and the duke read this document, they were instructed to leave it in the palace library.

After his signature, Baron Wexler had added a coda.

'Goddess, I think this is it.' The words escaped Seamus' lips before he could stop them. He looked up, but Walter was so engrossed in his own work he had not heard a thing. Seamus read the coda under his breath.

'A good thing I did not forward this to you yesterday as I had another visit from a godly form last night. I was instructed to add the following, word for word, in my letter to the duke. "When attempting to capture a being without a body, containing them in something like a casket is desirable. Traditional spells will not work, you need to find someone who works magic using images not words. To truly be rid of a god from your realm, you need to send them back from whence they came. This is the only way to restore the true balance."

'When I asked the god what this meant, I was assured a wizard would understand. At first, I thought he said *the* Wizard, but I must have misheard him. I have done as I was asked, and I beseech you to leave this in your library for future generations.

'Well, I am the Wizard and I am not sure I understand. How is it no god will tell me exactly what I need to do, but they are happy to leave instructions in a scroll for anyone to find?'

'Sorry, Seamus, did you say something?' Walter distractedly ran a hand through his hair as he looked up. 'I understand this work is boring for you, but there are only a few more scrolls to go. We must find something soon.'

'I found it, at least, I think I did. If I understand this hint correctly, if we face the god before he is here in his own form, we are to place the god's essence in the casket and send him home. We had already guessed that, but there is still nothing on the how.'

Seamus shoved the scroll towards Walter, venting his frustration. He paced the room while Walter read through the document, mouthing the words and running his finger along under each sentence as he went. Re-reading a particular section, the furrow in his brow deepened before he continued until the end.

'You know this may not be the document we were directed here to find. There might still be a scroll in this lot with some more explicit instructions.'

Walter's attempt to buoy his flagging spirits fell on deaf ears.

'Great. But if this *is* the document, we are little better off. If it is not, there is only a little time left to find the real one.'

Walter stood and placed the scroll at the far end of the table, not wanting to risk losing it. He calmly sat down and picked up the document he had been working on previously.

'Well, we will not know for sure until we complete our search, will we? Besides, look at it this way, we might also find something unexpected in these last few scrolls to help us out.' Walter returned to his study.

Seamus half-heartedly kicked a chair, thought about letting the rant in his head out, before making do with muttered curses as he sat back down. In is heart of hearts, he knew that scroll was the one they were sent to find. However, Walter was right. Before they spent any more time studying the document, they needed to be sure none of the remaining items from the archive section of the library contained anything useful.

Seamus added more wood to the fire, warming the servants dining room, before taking as seat at the large wooden table just as Liam placed down a loaf of bread. His cousin took the chair next to him, and started helping himself to food. The room was quiet except for the clanking of cutlery as they finished filling their plates with the collection of cold meats, cheeses, vegetables and fruit in front of them.

'Why so glum?' Emer asked, staring pointedly at Seamus once everyone was eating.

He silently cursed the growing closeness between them. It seemed not only to enhance her ability to read his moods, but also gave her the confidence to voice her thoughts.

'Do not tell me. You are going to work through the

night to find the scroll, and you are not happy.'

'No, we found it.' His tone sounded flat, even to his own ears.

'So, I ask again, why so glum?'

'Surely we should be celebrating?' Liam asked as he stood. 'Shall I find out if cook can rustle up some ale?'

Seamus reached out and grabbed a handful of tunic, pulling his cousin back into his seat. 'Apart from the fact I do not fancy a full day's ride with a fuzzy head tomorrow, the scroll tells us nothing more than we already knew. The god needs to be trapped in the casket. It does not tell us how. There are no spells or magic words to help. I feel like we wasted days looking for something that was no help at all.'

Although he tried to keep his frustration to himself, he gripped his fork so hard his knuckles turned white.

Walter paused, carefully placing his knife and fork on his plate, and said, 'To be fair, we only read the scroll once before double checking the last few documents to make sure we had the correct one. We did not have time to do more than scan the contents. Maybe there is more to it than the initial reading let on.'

Walter's ability to focus on the positive had never grated on Seamus' nerves as much as it did at that moment. He wanted to shout and yell and rail against the unfairness of spending days searching for a scroll that turned out to be no help at all. He could not understand how Walter did not.

Gripping his fork more tightly, he stabbed violently at the meat on the plate in front of him. As he brought a forkful of food to his mouth, he caught Emer's worried look before she attempted to hide it by turning her attention to Walter.

'Do you truly think the document might contain more? Maybe some secret message? Did you bring it with you? Can we look?'

Even Emer was hopeful. So why was he so despondent? Walter was right, they had only scanned the document. A second reading might actually reveal more information. Yet he could not bring himself to raise his hopes.

'I would not go as far as to say it might be hiding a secret message,' Walter said. 'But if you study things from a different angle, sometimes more is revealed. And yes, I did bring the scroll with me. I thought we might go over it after dinner.' His contribution finished, Walter continued methodically eating his meal.

I am full.' Emer started clearing away amidst Liam helping himself to more as the dishes passed him by. 'I will make us some tea, and we can go over the scroll together. Liam?'

'Give me a minute, I have not finished dinner yet.'

The girl's hard stare must have convinced him otherwise, because he stuffed the rest of the food on his plate into his mouth, and stood to help clear the table as he attempted to chew and swallow a few last morsels.

Seamus pushed his plate away. His hunger disappeared when the subject of the scroll's contents came up. There was nothing he wanted to do less than review the words he had read this afternoon, but nor could he leave this up to the others. After all, the scroll had been left for him and Aliah.

Closing his eyes to give himself a moment's peace,

they immediately flew open. Hold on, how did he know the scroll was meant for him? Was it just because it said the Wizard and Warrior needed to find it, or was there another reason?

With his eyes again closed he went over the words in his mind, and he kept sticking on the phrase, "thoughts not words". Of course there had not been a spell or a method for him to capture the god in the casket. During his trial, the gods explained how different his magical gifts were. He did not need gestures or words like other wizards, he only needed to imagine what he wanted and use the elements to make it happen.

He allowed a little relief to trickle through, then tensed again. His training enabled him to move objects, but how did you move a non-corporeal being like a spirit? He needed to concentrate on that, not re-reading the scroll.

Turning to Walter, who was still busy with his meal, he asked, 'Walter, have you ever heard of someone's spirit being bound?'

The older man paused, fork half-way to his mouth, and stayed stock still for a moment. Slowly he returned the fork to his plate and turned to Seamus. 'That is an odd question, and the answer should be no, no person should bind another person's soul. In reality though, binding is done relatively regularly.'

Seamus' face froze in surprise. 'Are you able to restrain someone like that?'

'In theory, yes, in practice, no. Although most wizards are able to bind a spirit, it is best performed by someone with healing gifts because so many things might go wrong.'

'So ...' Seamus encouraged Walter to go on.

'Umm, I am not really sure I should be passing this on, but I assume you are asking for a good reason and not just idle curiosity.

'Binding is often used by senior healers when someone has serious mental problems that place them, or those close to them, in physical danger. If the healer can isolate the source of the problem, they bind that part of a person's mind—or soul, if you prefer.'

'That sounds exactly like what I need.'

Walter chewed thoughtfully for a moment, swallowed, then continued. 'I am not sure I should be doing this, but, given our unique circumstances, I trust you to only apply this learning to our enemy.'

He placed his cutlery down again, giving Seamus his full attention.

'I assume your teachers showed you how to mind- link?'

'Yes.'

'Good. Now try and link minds with me. Excellent. Now, what can you tell me about the link you just made?'

'Umm.' Seamus frowned, trying to find the words to describe what was happening. 'Connecting with you is different to when I link with Aliah. You feel, well, it feels like a "Walterness" is surrounding me.'

'You are experiencing a full mind link. When most wizards connect, it is more like this.'

Seamus' sense of Walter changed, almost as though the wizard closed a part of himself off. Now he appeared more as a ghost than a complete person in his thoughts.

'Generally a link is agreed to, and the two wizards will create a space in their consciousness to allow another person in. This does two things, it stops the person linking from being overwhelmed by the other person, and allows each wizard to maintain some control over what they share.

'When a wizard needs to apply healing to a tortured soul, the interaction is much more intense than what you felt when you first joined with me, because the emotions the person is experiencing are so much more intense.'

Walter dropped his walls, once again appearing to Seamus as a full person.

'Now I want you to expand your presence in my mind, see if you can surround everything you perceive as my "Walterness".'

'You mean like when I first learnt to control magic and you taught me to move my magic in and out of my body?' Seamus attempted to put Walter's words into a context he could understand.

'Yes, although then you thought of your magic as a stream, this time I want you to flatten out your gift, like you are casting out a blanket and wrapping me up in it.'

Seamus imagined himself in Walter's mind, standing in front of what he perceived as Walter. He closed his eyes so he would not be distracted. He imagined himself walking around his projection of the wizard. Where he could not sense Walter's person, he saw a deep blackness and changed his direction. Once he completed the circumference, he floated over top to ensure he had an idea of the full height of the "Walterness". Satisfied with his survey, he imagined throwing a blanket over everything he saw as his friend.

'Walter? Walter? What is wrong?'

Seamus' eyes flew open and he found himself staring

into Emer's worried face. His gaze followed hers, and he saw Walter sitting quite still, eyes wide open, staring blankly at the wall in front of him. The only sign he was alive was the gentle rise and fall of his chest. As Seamus rose to check on the older man, he released his magic. The light returned to Walter's eyes and the wizard returned to himself.

Collapsing back into his chair, Seamus worked hard to stop his dinner from making another appearance. 'Walter, what did I do?'

'It is all right, boy, you went a little further than I thought you would be able to for your first attempt. None-the-less, you learnt the lesson I wanted you to learn.'

Walter serenely took the cup of tea Emer had poured for him, and waited for her and Liam to sit at the table.

'You expected me to do that? Or something like that?' Seamus was astonished.

'Well, yes, of course. Otherwise why would I have you do what you did? I must say though, those gods have been teaching you well because your skill is far in advance of where I estimated it would be.' Walter continued the conversation as if nothing much had happened.

Seamus was unable to let things go that easily. 'When I looked at you, it was as if you were no longer in your body.' Seamus' hand shook as he took a cup of tea from Emer.

'In many ways I was not. The blanket you threw over me hid my essence, or soul. I was not in any danger. I could have thrown the blanket off at any time as you had not secured it. I wanted to show you a way to identify my soul, and, as I found out when I taught you magic, you learn better by doing than by hearing.' Walter took a sip of his tea while Seamus fought to get his hands under control.

'Why ever would you want to do that?' Emer admonished them both. 'That is an awfully dangerous lesson. Seamus might have made a mistake and extinguished your light, or cut you off from your magic.'

'What?' Seamus stood and started pacing around the room, still fighting to keep his dinner inside. 'Emer, please explain.'

'If you had closed the "blanket" you placed around him and spelled it, Walter would have been like a zombie until you undid the binding. If you pulled the blanket tight and crushed him, his light would be gone and his body would continue on as a shell without a soul until it withered away.'

Seamus' hands clenched tightly around his mug. He had always feared the process of quietening, believing taking someone's magic was removing a little of what made a person who they were. Now he had almost done something worse to Walter. His stomach roiled at the very thought.

'Excuse me.' Seamus dashed into the kitchen, and through to the scullery. Reaching the stone sink just in time for it to catch his dinner.

Moments later, feeling wretched but a little more settled, he joined the others. 'Please explain to me the details of the process to cut someone off from their magic.'

He did not actually want to find out as just the thought of cutting someone off from their magic al essence made him sick to the stomach, but realised he must know details if he was to fight the god.

Liam passed him a cup of water, his eyes sparkling with mischief. At least someone appeared to be enjoying Seamus' discomfort.

'You realise what you just did is one of the ways they take away magic. You know, to quieten people?'

The shock of having his fears confirmed caused Seamus to knock the cup in front of him, spilling water across the table. His stomach clenched again, but he fought to control his emotions as he answered.

'No, well, sort of. After listening to you I thought it might be.'

Realising all this was truly new to him, Emer carried on a little more gently.

'To quieten a person with magic, you cut the link from their soul, or essence, to their magic. You get the same result if you hide the soul for any length of time. The connection weakens and eventually withers. Cut it off for too long, and the bond cannot reform.'

'Humph, a soul needs to be hidden for days, even moon-turns before that happens. And as I said, I was in control all the time. While he followed my instructions Seamus would not have been able to extinguish or damage my light. Now quit making the boy ill and let me finish my lesson,' Walter grumbled.

Emer made to say something else, then thought better of it. Concentrating on her tea, she allowed Walter to go on.

'When a person has a sickness of the soul or mind their essence becomes fractured. A healer will find the core of the person and repair or remove any of the fractures. The process is a difficult one, and always leaves the person less than whole. So it is only used in extreme cases.'

'Why was Seamus trying to find your essence anyway?' Liam asked.

'I believe because he is attempting to find some way to control a god who does not have a body. Am I right?' Walter asked.

Seamus nodded reluctantly. Although he now had an idea as to how he might isolate the god's essence, he was not sure he actually had the heart to do it.

'How do you know a god has an essence like a person?' Liam turned to his cousin.

'I do not,' Seamus admitted. 'But I have to start somewhere.'

'Perhaps you can ask one of your god instructors,' Liam suggested.

Raising his eyebrows, Seamus turned towards Liam, 'That is a surprisingly good idea.'

Seamus now felt in control enough to drink a mouthful of tea. When he finished, he stood and asked, 'Shall we take another look at this scroll?'

While Liam and Emer leaned over the kitchen table, pouring over the scroll's contents, Walter finished his meal and Seamus allowed his stomach to settle while sipping another mug of tea.

'Ahh.' Emer pointed something out to Liam.

'So that is why he wanted to know.' His cousin glanced up at Seamus, then back down at the document in front of him. Emer elbowed him in the ribs and pointed at something else. Liam shrugged and carried on reading.

'Did you translate the writing in the drawing?' Emer looked up at Walter and Seamus.

'What?' Walter had been daydreaming.

Seamus leaned forward to get a better look. 'The picture of the casket has writing? I thought it was just an elaborate sketch.'

'I would have been surprised if you recognised the words, but I thought Walter might. It is an extremely old form of our language, but most libraries still contain at least some scrolls written in it.'

Turning the paper to give Walter a better view, Emer moved to stand behind him. Running her finger along, she showed him where the writing was.

'Oh my, how did I miss that? Many of the documents I studied while at the Wizard Isle were written in the same language. Here, let me see if I still have my touch. It has been a while.' The room was silent as he concentrated.

'If I am not mistaken this is another version of the Wizard and Warrior Prophecy. Let me see...

"After the decimation and the fall,

When the new power rises

And the Wizard and Warrior meet,

Old and new blood will combine

With the two who are not what they seem.

The key is the Ember Casket, to trap and calm the chaos,

Or send it beyond to save one and all."

Emer stared at Seamus. 'Even if you missed the prophecy, this scroll is more useful than you give it credit for.'

'Really?'

'Yes, really. It confirms you need the casket. Obviously you now realise you need to put the god's essence inside, otherwise you would not have been fooling around with Walter and his soul. That lesson has also given you the bare bones of a plan to transfer his soul to the box.'

Seamus admitted to himself she was right, but did she have to sound so much like a tutor when she pointed things out? Elbows on the table, he cradled his chin in his hands.

'And …' Liam chimed in. 'It tells you placing the god in the casket is only part of what you need to do.'

Sitting upright, Seamus swung his head to look at his cousin. 'What do you mean?'

'Well, this bit here.' Liam indicated the coda at the bottom of the scroll. 'If I read it correctly, it says once the god is safely in the casket you need to find a way to get him and the chest he is imprisoned in back to the gods so balance can be restored.'

Surprise did not truly describe Seamus' reaction at that precise moment. Although his cousin was by no means stupid, he preferred physical activities to book learning. Still, how did Liam figure that out when his own brain skipped over it?

'He is right, Seamus. It is stated in the new version of the prophecy as well.' Walter leaned back. 'I wish we had taken the time to read the complete prophecy in the Sanctuary before we left. Knowing the thing in its entirety would be useful about now.'

'I had forgotten about that,' Seamus shook his head. 'Aliah and I asked to see it before our trials, but we were told we could not read it until the gods confirmed us in our roles. Afterwards, everything moved so fast I never thought to ask again.'

'Amelia and I were so caught up in the idea we needed to be back with you as soon as possible, we never thought to go through it either.' Walter's shoulder sagged.

'I think you are wandering off track.' Still in tutor mode, Emer moved so they could all see her. 'If you needed something else from the prophecy the gods would have found a way to let you know.'

Seamus chewed this idea over. The gods made sure Amelia found out about the casket and the scroll, so possibly Emer was correct.

'Besides, if there was anything else obvious in the prophecy documents my father would have told us. He knows that particular prophecy backwards and forwards.'

'All right, I believe you.' Seamus held up his hands for her to stop bombarding him with logic. 'There is only one more thing to worry about. I have a plan for moving the god to the casket, but how do I move him from this plane. Any ideas?' He waited for the others to speak. 'Anyone?'

The hush that fell over the room was so complete Seamus heard the plop of a dripping tap in the scullery.

'Nothing? Nothing at all? Not even a spark of an idea? Walter, maybe something in the library that might help? We still have a few hours before we need to leave.'

The older wizard shook his head. 'Sorry, although I understand the general principles, large scale transportational magic is beyond me. There are not many wizards able to move items beyond their line of sight, and even then, the objects are small like, umm, this cup of tea.'

'This gets better and ...'

BATTLE

Seamus stopped mid-sentence as something caught his eye.

'Seamus? What is it?' Liam asked.

'I thought I just saw ...'

It was as though he could see Dominic sitting in front of the fire, but there were no chairs there. As he tried to focus on the form of his Warrior, the room in front of Seamus disappeared and he was staring into a crackling blaze.

Seamus? Is that you?

Aliah?

Yeah! I did it.

Seamus found himself back in the kitchen looking intently at the grain of the wooden table in front of him.

'How odd,' he mused

Swiftly sitting bolt upright, Liam had his hand on the knife at his belt and wearily searched the room.

'What is happening?'

'Nothing, I am just tired.' Shaking his head clear, Seamus returned to the matter at hand. 'If we are not going to find anything further here, we may as well all get a good night's sleep. We have a long way to go tomorrow.'

Not waiting for anyone else, Seamus rose and left the room. Had Aliah really managed to contact him from so far away? If she had, then something good had come from today.

He was so engrossed in his thoughts he did not notice the guard in front of him until the man put out a hand to prevent Seamus from bowling him over.

'Pardon me, sir, but there is a man at the door asking for Boss Allum. I explained Mr Allum left this morning, but he is insisting on seeing someone.'

Seamus stopped in his tracks, waiting for his brain to catch up with what the guard had said.

'Umm, do we know this man?'

'Hardly, sir. He has an Arian accent, and he looks like he has not seen a bath in weeks. However, he is wearing wizard robes.' The guard's lip curled with distaste.

'Perhaps you can go and ask him what his business is, then I can decide whether or not to see him. I will wait in my father's office.'

It felt odd opening the door to the room his father ran the duchy from and not see his father seated behind the desk. Sighing, he plopped down in the nearest chair, then immediately stood. If he wanted to be taken seriously as the person in charge he could not sit there, but it felt odd to sit in his father's seat.

Wandering round behind the desk, he paused at a knock.

'Enter.'

The young guard opened the door and slipped in, closing it behind. Seamus nodded for him to speak.

'Sir, the man says he has come from the Carsten camp on the other side of the island. He says he was there as a spy for our side, and that he needs to speak to someone here to pass on some news before he leaves for the Wizard Isle.'

When Seamus said nothing, the guard continued, 'I can send him away, sir. I mean to try and gain entry with such a preposterous story ...' The guard trailed off mid-sentence when Seamus sat down in the duke's chair.

'No, no, bring him in. I want you to stand watch outside the door here, and send one of the other guards to fetch Walter, we will need him to verify this man is actually who he says he is.'

'Sir, I am not sure I should do that. He could be someone sent to spy on us, and I would be placing you in danger. The duke would never forgive me.'

Sitting as tall as he could in the chair, Seamus did what his father would in the same situation. 'You have your orders,' he said, and stared at the guard, challenging the man to defy him.

The ploy may not have worked with a more seasoned soldier, but the guard was new enough to the ranks that he did not yet feel confident to defy the duke's son. Moments later, he returned leading a balding, round faced man dressed in wizard black, who started when he saw Seamus sitting behind the desk.

'Oh, I am sorry, I thought I was being taken to whomever is in charge.' He moved as if to leave the room, but was forestalled by the guard shutting the door firmly behind him.

'That would be me,' Seamus assured the wizard. 'Please take a seat.'

The man remained standing.

'I have important information those defending Aria must hear, I need to talk to the person who is leading Hand's defence against Carsten, or at the very least, someone who can get a message to that person.'

An amused smile played around Seamus' lips as he answered. 'Once again that would be me. Perhaps if you would take a seat, we can introduce ourselves and that might clear things up a little.'

He waited patiently while his guest considered his options, sighed, and took the seat opposite Seamus.

'You are?' Seamus asked.

In a tone clearly telling Seamus the man would play his game, but only for the moment, the wizard answered. 'Braxton, Wizard of the Gold.'

Before Seamus could introduce himself, the door opened and Walter barged in. Glancing quickly at Seamus, his eyes moved to the man in the chair, and his face split into a wide grin. Braxton stood and embraced the older man, a look of relief clearly written on his face.

'Ah, Walter, I am so pleased to see you.'

'As am I to see you,' Walter answered. 'I have to say when Boss Allum told me you were working as a spy I had mixed feelings. The first was relief, because you had not gone over to the enemy as I suspected, but it was followed by concern, because your life was clearly in danger. Now I am pleased to see you back safe and sound.'

'Walter, I knew what I was getting into when I started this. Besides, you know me, as soon as things became sticky, I left. One of the Carsten truth sayers was showing an awful lot of interest in me, and I knew it was only a matter of time before I was found out. Besides, I have some interesting news I need to pass on. Perhaps you can take me to whoever is in charge. My boat leaves just before midnight and I do not have much time.'

Walter frowned, 'Person in charge? But ... Ah, Braxton, let me introduce you to Lord Seamus, Duke Damon's eldest son.'

BATTLE

Braxton at least had the grace to blush when he realised who Seamus was, but he was still not convinced.

'Walter, I am sure this young man is the highest ranking noble here, but I need to talk with someone who is actually going to be fighting in this battle and understands a little more about the real enemy we face.'

Seamus stood to protest, but Walter's laughter stopped him, and he sank back into the chair, realising the wizard had this all in hand. 'Why, Braxton, this boy is not only going to be fighting in this battle, but he is one of the two most important combatants for our side.'

Walter sat down, and Braxton joined him, still looking skeptical. 'I will have to take your word for that, Walter.' The wizard turned to Seamus. 'No offence, lad, but you are just so young, and this news is important for the safety of our realm.'

'I understand your concern. Perhaps it will help if I tell you I am in contact with both the king's forces in Port Marden, and the guard captain put in charge of defences here in Hand. At the very least I can pass on your message, at best your information might also help us with a plan we are cooking up to deal with the being pulling the Carsten Army's strings.'

Braxton considered Seamus' words, but still looked to Walter for confirmation before answering. Seamus suppressed a frustrated sigh, realising to assert who he was and his role in this war to a complete stranger was not the best course of action. If Walter had introduced him as the duke's son, then he had a reason to not name him as the Wizard.'

'All right, I guess this is the best I can do for the

moment given I have not got much time. I and two other wizards fled the enemy camp two nights ago, after Wizard Millard sent two battle ships to destroy the Wizard Isles. He was so incensed so many of our brothers had not joined him in his attempted coup, he decided they did not deserve to live.'

'Are there many wizards left on the isle?' Walter asked. 'I thought most were with the king's forces.'

'From what I can tell, there are maybe twenty wizards there, but I suspect the attack is against the wizards in training, the next generation,' Braxton answered.

Walter's eyes widened. 'Oh, no.'

'That is why we left. We could not get a message to them while we were still in camp as we would have been detected and our lives forfeit. We got through, and the school is being evacuated as we speak.

'We have a boat in the harbour. I am travelling with a weather magician, and another magician who can do some travel magic. Combined with my skills, we should be able to arrive at the isle before the Carsten ships. We will meet with the remaining wizards and rescue as much of the library as we can.'

'Even with your skills, they have had two days start on you. Are you sure you can make it there first?' Seamus asked.

'It will be close, but they have had to travel some way out to sea so as not to be detected by Arian forces. We can take a more direct route. Still, I must be on my way as soon as possible.'

'Wait.' Walter placed a restraining hand on the wizard's arm. 'I think good fortune brought you here today of all days. Am I right in remembering you had some skill in transporting magics?'

'Umm, yes. It is not my primary area, but I have some aptitude.'

'Before you go, could you please describe for us the process of moving an object from one place to another?'

Braxton appeared confused.

'I would not ask, but it is really important, perhaps more important in the long run than saving the library at the Wizard Isle.'

'Umm, all right. My primary skill is in elemental control; manipulating fire, water, earth and air. I can spell the elements to do more or less of what they do naturally, depending on the situation. While studying, I found if I spelled air to cocoon an object, I could then use the air to move something from one place to another.

'I know that is not strictly transportational magic as others with a true gift would describe it, but it works for me. Now, I really must be going.'

'Ah, Wizard Braxton, while the attack on the Wizard Isle is important news, I find it hard to believe that is the important news our military strategists cannot do without,' Seamus interrupted.

'Oh dear, you are quite right, I almost forgot. Millard and his goon Gaius have been searching for something, and they have had the magic users from Carsten helping them. I believe they are close to finding out where that something is, and once they have it, there will be full scale war. From the intelligence I picked up, I believe the main battle will begin in less than a six-day.'

'Thank you, Braxton, that is most useful. I will be

sure to pass the message on.' Seamus stood and shook the wizard's hand, then slumped back into his chair as Walter escorted his former pupil out of the palace.

His mind was buzzing with all he had learnt that day, attempting to fit all the pieces together. A bare bones plan was forming in his mind, and he was confident he knew what to do even though there were areas he needed to tease out.

However, there were two things that worried him. The first was he knew what he had to do, but what role was Aliah to play when the final battle came? He knew enough to know it would not be as simple as standing there guarding him while he fought the god, but he had no idea what else she would do instead. Nor did she, he suspected.

Then there was the news they had less than a six-day to stop the god before the final battle for Aria. This was all getting very real, and the desire to flee somewhere far from the war was growing stronger. The only thing stopping him was the knowledge that if the god came through to this world, nowhere would be safe.

9
A BUSY NIGHT

Heat scorched through her divided riding skirt, bringing Aliah back into Baron George's finest guest room. During her contact with Seamus, she had inadvertently wandered too close to the roaring fire warming the room.

'You did it.' Dominic's grin spread from ear to ear.

Absentmindedly moving back from the flames, Aliah sat down, still lost in her own thoughts.

'Hey, Aliah, you should be celebrating.'

Coming from afar, her tutor's words scarcely pierced

her consciousness. Something disturbed her about the way she joined with Seamus, and she needed to figure out why.

'I could feel Seamus, and I was drawing towards him, but something prevented be from getting through. Perhaps a lack of magical power? Then ... it was like a sort of bump ... and we connected, and he flooded my mind. I was so surprised I dropped the connection.'

Angrily she turned to face Dominic. 'You helped me?'

Although framed as a question, her tone suggested she already knew the answer. Before Aliah wound herself into full-blown anger, Dominic held his hands up in surrender.

'I understand you wanted to do it all by yourself, and you almost did.'

'Almost. Why did you not just let me fail? I am no shrinking violet to be put off by failure. I would have tried again.'

Weary from her magical training, she slumped in the chair, glaring at Dominic.

'There was more thought behind my actions than merely assisting you to join with Seamus. In my experience, it is easier to connect to someone you have joined with before. Remember when we started tonight, I asked if you could see or visualise a link to Seamus?'

'Yes,' she answered, unsure where this was going.

'When I connect with someone I have linked with before, I can see a faint trail to their mind, no matter how far away they are. Each time I connect with them the link to them becomes clearer. At first, I thought you might be able to see a path to Seamus, when I realised you could not, I decided to give you a helping hand to create one.'

'Oh.' Somewhat deflated, Aliah let the tension and anger drain from her body. 'I did not see anything leading me to Seamus when I was searching for him. Should I try again and see if I can find it now?'

'Maybe, but why not recharge your energy first? We can attempt another connection tomorrow. Perhaps it would be more beneficial to discuss what happened and see if we need to make some adjustments when you try next time.'

Skeptical about his motives, Aliah gave Dominic what she hoped was a piercing stare. 'Are you handling me?'

A chuckle escaped, and soon the boy in front of her was laughing out loud. 'Sorry, yes. You must appreciate sometimes it is easier to work around you than take you on directly.'

If she had had any energy left Aliah would have feigned annoyance, but in truth she was too tired to bother.

'I know. I sometimes react when I should think first. I am working on it.'

Dominic took some time to calm himself, and while she waited, Aliah replayed the process of making her link with Seamus.

First, she formed a clear picture of her Wizard in her mind. That was the easy part. Then she reached out and search for what felt like Seamus' energy. When a person stood near to you, it was easy to sense them. When contacting someone far away, your consciousness needed to keep expanding until you found the person you were looking for.

In theory it sounded simple, in practice it was not so easy. Between her and Seamus lived hundreds upon hundreds of conscious minds—animals as well as people—not to mention the tiny pinpricks of light she assumed were insects. Some of the larger lights were dull and uninteresting, but others were bright and shiny. The difficulty was not to be drawn off track by the more interesting glowing balls.

Finally she found a luminous presence, pulling her towards it like a magnet. Drawing closer, the "Seamusness" of the light washed over her. Excited at having found her destination, she rushed forward only to find she could not penetrate his mind.

Almost overcome with frustration she thought about withdrawing when, suddenly, they were linked. Instead of the gentle contact she planned, Seamus said her name and had blundered into her head.

Now she realised Dominic had given her a nudge, there was no longer a mystery about how she connected. All she needed to work out was how Seamus managed to overwhelm her by simply acknowledging her presence. Dominic's laughter was back under control and he was ready to answer her questions.

'Much as I hate to say it, you are right, I need to understand what happened. When I linked with Seamus, I caught a brief glimpse of where he was, I am sure he was at the table in the palace kitchens. There were some people with him, I guess Emer and Liam, but I cannot be certain. What worries me is when I join with you it is like entering a house. You allow me to come in and the space is welcoming.

'The moment Seamus was aware of me he filled my head with his presence, and I lost control. I spoke to him but he seemed unaware of anything I said, so I shut down the connection.'

She closely watched Dominic for his reaction, but he continued staring into the fire.

'Did you hear me?' Aliah attempted to keep her temper under control, but it was not easy when being ignored.

'Yes, I am thinking.'

'Oh, you could have said.'

The moment the words escaped her lips she realised she sounded like a petulant child, and wished to take them back. This new closeness with Dominic unsettled her. Should she treat him as a friend, a tutor, or a guard? None of the traditional roles seemed quite right to describe their new relationship.

'Aliah, are you there?'

Goddess! Her face warmed with a blush. Had he guessed she was thinking about him? Did he see her blush, or would he assume heat from the fire caused her to turn red?

'Yes, carry on.' *Argh, how formal.* Now he would know something was up. *Just calm down and stay focused,* she commanded herself.

'Normally the person who initiates contact stays in control of the process. Perhaps Seamus took over because his magic is really strong, or maybe it is because your sword and his wand support the link?

'We need to work on your defences before we try again, otherwise you will never be able to communicate clearly with him. In the normal course of things that would not be a problem, but if you need to pass on a brief message you might run into trouble.'

'Oh. So I did not do anything wrong.' Relief flooded through her, giving hope she might actually be able to do this, eventually.

'I am sure your linking will improve with practice. Now, I believe rest is what you need as we are meeting early with Baron George again tomorrow to finalise details before heading to Rasmussen's.'

With Dominic's departure, Aliah found herself feeling more alone than she had in a while. Without Seamus who would talk through the days' events with her and figure out what it all meant. Without Daniel, who was still not recovered from his stomach problem, and was in bed resting for tomorrow's ride. Amelia and Boss had their heads together over something and she thought maybe Dominic would stay after their lesson. Even his know-it-all comments would be preferable to this loneliness.

Something had definitely altered between the two of them, and she was not sure she liked it. Yet, things could not return to the way they were either. Annoyingly, she should be concentrating on their more pressing problems, but thoughts of Dominic and the changes between them filled her head.

A yawn escaped as she stood and picked up her travel pack. Exhausted, she decided to take Dominic's advice and get some sleep. There would be plenty of time for her to worry this through while they travelled tomorrow.

BATTLE

Mulling over things in his head, Seamus realised he was in for a busy evening as he urgently needed to speak to two people and a god. First things first, he sent out a prayer to the gods, asking for another extra training session. That done, he searched for Emer and asked her to pass on the information he gathered from Braxton to her father, ensuring the king would remain informed.

He did not ask her to pass anything on to Amelia for Daniel yet, he believed he had that message covered. All he had to do now was wait, and he had to wait for quite a while for a god to appear.

'You have need of us again?' the god asked. 'Are you still worried about not being able to train with Aliah?

Instead of answering, Seamus launched into a series of questions coming from his discussion with Walter over dinner, starting with whether or not it was possible to link with a god's mind in the same way you could with a human one.

Not really knowing what to expect, he was taken by surprise when crystalline tears streamed down the warrior god's face as she tried to hold the laughter in and answer Seamus' question.

'Young Wizard, you are indeed strong for a human, but you are not strong enough to enter a god-mind. Here, let me show you.'

Feather-light, the god reached out and touched his cheek with her hand, gently drawing him towards her mind. Before he was anywhere near the core of the god, light over-whelmed him and Seamus mentally pulled back with such a force his consciousness snapped back into his own head with an almost audible thud.

'What did you see?' asked the god.

'Colours so bright I could hardly bring myself to look at them. I was not even totally in your mind and I felt like I was standing on the edge of an abyss. I knew if I went any closer, I might never be able to return to myself.'

Settled safely back into his own mind, worry overtook the awe. How would he ever be able to force the god into the Ember Casket if he was not even able to look at him?

'There is more you wish to ask?'

'I fear the task you have set me is insurmountable. I know you cannot discuss any details with me, or tell me what to do, but how am I to control an entity such as you for long enough to force them into a chest, presuming you have not spelled it so he will enter himself when he is close by?'

The god tapped an index finger on her lips as she thought how to answer, or perhaps she was communicating with the other gods.

'You are correct, I am unable to instruct you in what you have to do, and no we have not set a trap for our brother. However, what I can do is tell you a little about we gods in general, which may assist you in your preparations.

'For one of us to come and teach you each night in corporeal form it takes the combined will of all seven of us. We are hundreds of times stronger in this form than in any other, therefore our lights shine brighter.

'The trial you undertook was on a mid-plane. When the veil is thin, we can appear there in ethereal form, and communicate using our minds with those of you on this world with very little effort.

'Once every hundred years or so, the veil between the

worlds thins enough so we can project an ethereal form onto your plane of existence using only a little of our energy. In that form, we are able to communicate with your kind, if invited in we can even share a physical body. With an especially weak mind, we might even take over a body if the mind occupying it is weak of will.

'What we cannot do is move our physical selves from our world to your world, or even to the mid-world, without an exceptional amount of magical power.'

The god was silent while Seamus mulled over what she said. Knowing the god could not confirm or deny anything specifically to do with her brother, Seamus noticed when she spoke there were often micro reactions indicating whether or not he was on the correct path. A small tightening of the lips when he was wrong, or a twitch at the corner of her mouth that was almost a smile when he headed in the right direction. Speaking his thoughts out loud, he watched his teacher's reactions.

'Mmm, if I understand what I heard correctly, you are here in physical form so your light is very bright. If I had attempted the same exercise during my trial, I would not have found your essence to be so all-encompassing.'

Was that an almost smile?

'Continue,' the warrior god commanded.

'If I came across you in ghost form on this world you would be even duller in appearance, perhaps much closer to the essence of a human.'

'How dare you even suggest my essence could ever be close to a human's. I would still be brighter by far.'

Although the god appeared to be boasting, Seamus took note of the information she was passing on.

'If it takes seven gods to send one of you to train me for even a few candle-marks, it stands to reason it will take an equal amount of power to send a god back to where they came from.'

Click, click, click. Pieces fell into place. 'I am looking for an artefact to contain a god-mind. I am thinking perhaps the chest contains a magical boost, enough to send the god back to where he came from.'

Perhaps a slight surprised rise of the eyebrows there?

'Oh no.' Seamus' stomach lurched as more puzzle pieces fitted together. 'If the chest holds enough magic to send the god away, it also holds enough to bring the god into this world. Whoever gets to the chest first is likely to win at least the first round of our battle.'

Sadness swept so swiftly across the face of the god, he almost did not see it. Defeat seeped through him as he realised the full extent of the task before them. They had to beat the god in a race to an object of power, then use that object to send him out of this realm of existence. A small misstep and he could actually end up helping the god to come here in all his glory.

No matter the gods said they would be able to fight their brother even if he was physically on this world, with the Ember Casket in his hands, where would they find enough power to send him home?

Sinking to the ground, he held his head in his hands, going through everything he had learnt again to see if he could find any glimmer of hope. There it was, a dull light flickered in the recesses of his mind. *I know his name.*

As if she read his thoughts the god asked, 'Have you

another question for me, or shall we train?'

'Wait a moment, I need to think this through. When we worshipped you all, and called you by your given names, a link must have been created between you and the people who prayed to you. Perhaps it not only kept balance between the worlds, but did it also make it easier for you to move between the them?'

'It was a very long time ago, but yes, that is correct. When we were worshiped in all the lands equally, the veil between the worlds was thin enough for us to have full contact with your kind.

'Now few of us are worshipped in your world, and some not at all. The balance is not as strong as it once was, and it is more difficult for us to contact you.'

Slowly the small light was growing brighter.

'So … if a god was no longer worshipped here and people had forgotten their name, there would be no link. If one person was to own the name and be the only person to call it, there would be a strong link, perhaps almost tethering the god to that person?'

The god in front of him was completely motionless, as if she dared not give anything away at all. Seamus knew he must be onto something, but he was not quite sure what. He needed to think through how to use the small advantage he unearthed.

While his mind whirred with all these new thoughts, he asked the final question he had for the god.

'Can you help me connect with Aliah?'

The god considered his request. 'I could, but I think your mind is too distracted to communicate effectively. When you have settled down, and your mind is quiet, you can look for your link to Aliah. When people have linked before it leaves a trail to that person. The more you connect, the clearer the trail. If you can follow that link and find your Warrior you can try connecting like you did here.

'If there is nothing else, I need to return. We have preparations of our own to make. Would you like me to send you to sleep before I depart?'

'I have things to do, so I am fine, and I cannot think of anything else to ask,' Seamus responded distractedly. 'Thank you for coming.'

'You are welcome,' the god said as she winked away.

Exhausted, Seamus flopped down on the bed and thought through what the god said to him about people and energy. At first, he cast his mind out around the palace and found little balls of light. From their positions in relation to each other he could work out who each of them belonged to.

Leaving the confines of the building, he was overwhelmed by the sheer number of lights in the half-deserted town of Port Hand, and he retreated back to his room in frustration. When Emer spoke of connecting with her father she made it seem easy, almost as easy as he and Aliah connecting when they were together. He knew if there was a way to filter out the other lights and just concentrate on Aliah, he would be able to recognise her.

Clearing his mind again, he thought only of Aliah and let his consciousness leave his body. As he disconnected, he glimpsed a gossamer thread of light. Wondering if this was the connection to Aliah the god described, he followed it.

Racing along the thread, he soared above all the other consciousnesses until he spotted a glow he recognised. Relief filled him, and he rushed towards her, slamming into her mind.

ALIAH.

Seamus? She was groggy, telling him he had probably woken her up.

His elation at finding her was soon superseded by surprise as he felt himself violently pushed out of her presence.

Back in his room, frustrated, he tried again. He was able to find Aliah more easily this time. Rather than rushing in, he imagined himself whispering her name.

He watched a small opening appear and he rushed forward, only for it to close before he could enter.

Aliah?

The opening appeared again, and this time he moved forward at a gentler pace.

Hello, Seamus.

Aliah? What was that all about?

If you remember, the gods told us there are rules for entering people's minds. In fact …

Rules? Seamus asked.

Yes, remember, you ask first if you can make a connection. Then you do not just barge in, you enter respectfully.

Oh. Right. You were making a point.

Ignoring him, Aliah continued. *And, when you enter, you hold some of yourself back so you do not overwhelm the other person.*

That seems sensible. But am I really linked with you? This feels different somehow?

It is. We are not fully linked, but we are communicating.

You seem to have learnt a lot from Dominic, Seamus commented.

How did you … the gods.

Yes. Anyway, I am pleased I have made it here. Did you just yawn?

I am exhausted. Why are you here? I hope it is not only to see if you can? Travelling for days on end is tiring and I really need to get some sleep, Aliah answered dozily.

No. Well, yes, but also to pass on news. How did you go today?

Not so good. Baron George is lovely, and we have his full support. On the other hand, Baron Tappit was, well, let us just say he is not very nice. We did not manage to secure his troops yet, but we have a plan.

I met Baron Tappit once, not long after his brother died, and I know what you mean about him. We do need his troops though.

As I said, we are working on it. Fortunately, Baron George has been most helpful. He is such a dear man. What is your news? Aliah asked sleepily.

We had an unexpected visitor today. Boss' spy friend.

What? Why? Aliah's mind was now fully alert.

He is heading back to the Wizard Isle, it seems they are soon to be under attack. Apparently Millard wants to be rid of all opposition, both present and future, Seamus updated her.

Will he be able to get back to the other wizards in time?

BATTLE

He has ways of getting there. Although that news is important, he had more. Now Aliah was more fully awake, he decided it was time to tell her the worst of it. *From what he said, I believe the god and Millard are looking for the same chest we are, and once they have it, they intend to launch the final attack. He said they know where it is and we will be fully at war before the end of this six-day.*

He paused and waited for Aliah to process the news before continuing.

I am thinking in light of this new information, you should head directly to Baron Wexler's and meet me there. Leave the others to finish rallying the troops.

Whoa, Seamus, slow down. What has changed so dramatically to make you think we should alter our plans?

Aliah appeared much calmer than Seamus expected her to be. Did she not see how important it was for them to be together now?

The time for our battle is drawing close, we should be together, Seamus said.

Do you feel that is important? You know what I mean by feel? Is this a premonition sort of thing?

The question made Seamus stop and think.

Seamus? Is this something we have to do, or are you worried about us being apart?

It is more something I would feel better about, if I am honest, Seamus eventually admitted.

When I left, you were all right with my going. What has changed? Do you need my help planning for the final battle?

Again Seamus paused before he answered, trying to

be clear about his concerns.

I think I know what needs to be done. We need to find the chest, bind the god and send him home using the power the chest contains. I also have an idea on how I might do that.

Then what is the problem? Aliah interrupted.

The prophecy and the gods have always said we need both a Wizard and a Warrior to defeat the god. I cannot see what your role is meant to be in all of this.

Ah, and you think if we are together my role might just suddenly appear? Aliah's voice seemed amused.

Well, I suppose that is one way to put it. I was thinking perhaps by talking with you I would more clearly understand what you will be doing while I am taking care of all the magic stuff.

Seamus, sometimes you do make me laugh. Firstly, have you considered my role might actually be what I am doing now, making sure the island is not over-run by Carstenite soldiers so we can access the chest and prepare for the battle? Aliah did not wait for him to answer before continuing. *Secondly, what are we doing right now? Talking. We can go over things any time you want now we know we can contact each other. And, finally, you know any battle plan only holds up for the initial engagement, after that you are merely reacting.*

There was silence as Aliah waited for Seamus to respond. While he thought about what his friend said, he hoped this new sort of link did not let her know how stupid he felt.

Seamus? Are you all right? You may be wondering if you overreacted a little, and I think you are probably kicking yourself right now. Well, stop. You take your role seriously, I know, and it is good for us to talk like this. It will give you perspective.

Seamus sighed. It seemed Aliah did not need a mind link to know what he was thinking.

Thanks, Aliah, I do feel a little better. Now, if I think about it a little more clearly, we are going to meet up in two days and that should still give us time to finalise our plan before we face our enemy.

It will, now stop worrying and get some sleep.

Good night.

Good night, sleep well.

As Aliah pushed him from her mind, Seamus cursed, he had meant to tease her a little about training with Dominic. The thought made him laugh out loud as he realised just this small contact with Aliah had lifted a weight from his shoulders, and now he might actually get some sleep.

Cowering behind the solid oak door he had imagined in his mind, Gaius looked out through the tiny knot-hole in the wood, the only view of the world he allowed himself at the moment.

'I found it.'

Millard stood triumphantly in front of the form of his former pupil.

'The casket is not far from here,' the wizard informed the god.

'We must go and collect it immediately.'

Reverberating through his body, the god's response emanated pleasure and anticipation.

'I am not sure that is the best plan,' Millard advised.

If the god had not been so intent on crushing Gaius as he took over his body, he might have retained access to his memories. Gaius knew the look on his old master's face. Millard was up to something, something likely only to benefit himself.

The young man drew away from the door, surrounding himself with the darkness of his hiding place. For a moment, he allowed the hurt inside to take over. His former tutor had not so much as tried to find out if he were still alive inside the body he once owned. In fact, Gaius finally admitted to himself the wizard's reaction to losing his apprentice was not sadness, but clearly relief at not having been chosen to host the god himself.

As he drew further inside, Gaius wallowed in self-pity, bemoaning how he had ended up in this position. He spent so much energy on his own bitter quest for power, it had blinkered him to Millard's manipulation of his life. The man encouraged his isolation from children his own age, and helped him build his cloak of superiority. He had been flattered someone holding so prestigious a position had shown an interest in him, and he allowed that to blind him to all the signs the older man used him only to further his own ends.

Mentally he pulled himself back from the path of remorse, and forced himself to return to the tiny opening. The past was just that, in the past. He needed to focus on the present, which meant gathering as much information as possible if he was to take advantage of any opportunities to gain his freedom.

'Let me go and retrieve the chest for you as I promised I would. I will be able to sneak in and out before anyone realises I am there. In the meantime, you will be able to focus on your main problem, the Wizard and Warrior.

'As you pointed out on numerous occasions, I am no match for them. If you decide to act on the intelligence we received from our friend in their camp, you would clearly be best placed to take one of them on.'

While Gaius realised Millard was up to something, the god preened as the wizard flattered him into agreeing to his plan.

Fool. The thought leapt into Gaius' mind before he could stop it.

The god's focus turned inwards, searching for the origin of the word that popped into his head. Moving swiftly, Gaius pushed the plug into the hole just before the god's inner eye swept across his barrier.

You are the fool, he chided himself as he trembled in fear. *He must never find out you are still alive, or you will never escape.*

10
DIPLOMACY IS RESURRECTED

Dappled sunshine draped itself across the bed like a quilt. Stretching cat-like, Aliah allowed herself the luxury of a moment more of blissful relaxation before forcing her weary body out from under the covers. She hardly remembered the last time she stayed in bed until she woke naturally, rested and able to face the day. No use complaining though, there was work to be done.

When the maid appeared to open the curtains, she left some warm water for washing, and a pot of tea. Most civilised, Aliah thought, as she washed and dressed herself quickly so she was able to take a moment to sit and enjoy the refreshing beverage.

With almost perfect timing, just as she finished the last of her drink, there was a knock at the door. Daniel entered, looking much better this morning. The dark smudges under his eyes were barely noticeable. Aliah attempted to hide her relief with a cheerful, 'Good morning.'

'Shall I gather the others for the meeting?'

'Yes, it is time. Are the horses ready?'

'Boss and Pauley are in the stables as we speak, making sure everything is set for our departure. Would you rather I took your belongings down, or would you like me to come to the meeting?'

His tone suggested he would prefer not to attend the breakfast arranged by Baron George last night. Using the pretext of needing to finalise everything they agreed to, it was more an opportunity for the lonely baron to spend time with his guests than to rubber stamp everything.

'You can take my things down, and anything the others need as well. Although I should make you have breakfast with us, you know. The baron is a lovely man, he just wants some company. It is not his fault he recently lost his wife, and his two sons are off fighting with Duke Damon. With the help he is giving us with Baron Tappit, a quick breakfast is the least we can do.' Aliah spoke as she followed Daniel out of the room and down the stairs.

'I am a soldier, Aliah. I only ever wanted to be a soldier. I wish you would stop trying to mould me into something else.'

Daniel's words were sad and heavy, causing Aliah to pause and remember Dominic's words from the night before.

BATTLE

'Daniel, is everything all right?'

'Of course, silly. I just want you to realise I am happy doing exactly what I am doing. So stop meddling and trying to change me.'

'If you so order, captain, it shall be done.'

Parting company at the door to the dining room, Aliah's eyes pierced her friend's back as he carried her travel pack out to the stables, almost as though she wished she could see into his very soul. Something niggled her about Daniel's behaviour lately. Try as she might, she could not place her finger on what it was. Shrugging with defeat, she plastered a bright smile on her face and opened the door.

'Ah, Princess, we were just wondering when you would turn up.'

A middle aged man, still in his prime with a homely face, beamed as she entered the dining room. Dominic turned in his chair to say good morning, then promptly turned back to his meal and attacked it as though he would not see another for all eternity. Sitting down beside Amelia, a servant brought her a full cooked breakfast, the size of which she would not be able to eat even if she sat at the table all day.

'Dig in, my dear. Do not feel you have to eat it all. The servants are used to catering for my boys, who eat every meal as though it is their last,' the baron joked. 'I was in the middle of recapping what we talked about yesterday when you entered, so I shall start again.

'This morning I dispatched a rider to Baron Tappit with a message directing him to get off his butt and send some men to this fight. I worded it in terms he will find very difficult to ignore. He is not a bad lad, but he has a tendency to only stir himself if everything is guaranteed to turn out in his favour.

'Half of my men are preparing to ride out today, and will meet with you at Rasmussen's. They will give you enough time to talk to the baron and gain his agreement first, but in good time to add a little pressure if he is being indecisive. Although, given his holdings are closer to the enemy camp, I doubt he will need the extra incentive.'

'Why, Baron George, you have been busy this morning, and here I am just out of bed.'

Aliah overdid the compliments, but the baron's blush of pleasure made it well worth the extra effort.

'Is there anything left for us to do?'

Baron George's face clouded over and his tone became serious. 'My dear, you are already doing more than we could ever ask of you. You are all going to face our enemies and put your life on the line for Hand, and Aria. The little I am doing pales in comparison.'

'Bet that took the wind out of your sails,' Amelia said under her breath.

'Wow, Aliah, great way to change the mood of a celebration meal.' In contrast, Dominic's teasing comment was loud enough for all to hear.

'Please show some manners, young man. It was I who changed the tone, because I cannot believe you all, and my own sons, are being forced to fight for our way of life. I never thought I would see the like in my lifetime. My poor Clarissa will be turning in her grave.'

A chastened Dominic returned to his meal. However, finding she no longer had much of an appetite, Aliah laid down her cutlery. 'Baron George, we will do our best to make sure you and your people remain safe.'

'I know you will, my dear. What I worry about though is you placing yourself in such grave danger.'

Amelia took Aliah's hand, as if she sensed the worry churning in her stomach. Daniel was not well, something had changed with Dominic, and now this dear man expressed heartfelt concern for her safety. The morning started so full of promise, and now she felt as though everything was slipping through her fingers. A knock on the door prevented her from completely falling into melancholy.

Daniel popped his head around and grinned. 'Everything is ready when you are, Princess.'

'I wish you had more time to spend here, but I appreciate you must be on your way.' Baron George was the perfect host as he stood and accompanied them to the door, easing their departure with a practiced hand.

Aliah was not just being polite when she spoke of her sorrow at leaving so soon. In the baron's warm, capable presence, she could let someone else take care of the details, and the impending battle seemed so very far away.

Aching muscles in her bottom creaked, forcing a groan from her lips as she hauled herself into the saddle. Unaccustomed to two days hard riding, her body protested at the thought of more of the same. Glancing at Amelia, she found her friend sitting straight backed and relaxed on her mount. Moving her horse closer to the older woman, she touched her gently on the arm to gain her attention.

'You are looking sprightly this morning, Amelia, it would not be a result of some practices forbidden on Hand, would it?' she joked conspiratorially.

Inclining her head towards Aliah, the woman also spoke in hushed tones. 'You mean to say you are not using that sword of yours to give you energy and soothe your aching muscles?'

Bewildered, Aliah stammered. 'I … I never thought to. Would that not be cheating a little? I mean, using the sword for my own benefit seems against the god's intentions when they gave it to me, you know, to save Aria.'

'Sometimes I forget you are a child, then you make silly comments like that and I remember how young you still are. Aliah, you are gathering defences to fight Aria's enemies. At any moment they might appear and you need to be fighting fit to face them and survive. Under the circumstances, I would say using your sword to maintain your strength and agility is your duty, not some sort of a short cut.'

Amelia's words hit her like a slap, and she cringed at her own stupidity. She had been gifted the sword to aid her on her journey, of course the sensible thing to do would be to use its powers. Reaching forward, she undid the soft leather covering the hilt and placed her hand around it. Immediately a healing warmth spread through her body. By the time they were ready to leave, she felt revitalised and her aches had almost disappeared. Now ready to face the day, she rode until she drew up beside Dominic.

'Are we to work some more today while we ride?'

'How can you be so cheerful? We worked late into the

night, and with our early start ...' His words trailed off.

Aliah took a close look at her friend and realised he too had been burning the candle at both ends. Sure he continued working once she took to her bed, she regarded the dark bruises under his eyes and his grey pallor. Her friend was exhausted.

Once again, she placed her hand on the sword, then reached out with her mind to find Dominic, just like she did when they practiced mind to mind communication. Sensing his barrier, she pulled a trickle of healing magic from her weapon and guided it towards that barrier.

'Hey, what are you doing?'

Concentrating only on the task at hand, she ignored his question and kept feeding him the healing strength until he no longer looked grey and the weariness around his eyes was almost gone. Releasing the sword, she found herself face to face with a very angry Dominic.

'What do you think you are doing?'

'Giving you energy. From the look of you, you needed a boost.'

'I do not need your energy,' the spy forced out through gritted teeth.

Annoyed at his reaction, and not understanding why he turned this into a big issue, Aliah's own temper flashed.

'Do not be such a baby. I did not deplete my own resources to assist you, it came from the sword. And rest assured, it would not have allowed me to continue if I was doing anything wrong.'

'You think that is why I am upset?' Her companion stopped his horse and she followed suit.

'If you are not worried about me, why are you so grumpy?'

'You broke through my personal barriers without my consent.'

'I did not.' Indignation fuelled her anger to new heights. 'You told me that was incredibly intrusive, so I have been careful to respect your boundaries and not enter your space unless invited.'

Confusion clouded Dominic's face. 'How did you feed me energy then?'

'I fed the energy to your actual barrier, your body absorbed it and did the rest.'

Smirking, Dominic said, 'I might have known you could not get through my barrier by yourself.'

Kicking his horse, Dominic headed off after the others. Resentment and rage warred inside of Aliah. All he thought to say was a smart comment. No word of thanks. No apology for falsely accusing her. How dare he treat her gift like that! And how dare he underestimate her abilities! She would show him exactly what she was capable of.

Without thinking, she sent her thoughts after Dominic, quickly found his barrier, slipped through and into his mind. Instead of the normal bland room he allowed her into previously, she found herself in a rainbow coloured cloud. Before finding herself booted out, she learnt why entering someone's mind unasked was such a mistake. His mind was filled with an overwhelming sense of loneliness and anger. Then, behind his fury at her actions she found admiration, exasperation and ... love.

Thoughts in disarray, she found herself frozen in place, not quite knowing what to do next. When she came to her senses Dominic was in front of her, his face carefully schooled to give nothing of his emotions away.

'Oh, Dominic … I …'

Before she completed her thought, the boy who was in love with her cut in.

'Do not say a word. Those were my private feelings. It was my decision whether to share them with you, or to keep them to myself. You have taken that choice from me and that makes me beyond angry. I am also saddened because I can no longer trust you enough to carry on with your training.

'As we need to focus on making sure Aria is not overrun by a god, I do not have the luxury of walking away from you, which is what my gut is telling me I should do. So, for now, we will pretend this moment never happened.'

Before Dominic could steer his mount away, Aliah did something she did not know was even possible to do. Reaching out with her mind, she grabbed what she could of Dominic, and drew him back into her, laying herself bare.

Apologising the only way she knew how, she allowed him to experience her shame at her own actions. She let him know of her own confusion, of her desire for his good opinion, and how she thought she was a better person with him around. She allowed him full access to all the other confusing emotions and feelings swirling in her mind. More importantly though, she showed him how devastated she was knowing she had lost their friendship because of one act of pique.

Loneliness overtook her as he withdrew from her head and met her gaze with his own.

'I am still angry with you,' he said, and paused for a

moment as if carefully considering his next words. 'In time, I might forgive your intrusion into my thoughts, but it is clear we have much more to consider, and perhaps even more to talk about. This is such bad timing.'

Oh no, Aliah thought. *I have lost him before I found out if we have a future together. I am such a fool.*

The silence drew out to an uncomfortable length, before Dominic finally said, 'We should forget this ever happened,'

Embarrassment and confusion raced through her. She was not sure she heard him correctly. 'You want us to forget everything?'

Dominic placed a hand on her arm. 'I mean to say, we need to move beyond your thoughtless breach of protocol, and mark it up to a learning experience. If you promise never to do such a thing again, I promise to try and move past it. But, if you really want us to forget everything, we can do that too. We can agree to never speak of today, and what we have found out about each other, again.'

'No,' Aliah gasped as he finished speaking.

'Good, because it is not what I want either.'

Hope fluttered in the pit of her stomach, but she pushed it back down.

'What do you want?'

'I want to be back in Bannock courting a girl I rather like, finding out if she is the one who will cause me to set aside my wandering ways and settle down.'

The words were tinged with sadness, and Aliah understood why.

'That would be perfect, but it is not going to happen any time soon, if ever,' she said.

'So, what I want and what I must do are two different things. What I must do is make sure my Princess Warrior is as prepared as she is able to be to face and defeat a god. If I do that, then I may one day get my wish.'

'I can see it is in my best interests to make your wish come true.'

'Hurry up, you two.' Daniel, who had been riding rear guard, dropped back to join them. 'Quit mooning about, Baron George's men have nearly caught us up. If you do not pick up the pace, they will beat us to the Rasmussen place.'

Dominic was first to break eye contact, before he fell in beside the guardsman he said under his breath, 'If you ever enter my mind without permission again though …' He left her own imagination to fill in the blanks.

Although his tone was playful, Aliah heard the steel beneath the words and her stomach churned as shame at her actions arose anew. Although now a hopeful butterfly also fluttered in there as well. Pushing both feelings aside, Aliah nudged her mount and rejoined the others, ready to focus on the task ahead.

Aliah shifted uncomfortably in her saddle, happy to see the end of the day's journey in sight. They had kept a steady pace all day so as to maintain a reasonable distance between themselves and Baron George's men, barely even stopping for lunch. Her body was so weary, she had resorted more than once to drawing some energy using her sword, but refrained from offering a magical boost to anyone else.

As their party clattered into the stone courtyard in front of the baronial manor, they found Baron Rasmussen already there, seemingly mustering his men. It reminded Aliah of Robin's quick rundown of the baron, who had recently been awarded the vacant property for services to the duchy. It had only been a few moons since he left his post as Guard Captain, and brought his wife to this remote spot.

The tall, well built man flicked his blond hair out of the way and looked about in surprise as they entered. However, gratitude soon filled his blue eyes as he heard they were followed by a guard contingent from his neighbour.

'Your arrival could not have been more timely. One of my patrols arrived back a short while ago to report unusual activity by the pass to the costal lands. They believe some men may have passed through last evening, or perhaps early this morning.

'I am about to send these men out to begin securing the top of the track, while the bulk of my men prepare to leave in the morning to begin fortifying in earnest. I would welcome the assistance of the guards you say are coming from Baron George, as my men alone would not be able to hold the pass from a serious attack for long.'

'Perhaps we might ride along with you and be of some assistance ourselves,' Aliah offered as the baron helped her down from her mount.

From the look on the baron's face, Aliah understood he was struggling with something, and waited more patiently than she was used to for his response. When it was not forthcoming, she said, 'You can be direct with me, if you think we will be more of a hinderance than a help then I am prepared to hear your reasoning.'

Smiling with relief, the baron took her arm and escorted her towards the hall.

'I do not know how many men slipped through the pass, and I am only sending out a small force tonight. I would rather they concentrated on the job at hand than being worried about the safety of such an important person as yourself, Your Highness.'

Aliah laughed at his forthrightness. 'Baron, while I can look after myself, I appreciate your concern, and will abide by your direction.'

A slight blush rose to the baron's cheeks, but he surprised her with his next comment. 'I am sure Baron George's men would welcome the opportunity of a night's rest before engaging the enemy, and you yourself might like to enjoy the luxury of a bath before eating tonight. Then you can all ride out with the rest of my men in the morning, feeling refreshed and ready to face anything.'

Laughing out loud, Aliah could see why Duke Damon had raised this man to his current position, and she responded, 'Baron I think you have missed your calling. You would fit in well with the diplomats at my father's court.'

Embolden by her response, the baron pushed his hand a little. 'I hope you will forgive me, Princess, but with your leave I would like to ride out with my men to see what is going on for myself.'

Aliah smiled. 'Baron, in times of war the people's safety must be placed before social niceties. I am sure your wife will see us well looked after, and you no doubt would not be such good company worrying about what is going on elsewhere.'

Bowing, and thanking the princess, the baron quickly excused himself as the baroness deftly took charge and saw them to their quarters.

She chatted non-stop to Aliah as she escorted her to her rooms. Born in Port Hand, she was not yet used to life on the quiet plateau, so took great pleasure from their company. By the time Aliah arrived at her room she found there was already a wooden tub inside, and a maid had begun the process of filling it with hot water.

Sighing out loud, she thanked the young woman for her thoughtfulness. Closing the door behind her, Aliah intended to make the most of this little luxury. So relaxed was she, she was still in the tub herself when the dinner going sounded.

Having rushed to meet with the others, Aliah was able to relax during the meal as Daniel and Dominic plied the young woman with stories, each trying to capture the pretty girl's attention. She and Amelia politely answered questions, and made the occasional comment when required, but both were clearly exhausted.

Aliah excused herself early saying she was tired from the constant travel. She had not found the opportunity to tell anyone she had been in contact with Seamus, and that was really why she was going, because she wanted to talk with him tonight before she was too tired. Amelia had looked at her with concern, but said nothing, and Aliah promised herself she would explain everything tomorrow.

Back in her room, she stilled her mind and reached out for Seamus.

11
MAGIC IS ALIVE ON HAND

After his nocturnal activities, Seamus spent sleepless hours pondering how to place the god in the casket and send him back at least to the mid-plane so the other gods could deal with him. He almost had it worked out, except he did not yet know how the name fitted into it all, nor had he had any inspiration as to what Aliah would be doing while he fought the god.

Forcing himself to rise as sunlight crept through a gap in the curtains, he hurried to join the others in the stables preparing for the journey ahead. Once on the road, instead of enjoying his first opportunity to be outside in days, Seamus sunk deep into his own thoughts, determined to work out how to use the last piece of the puzzle. He also still needed to formulate a Plan B for defeating the god, if they failed with the casket and he made it to Aria.

Would it be possible to somehow use worshippers of the goddess if the god managed to reunite with his physical form? Then an idea hit him, worshipping a god made a connection and thinned the veil between worlds. Seamus realised it was no mistake Aria was the site chosen to battle the god. Worship of the goddess was strong here, so perhaps the veil was thinner. Was there some way he could use that to their advantage?

'Seamus? Seamus? Are you all right? You are not really with us this morning.' Emer had pulled her horse up alongside his.

'I am sorry. I have just been imagining my meagre magical abilities coming up against the enormous power of a god in all his glory. Every time I think about us facing down such a formidable foe, all I imagine are mice nibbling at the feet of a giant. At any time, he might decide to simply blast us with a fireball, and it is all over. I cannot see myself coming out of this alive.'

Shoulders slumped, Seamus avoided looking at Emer, not wanting to face her disappointment in him reflected on her face. A gentle hand was placed on his arm. Understanding—that was even worse. The hand gripped his arm tightly, almost painfully.

'I loathe self-pity, pull yourself together. If the gods thought an all out battle was needed to defeat our enemy do you not think they would have the sense to ensure you were given enough power to fight him head on. They are seven of the most powerful beings in the universe, yet they were unable to stop him.

'This suggests something different is needed to defeat him. Your magic is different, something never given to another human, and you yourself are different. You and Aliah have unique powers, and unique ways of approaching things. Perhaps you should spend less time worrying about what you cannot do, and more time thinking about how you can use what you have to your advantage.

'A single rumour can bring down a leader more effectively than an army. So we mice can definitely bring down a giant.'

Seamus found the courage to look up into Emer's face and saw, not anger, but determination written there. Straightening his shoulders and sitting more erect in his saddle, he decided there and then to stop feeling sorry for himself and start believing there might be a way for them to win this battle.

Sometime later, as grey clouds threatened rain, they arrived at the entrance to Baron Wexler's estate. The tall wrought iron gate was locked closed, guarded from inside by four burly men who did not look welcoming at all. With his new found confidence, Seamus urged his horse forward and took control of the situation.

'I am Lord Seamus, and I wish to speak to your master on behalf of the Duke of Hand.'

Under any other circumstances his words would have caused the gates to be swept open and he would be beside a fire, drink in hand, in less than a candle-mark. In this instance, the men did not move a muscle.

'Did you not hear Lord Seamus?' Liam moved his mount alongside.

'We heard, but we have our orders. No one is to enter the estate until morning.' The man who spoke left the group and approached the fence. 'You are welcome to make camp where you are, and tomorrow I will escort you to the baron myself.'

Flummoxed by the response, Seamus was unsure what to do next. 'Why? Why can he not meet with me now?'

'That is his business.'

In the face of such obstinacy there was no obvious path to take. Turning around, Seamus rejoined his companions.

'What now?' Emer asked

Unsure whether to be annoyed at being denied entrance, or relieved he had not needed to face the baron today after a sleepless night, Seamus considered options as he surveyed their surroundings. The forest they had ridden through for the last candle mark or so thinned out near the gates, and the wrought iron fence surrounded the baron's land for as far as they could see. Beyond the boundary, tussocky hills led down towards the coast.

'How much do you want to bet the baron could not afford to put such a high fence around the entire boundary of his property?'

'You are thinking of sneaking in and finding out what he is up to?' Liam's eyes glimmered with excitement in the fading light.

'Are you sure that is wise? It is a very confrontational thing to do.'

Walter, as ever counselled caution, but Seamus was

not ready to listen. Although part of him wanted to delay the meeting and get some sleep, he knew their cause would be better served by confronting the baron tonight. Besides, after days stuck in a library his body longed for some action. Then there was this nagging feeling he had had for the last candle mark or so, a feeling he really needed to meet with the baron today.

'Come on.' Turning his horse to the left, he headed off along the boundary line. For the benefit of the guards he threw back over his shoulder, 'We should find a more secluded spot and set up camp for the night.'

Skirting the tree-line near the barrier, they rode for another candle mark without finding a break in the fence line. As the sun began to set, colouring the sky with crimsons and purples, they came to the end of the enclosure.

Groaning, Seamus halted his weary horse and slid from the saddle. Leaving the animal to nibble on some grass, he walked towards the edge of the cliff and looked down. Iron spikes continued more than a body length down the face of the cliff. Below was a sheer drop into the swirling rocky depths of the sea.

'Who would have thought the baron would fence his entire property?' he said the words mostly for his own benefit. 'What a waste of time. We may as well make camp for the night and go and meet with Wexler tomorrow as the guard suggested.'

As he said the words, Seamus still searched for another way in. He could not shake the feeling it was important he reach the baron tonight. Walter joined him, staring out to sea.

'If you are intent on finding out what the baron is up to, I believe I can help.'

Unwilling to raise his hopes, Seamus cautiously asked, 'How?'

'I can bring a tree from the forest down on top of the fence and we can use it to climb over.'

'Could you not have suggested that before we rode all this way.' Unable to keep the frustration from entering his voice, the hurt in his friend's eyes made him instantly sorry for snapping.

'I was not sure breaking in was our best course of action. Also I did not really want to use magic in broad daylight on Hand.'

'I am sorry, Walter. I spoke thoughtlessly,' Seamus apologised. 'Your suggestion is a good one. Let us set up camp and eat something. When it is dark, we can bring down your tree and take a look at what the baron is going to such pains to hide. You can remain behind if you do not approve.'

Leaning back against the trunk of a tree, Seamus gazed into the fire. His belly full, he no longer felt such a burning need to enter Wexler's domain. It would be so easy to curl up in a blanket by the fire and get a good night's sleep. Still, a niggling thought pestered him, compelling him to move.

Just as he was about to stir himself to action, he felt a tugging at the edge of his thoughts. Something had been nagging him all day, but this was different. Almost as though someone was knocking to get in.

BATTLE

Aliah?

As soon as he thought her name, there she was, inside his head.

What is it, is there something wrong? Seamus asked, sensing Aliah was not her usual self.

No. Well, yes, but nothing you can help with. Nothing to do with our upcoming battle, she was quick to reassure him.

Seamus was not so easily put off. *Anything that has you so worried I can sense it, needs to be dealt with before we face the god. If we are distracted when we fight him, it will lessen our chance of success.*

It is … well, it is personal.

I can help with personal.

Umm …

Aliah, what did you do to Dominic? I knew it would not be easy, you two mind linking, especially given the way you feel about each other.

What do you mean? Aliah was immediately defensive.

Laughing, Seamus answered. *Well, given the fact you like each other, it cannot have been easy.*

You knew?

Aliah, we all know. I think you were the only people who had not acknowledged the fact. At least now it is out in the open.

Oh, Seamus, I broke into his mind and that is how I found about his feelings for me.

Although Seamus felt her shame at the action, he could not stop himself. *You did that after lecturing me about over-taking a mind.*

Waves of shame rolled of Aliah, and Seamus regretted his words.

We are all entitled to one mistake, and I can tell from how you are now you are unlikely to make the same one again. Dominic will forgive you given time. You need to stop beating yourself up and forgive yourself.

Rather than continuing the conversation, Aliah changed the subject, clearly not yet ready to let herself off the hook.

Are you with Baron Wexler?

No, we have not been let onto the baron's lands. Something is up here.

Oh? Are you going to do something about it? Aliah asked. *It is kind of urgent we find out whether or not the chest we need is there.*

Thank you for stating the obvious. As it happens, we are planning to break in soon and find out what he is hiding.

Aliah chuckled. *I bet Walter is ecstatic about that.*

Not really, he would like us to wait until tomorrow.

I bet he would. Are you totally sure you should not wait? I mean, much as we are on a strict timeline here, we do not want to get off on the wrong foot with the baron.

Seamus considered his response, he found it hard to put into words the need he had to find out what was going on tonight. *Maybe it is premonition, or maybe it is just a gut feeling, but I think I need to find out what is happening today. I will be careful though, and try not to do anything to upset the baron too much.*

If we carry on talking there will not be much of the night left for you to break in. I should let you go, Aliah said.

Yes, I guess so.

Seamus was reluctant to break contact. Everything always seemed so much clearer in his mind when Aliah

BATTLE

was near.

Seamus, thank you. Aliah's voice broke into his reverie.

Huh?

Thank you for listening, I feel so much better now. Let me know how you get on tonight if you have a chance, otherwise I will see you at the rendezvous the day after tomorrow.

With that she was gone and he was left alone again, wondering what on earth he was doing. Reluctantly, he drew his gaze back to the fire. As he did, the nagging feeling he had been experiencing returned, and he sighed as if he carried the weight of the world on his shoulders.

Turing to the man seated beside him, he said, 'Walter, it is time. Can you please bring down the tree for us?'

'I am sure with your magical training you are able to do it yourself now I have given you the idea.'

About to agree, Seamus stopped himself. When he attempted to clear a path in a forest to escape pursuers once before, he had been flooded with the pain the vegetation endured as he forced it to do something against its nature.

'I think it best you do it. My magic connects me to the earth in some way, and I suffer the consequences of any such magical actions,' Seamus explained.

'Interesting, yet you suffered no backlash when you used magic on a living being when you struck down the King of Carsten.' Walter stroked his beard as he considered the implications.

'This is not the time to discuss magical theory.' Emer pulled Walter's attention back to the task at hand as she stood and picked up her sword and knife. 'If we are to survey the lay of the land and still get some sleep tonight, we need to get moving.'

Liam joined her, and Seamus unwillingly rose and reached for his own weapons. Having placed a knife in the sheath at his side, one in each of his boots, and a fourth in a special sheath on his forearm under his shirt, he was ready to go.

'I will take you up on your offer to stay behind,' Walter informed them as he motioned for the three youngsters to stand behind him. 'I am too old for daytime rides followed by night-time adventuring. Besides, I am still not sure this is the best way to get the baron on our side.'

Lowering a sturdy tree onto the fence, Walter held it in place while Liam led them upwards. Tying a rope to one of the branches hanging over the other side, Liam shimmied down, followed by Emer.

Before he climbed up, Seamus turned to Walter. 'I know you do not approve of what we are doing, but I cannot help thinking we need to be here tonight. I am sure something important is going to happen. Keep your eyes and mind open, we may need your help.'

'I will try not to fall asleep, but these old bones are weary after travelling today, so I cannot promise anything.'

Chuckling to himself, Seamus hurried up the tree and dropped down over the other side. Before catching up with the others, he heard the earth groan as the older wizard placed the tree back in its original position.

The estate on this side of the wall was similar to the untended countryside on the other side. Near the costal cliffs the grass was short and scrubby, changing to pasture moving more inland. There were small copses of trees dotted around, intermingled with groups of hardy shrubs. A quick scan of the area showed nothing was moving in between the trees, and Seamus was confident they were alone for the moment.

'Do you smell that?' Emer asked as Seamus joined them.

Sniffing the air, he caught a whiff of something, but could not make out what it was. 'Sort of.'

'A large fire has been lit close by, or a number of small ones. Somewhere over that way.' She pointed along the coast. 'Should we head over there, or sneak up to the house?'

Seamus did not hesitate. 'We head for the fires. All day I have had a niggling sensation. When I try to reach out, the energy around me feels strange. Something is up. I aim to find out what, and it is more likely to be at the beach than in the manor.'

'What makes you say that?' Emer asked.

'Well, I think we would be able to see lights on in the manor from here, and yet it is dark. Besides, I just have this feeling,' Seamus responded.

Beside him Liam tensed, then shrugged as if trying to loosen his limbs. 'I always thought I was all right with magic. When I thought about people having it, I felt no fear like some on Hand.

'In practice though, I find it gives me the heebie jeebies. All this talk about feeling and sensing energies around us unsettles me.'

'Why did you not say anything Liam? I had not realised it made you uncomfortable to be around me. I would have sent you with Aliah, and asked Boss to come with us if I had known.'

Seamus' concern for his cousin's wellbeing overrode his disappointment at Liam not being able to accept magic as a part of him. Pausing briefly to punch Seamus on the arm, Liam laughed.

'You dolt, if I had grown up with magic around me, I would find it as normal as swinging a sword. It is only fear of the unknown, and I will not allow it to control my life. Besides, my place is by your side, and being jittery about something so silly will not stop me from being with you.'

'If you boys have finished having your moment, I think it would be a good idea for me to change and range ahead,' Emer interrupted them. 'With my improved night vision in wolf form I should be able to scout out any problems.'

'Oh, yes, of course. Sorry, I should have planned this better instead of focusing on the fact I wanted to find out what we were being excluded from.'

'It is not up to you to think of everything, we are a team, remember?' Emer changed as she spoke, then, with a flick of her tail, her wolf form strode off into the night.

'That is so amazing. Why is your magic not as incredible as Emer's?'

'So sensing things is creepy, but totally changing form is not? How is it I never noticed how weird you are?'

Continuing their whispered banter as they walked, calmed Seamus' nerves, making their outing seem more like an amble along the coastal cliffs than a midnight mission to find the cause of a disturbance in magical forces. So engrossed were they in trading insults, they started and banged into each other when Emer-wolf appeared in front of them. She changed back before reporting.

BATTLE

'A little further ahead is a path winding down to a cove. On the beach are about four or five fires, with a handful of guards sitting around each one. At first glance, it looks like they are having a relaxing meal, but they are all fully armed, and they search about as if expecting an attack.'

'Could you see anything to tell you why they are gathered?' Recovering from the collision first, Liam was also quicker to begin assessing the situation.

'I could not. A wolf atop a cliff face observing activity would be considered quite normal. One walking on a sandy beach, not so much.'

Not to be outdone by his cousin's recovery speed, Seamus felt the need to contribute his wisdom. 'We will not be able to see anything from the top, one of us needs to go down and find out what is going on.'

'I can quietly slip down and look around.' Liam made as if to go.

'I am not sure you are our best option,' Seamus placed a hand on his cousin's arm before he moved too far away. 'With so many fires in a confined space, I assume the cove is well lit with no shadows for even the most agile of boys to hide in.'

'That is correct. They are strategically placed to ensure the guards can see anyone approaching from land or sea.'

'So a wolf on the beach would be remarked upon, as would an eagle flying at night?'

'Yes, Seamus, this is one time when my animal forms will not be of any help.'

'I would not say that. As a wolf, your improved vision will be useful helping Liam guard the top of the cliff while

I go down and find out what is happening on the beach.'

A snort escaped from Liam, and he placed a hand over his mouth to stop any more getting out. When he regained his composure, he removed his hand and spoke. 'If I cannot sneak in there, Seamus, how do you expect to? When it comes to stealth, you are like a stampeding horse compared to my mouse.'

Although he would like to deny the charge, Liam was correct. In normal circumstances, the shorter, slighter boy was far better at moving undetected. In this instance though, he believed he might have an added advantage.

When he found out Dominic was able to blend into the background, he had tried to mimic the ability using his own magic. Unable to disappear like the spy, he asked for a lesson. No matter how hard he tried he could not do it. Not even when Dominic let him in on the secret words he used when he first found out he had the ability to become invisible. Saying, "you cannot see me" had no effect at all for Seamus.

Since then, he had been trying to find a way to make himself invisible at will using his own magic. If he could not blend into the background, he wondered if his ability to connect to people might be used to influence their minds, convincing them they could not see him.

Having moved stealthily to the edge of the cliff over-looking the cove, Seamus pondered some more how he might influence the thoughts of others as Emer changed back into a wolf. Shrugging his shoulders, he decided there was no time like the present to try. In his mind he formulated an idea; "Seamus just disappeared before my very eyes". Once the thought emerged crystal clear in his mind, he took hold of it and gently pushed it out towards Liam and Emer in much the same way he pushed his mind out to connect with Aliah.

Liam looked at him quizzically, but it was clear he could still see Seamus. Pushing a little harder he was rewarded with a look of complete shock on the other boy's face. As Liam searched around, Seamus turned to find Emer's head cocked to the side.

What are you doing to Liam?

I told you both I disappeared. Seamus mind spoke to her so as to remain silent.

You did? I can still see you, but your body is shimmering, like my eyes cannot quite focus on you. Perhaps your trick does not work as well on animals? Or maybe on magic users. It is risky to assume there will be no magic users below.

I think it will be worth the risk, unless you have a better idea.

'Seamus?' Liam hissed loudly, 'Where are you? This is not the time to play tricks.'

Releasing the thought, Liam stumbled in shock as Seamus appeared before him. Reacting quickly, he grabbed Liam's arm before he fell back over the edge of the cliff.

'What the goddess are you playing at?' If they had not been trying to stay undetected, Liam would have yelled the words. As it was, he hissed them loud enough to startle Seamus.

'Calm down, would you? I needed to find out whether I was able to creep through the guards without them seeing me. This is new, and I thought it would not be such a great idea to find I could not do it in the middle of hostile guardsmen.'

'Well, you might have warned a soul rather than scaring them half to death.' Grumbling, Liam attempted to regain his composure. 'I guess you are the best to find out what is going on, after all.'

Will you be able to influence so many minds? Emer-wolf asked.

'Emer just asked if I would be able to convince a number of people I am not there. It is a good question, and the truthful answer is I am not sure. Perhaps for a short time—time enough to find what I need to, I hope.'

'Most days I am a little sad for you,' Liam mused. 'You have to stay away from your family because of your magic, you have this great destiny to fulfil and your life is constantly in danger. Then you do something incredible like you just did, and I come down with a huge case of envy.'

'I would gladly switch places. Just say the word and I will ask if the gods would agree.'

Holding his hands up in front, Liam shook his head. 'No, I am good.'

Once again, Seamus, while this bonding is all well and good, can we please do what we need to and get out of here? I sense a change in the air, and I think the sooner we are on the other side of the fence with Walter, the better.

Emer's anxiety caused Seamus to pause, maybe Walter was right. In light of their larger goals was it sensible to go rushing into danger tonight? Emer flicked her tail and headed off into the night. Liam followed after.

'I guess we are doing this,' Liam said as he departed.

'I guess we are,' Seamus affirmed, realising the decision had been made for him.

A warm orange glow from the fires below lit the pathway

down to the cove. Emer led them to a clump of scrub large enough for them to hide behind while they surveyed the scene below.

'Look,' Liam pointed. 'The fires are arranged in a semi-circle around that particular part of the cliff. That formation is common in military training books. I would say they are guarding something along the wall.'

Nodding his head in agreement, Seamus plotted the shortest way through the groups of men to the point in the centre of the arc of fires.

'All right, wish me luck.'

Do not cast your thoughts until the absolute last minute. Bending so many minds to your vision will quickly drain you, so you need to limit the amount of time you send them.

Emer sent her warning as he reached the beginning of the path. Trusting her experience with magic, instead of walking down, he dropped to his bottom and slid towards the beach.

The trip down took longer than walking, but it was worth it to conserve his magic. At the last bend before the cove, he stopped. In his head he started forming a thought; "I cannot see anyone walking through the fires".

Screwing up his face, he scrubbed that idea. Surely it would suggest they should be looking for someone, and they might look all the more closely. This was going to be harder than he thought. Perhaps he should have planned this better before starting out, maybe even tested it on Liam some more.

Running through ideas in his mind, he eventually found one he believed might work. Closing his eyes to concentrate, he began forming an idea; "What is that noise? Is it oars?

Someone is coming to attack us from the sea". He lay on his stomach and popped his head around a tussock, looking towards the first couple of groups of men.

He let the thought go. Gently at first, then with more force as he saw a few of the men turn and peer out to sea. When all the guards in his line of sight were looking away, he rose to his feet. Fortunately, he was greeted with the sight of everyone on the beach searching the ocean for something. Not knowing how long the illusion of an invasion from the sea would last, he rushed towards the area Liam previously pointed out.

As he drew closer, he spotted a cave entrance. Not much taller than him, and very narrow, he turned sideways to enter. The flickering glow from inside told him whatever he searched for was likely to be in there.

Once through the opening, the tunnel widened a little and natural steps in the rocks led upwards. Torches were spaced at regular intervals, illuminating the pathway. Steadily climbing, he slipped on seaweed and sea slime left by the tides, sometimes losing his footing. The steps rose until he passed the high tide line and the path cleared of debris.

Turning a corner, the path widened out into a cave so enormous he could not make out the roof, let alone the other side. In the centre stood an altar, and before the altar, with his back to Seamus, knelt a man dressed in plain brown robes. On hearing his footsteps, the man rose to his feet and turned.

BATTLE

Squinting into the shadows, the man by the altar asked, 'Are you real, or an apparition?'

'Oh, sorry.'

So engrossed was he in reaching his goal, Seamus had forgotten to release his mind cast. A mistake he fixed immediately.

'Definitely real,' the stocky grey haired man acknowledged moments later. 'Seamus, I believe, I am Gareth Wexler. You certainly took your time getting here.'

'You knew I would come?'

'I have been calling out to you all day, asking you to come. I was unsure whether you could hear me. All I could do was hope you would respond in time.'

'How?' A flash of inspiration. 'Your family has the gift of calling. You used magic to draw me here. That explains the feeling I have had most of today.'

Sheepishly the man shrugged his response. 'Guilty as charged. If you felt the pull, what took you so long?'

'Your ... your guards turned me away at the gates.'

'What?' The baron was genuinely surprised.

'When we arrived earlier this evening, the guards at your gates informed us you were not available until tomorrow. I am only here because I had a strong urge to find out what was going on.'

Baron Wexler's amiable countenance changed to concern, then outright fear as he glanced around the cavern, nervously checking the shadows.

'Come. I suspect we shall soon have visitors, so we had best get this over with.'

'You can just give me the casket and I will go.'

'You must know by now nothing to do with the gods

is that easy. There are two sets of instructions I am to pass on before I hand you the casket.

'If you have chosen to fight the god before he appears and cast him from this world, the first thing you must do is bind him securely, making him as small as possible, before placing him in the casket.'

'I guessed that. Can I please just take it and go?' A deep sense of foreboding ran through Seamus, causing him to forget his usual good manners.

'The next is the most important piece of information you need so, no, I will not hand over the chest my family has guarded for generations until I have completed the task I have been set.'

With little grace, and more than a little impatience, Seamus offered, 'Go on.'

'After you capture him, the god must leave this plane. One of the gods took me between the planes a few nights ago so I could describe the experience to you.'

The baron shivered from head to toe as he remembered.

'The god appeared in my room, sat on my bed and began explaining the universe is like an onion, made up of many layers. We live on an outer layer, the gods inhabit the innermost one. In between each layer is a skin shielding it from the others. As you move towards the middle, the protecting membrane gets thicker.

'Having told me this, he pushed me from this plane to the next and pulled me back. He asked me to describe my experience. I did, and after that he instructed me to call you today and repeat what I told him word for word. I will do that now.

'As I was pushed from our world, I hit what appeared

to be incredibly dense water. I sort of squelched through it like when you pull your foot out of mud. For a brief moment I was encased in the substance, then there was a popping sound, and I was on the other side. When he pulled me back through, the whole thing happened in reverse.'

Closing his eyes, Seamus tried to imagine the journey. 'Was your body transported?'

'Oh, that is an interesting question. Let me think. It did not feel like I was moving, it felt more like I was dreaming or imagining what was going on. Does that help?'

'Yes, you have no idea how much. You have given me the final piece of the puzzle I need to rid the world of the god presence.'

'I told you the second part was the most important. Now, although there is much I wish to ask you, I appreciate time is short ...'

'Wait, wait a minute.' Seamus stopped the baron. 'All your instructions are about dealing with the god if he has not joined with his body. Have you nothing to offer should the god arrive in his full form?'

Pausing before he answered, the baron said, 'My family have guarded the casket and we have kept the law of how the Wizard and Warrior are to use it. I guess the gods assumed if we gave it to you, you would know what you needed to do.'

Seamus nodded. 'That makes sense. I am sorry this meeting has been so short, but I must really go now.'

'Perhaps once this is over, we can compare—who are you?'

Seamus turned, following the baron's gaze and audibly gasped when he saw who stood behind him.

'I hoped to be a little quieter, but it does not matter. The chest will still be mine, regardless of who guards it.'

With a flick of his hand, Millard sent a wave of power. Without thinking, Seamus threw up a defensive wall of air around himself and Wexler. He was not quick enough to save the baron. Millard's attack flung the older man against the wall. Crashing to the floor, the old man lay motionless. Running to his side, Seamus was pleased to see him still breathing.

In the moment he looked to the older man's safety, Millard made it to the chest and reached out to pick it up.

'I would not do that if I were you. You know what happened last time we met,' Seamus threatened as he wondered what he would actually do if Millard ignored him. Almost as if he sensed Seamus was not prepared for this confrontation, the wizard scooped the chest up in one arm as he flung a fire bolt from his other hand. Seamus managed to roll away just in time. Jumping to his feet, he paused, glancing down at the injured man beside him.

'Ah … what?'

Baron Wexler attempted to raise himself up on one elbow in time to see Millard slip through the opening. 'What … what are you waiting for, boy? Get after him. Send one of the guards of the brotherhood to me if you get a chance.'

As the baron lay back down, Seamus took off after the man who had stolen the one thing he really needed to dispel a god.

BATTLE

Close on the wizard's heels, Seamus urged his legs to pump faster. His body was slow to respond, appearing sluggish, almost as if he were running through water or very thick air. Of course, Millard had learnt from their last encounter. To avoid a confrontation, he must have cast a spell to slow Seamus down.

Pausing, Seamus called air to himself and created a defensive shell around his body. He imagined it moving outwards, giving him enough room to take a long stride. Walking forward, he practiced moving the bubble as he walked, then ran. Freed from the wizard's constraints, he now used his youthful speed to return to the cave opening.

As he approached the exit, the ring of metal striking metal filled the night moments before something bounced him back, off his feet and onto his butt. Standing, he checked for injuries and wondered how to bypass Millard's new spell.

Shaking his head, he laughed at his own foolishness. This was not the wizard's doing, it was his own. His shield would not fit through the narrow gap. Dropping it for a moment, he turned and wedged himself through, hurriedly raising it again while he surveyed the mayhem in front of him.

Emer? Can you tell me what is going on?

Phew, we wondered if we had lost you. I watched you enter the cave. Then, from out of nowhere, soldiers appeared and rushed down to the cove. We stayed hidden, waiting to see if you needed us.

Did you see Millard enter the cave?

Millard? Are you sure?

Did you see him? Seamus asked impatiently,

I saw another shimmer after you disappeared into the wall, but then the fighting distracted me.

Seamus had no time to soothe her regrets. *Do you see him now?*

No. Seamus did you get the chest? Emer asked.

He has it, I need to find him.

Wait, Liam has just seen you. He says the only way out of the cove is up the path. Head that way and we will cut him off up here.

Heeding his friends' advice, Seamus ran towards his escape route, strengthening the shell around him to ensure any arrows or stray sword jabs slid away, leaving him to concentrate on weaving through the battle zone.

By the time he reached the pathway, a handful of Wexler's guards were in front of him, chasing a couple of fleeing intruders. Allowing his hand through the protective barrier, Seamus tapped one of them on the shoulder. Startled, the man turned and raised his sword ready to strike.

'Stop. I am Lord Seamus. The baron sent me. He is in the cave, injured. You need to send him help.'

'How do I know you are who you say you are? This could be a trick.' The guard turned as if to follow the others to the top of the cliff.

'I do not have time for this.' Seamus grumbled as he sent an image of the baron asking Seamus to get help to the guard.

The man paused, looked back towards the cave, then

up the path, undecided on whether to help stop the intruders or help his lord.

'My friends are at the top of the path. They will help stop the thieves. Go to your master.'

Although his face wore his doubt like a beacon, the guard decided to help his baron. 'Thanks for the warning, I will go to our brother.'

Seamus wasted no more time, dodging around the guardsmen he began his ascent. As he reached the top, he found Liam and Emer, returned to human form, fighting beside the baron's men.

'Millard slipped by us, he headed back the way we came.' Liam managed to get out before turning to block a blow to the head.

Leaving them to their task, Seamus sped off along the coastal path, keeping his shield up just in case. About a quarter of a candle mark later, he saw a shadowy figure in front. He put on a burst of speed but, seeing his pursuer gaining, Millard did the same.

Unable to make any ground, Seamus would have sighed with relief if he had any breath to spare as he made out the dark shadows of the fence line.

Walter, can you hear me?

No need to shout, boy.

Walter, no time I need …

It is all right, I see what is happening. Wait a moment. Done.

As she watched, Millard's feet lifted from the ground and in the blink of an eye he was flat on his back, almost as though someone had tackled him round the ankles.

Standing, still clutching the stolen chest, he rounded

on Seamus, teeth bared, snarling. So strong was the hatred rolling off him, Seamus could almost see it.

'Still on your crusade, boy? You will never win. You cannot win against a god. I was sure you would have figured that out by now and run away, tail between your legs.'

'Then you do not know me or Aliah well. Can you not see if we stand by and do nothing the world as we know it will disappear into despair? You must realise the god has no intention of sharing power with you. Once he is in his own body and in this world, he will no longer need you as his minion.'

A look of cunning crossed the magician's face. It was so quickly replaced by his usual superior demeanour, Seamus was unsure of whether it had been there in the first place. 'You could join me, and together we could make sure the god never controls our land,' Millard offered. 'Together we can send him back to Carsten. They deserve him for trying to invade Aria.'

While they were talking, Seamus dropped a knife from its sheath into his hand while he worked out how to wrest the chest from Millard before he found a way to escape and deliver it to the god. Then it dawned on him, Millard had no intention of handing the chest over to anyone.

This changed everything. Now he needed to get the artefact back before Millard decided to use it for his own ends.

Seamus, do you realise he is quite mad?

Yes, I know. Let me concentrate. Protect yourself any way you know how, just in case.

'Millard, you and I both know our god friend will not give up that easily. He would hunt us for the rest of our days. How about you help Aliah and I rid the world of his presence, and we can talk to her father about reinstating you to your position on the Wizard Isle? Or perhaps he can find you a barony if you prefer.'

A glimmer of hope flickered in Millard's eye. Appealing to his need for recognition seemed to be working. Regrettably, the look left as swiftly as it appeared, replaced by a shining mania.

Walter, he is really unhinged. This is not going to end well.

'I am worth more, boy. I set out to be ruler of this great nation, and I shall settle for nothing less. Watch and learn.'

Swinging the casket round in front of his body, he rested his other hand on the top.

'Wait, Millard. You do not know what you are doing.'

'In here is enough power to turn me into a god. I will be the most powerful being in all of Aria.'

Jerking the lid up, a golden glow spilled from the box, covering Millard. Dropping the chest to the ground, he swung his arms out wide, and looked up at the sky as he opened himself to absorb the power released from the magical artefact.

'Ahhh ...' a sound of pure bliss escaped from his lips.

Seamus, frozen in place, watching his chance of dispatching a god drawn into the mad magician. At the same time, he reached out with his own gift, attempting to close the lid of the chest before Millard released all the stored energy. Neither air nor earth were able to help him as the power being released from its centuries old prison was too strong, thwarting every attempt. Mesmerised and unable to prevent what happened next, Seamus stood by, hopelessly watching his chance of saving Aria slip away.

'Ahhhhhhh ...' The noise was no longer one of joy, but a rising screech of pain as the wizard's face contorted to reflect his inner battle.

Millard's body was not capable of taking in the torrent of energy it called forth, and had begun to expand and bloat. The wizard's eyes widened in fear as he realised the inevitable conclusion to his action only moments before his body blew apart.

Blinded by the explosion, Seamus belatedly threw up a protective shield. Ringing in his ears blocked out any noise, and as his eyes adjusted to the darkness, he realised he now stood at the edge of a gaping crater.

Walter? he urgently sent out.

You are yelling again.

Walters grumbling tones were drowned out by the buzzing in his ears as it became a roar, and he tingled all over from the top of his head to the tips of his toes. The world tilted, then went black as he slipped into unconsciousness.

12
DISASTER STRIKES

'No ...'

The god released the word with such force, Gaius was hauled from his prison and into his mind. Cringing and making himself small so as not to be seen, he slunk back into his cell and shut the door. He need not have worried, the god was clearly in too much of a state to notice his presence.

'You fool, Millard, what did you do?' he shouted to the moon. 'I knew you could not resist looking inside and stealing some of the magic for yourself. You released so much I can feel it from here. Will there be enough left for me to come through?'

What had Millard done? Opening the door a little and peeking out, he allowed his senses loose for the first time in a while. He was bombarded with a multitude of magical pin-pricks, the like of which he had never experienced before.

Basking in the essence, he pulled some into himself, and squirrelled even more away in his prison. He needed to be prepared for any eventuality, and this magical energy might come in handy.

Time passed and the energy levels dwindled. Aware the god had stopped his wailing, Gaius closed the door and hunkered down, trying to piece together what happened.

The god's sense of loss overwhelmed him. What might cause such intense feelings? The casket? Then it hit him.

Millard, the sly old dog, had opened the casket and used some of the power for himself. What he felt must have been the dregs of magic the wizard had been unable to absorb. How much had the wizard released? It must have been a lot to have reached them from so far away. How big a setback was this?

Apparently the god thought it was a major one. He muttered something about having to gather additional magic to refill the casket, and how this might delay his plans.

Finally he calmed down, and turned to the small force he had been travelling with. They had spent the night hidden not far from the top of the pass. The god informed them today's operation would go ahead as planned. It was critical to their ultimate success, especially now.

BATTLE

As they busied themselves, the god continued to mutter under his breath about how he would punish Millard for being so wasteful when they met up tomorrow. Still, this was a minor set back, he told himself. Things would just take a little longer. He would need to gather a little more magic before he was able to be reunited with his own body.

Gaius smiled, he had more time now. Time to plot for the return of *his* body.

Aliah sat bolt upright in her bed. Shaking her head to clear away the sleep, she wondered what had scared her enough to drag her from a deep slumber. There was nothing obvious in the room, but she could not shake the feeling something was different with the world.

After tossing and turning for around half a candle mark, she could stand it no longer. Rising quickly, she dressed, packed and took her gear downstairs only to find the others waiting for her in the half light.

'You felt it too?' Amelia asked.

'Yes, what was it?'

'I do not know. I felt a huge shift in the future. Everything is now poised on a knife edge. I can see thousands of possible futures, but none clearer than any other. Every action from here on in decides Aria's future one way or the other.'

'To me it sounds as if nothing has changed.' Daniel grunted as he dropped his pack to the ground.

'Oh, there was a massive change. Before there were

one of two futures; the god won, or we won. It is now as if those futures have been shattered into a thousand pieces and anything might happen.'

A frown creased Aliah's brow. 'What might cause such a change? What do we do now?'

Amelia shrugged her shoulders. 'Perhaps in one way Daniel is correct, we go on as before.'

'Breakfast is served.' A maid interrupted their discussion.

The baron met them in the dining room, and briefed them while they ate. Blockade building had started, but footprints in the area indicated a large force left the pass sometime the day before, heading around the coastal path towards Port Hand and Wexon. He suggested they stay with his guards until the pass, and that they pick up some tents for the next part of their journey.

With their party re-provisioned, they headed to the stables to find only six horses waiting for them and Robin standing, head down, looking decidedly sheepish. At their arrival he straightened up and told them his news.

'I am not continuing with you. By introducing you to the barons and working with you to ensure the pass cannot be used to invade Hand, I fulfilled my duty to the duke. Now I wish to return home.'

Aliah's initial reaction had been to let Robin go, but Dominic placed a hand on her arm, preventing her from speaking.

'Robin, we still have much to do, and we may need your skills with Baron Wexler.'

Pauley and I are sure he is up to something, and at least if he is close by, we can keep an eye on him.

'I appreciate your having so much faith in me, but my

relationship with that particular baron is not good. I fear I would be more of a hinderance than a help. Besides, my mother has been unwell. I left her in the care of others while I travelled with you. It is now time I returned home and saw to her myself.'

We cannot force him to come, Dominic, especially not if he has a mother to care for. That would make him suspicious and, if his story is true, it would be downright mean.

'Of course you must go to her, Robin. We really appreciate all you did for us. I hope your mother is better soon.'

As Aliah shook the man's hand she thought she caught a look of fear in his eyes, and perhaps a little sorrow. She had no time to follow up though as Rasmussen's guards were already mounted and filing out of the courtyard.

During the first part of their journey Dominic made his displeasure known. He and Pauley had been unable to find out what the man had been up to, and the spy grumbled most of the first candle mark about how now they would never know. When Aliah remarked they should be pleased he was no longer with them as it was one less thing for them to worry about, he gave her such a withering look she decided to ride with Amelia.

At various times during the day, Aliah let her mind spread out to find Seamus, wanting to ask if he had met with the baron, and wondering if he knew what had happened overnight. She was unable to find the link to him.

With Dominic in such a bad mood she did not want to ask him what might cause this to happen, and she certainly did not want to worry Amelia about her nephew. Besides, everything was strange today, and they had only ever made contact at night before. She would try again after dinner before she raised any alarms.

As the sun slipped lower in the sky and the air began to cool, Aliah sighed with happiness as Captain Williams called a halt to their journey. The young guard rode to the back of the column, to where Aliah and her party had been travelling that day, and stopped.

'The pass is up ahead. I sent the first watch forward, and we will make our camp here. You are welcome to stay with us tonight.'

Aliah did not even wait to ask the others before giving her answer. 'Thank you, we will be happy to join you.'

'Aliah,' Daniel stopped her from continuing. 'We are close to the meeting place, perhaps we should press on and make camp there.'

Trying hard not to glare at him, she forced her body to half turn in the saddle. 'We have been riding since sun-up. I think breaking now and starting fresh tomorrow would be best for those of us unused to spending days in the saddle.'

Admitting defeat, the Arian guard drew his horse alongside his counterpart from Hand.

'If you could direct us to a camp site out of your way, we will make use of the tents your lord kindly sent for us.'

Captain Williams showed Daniel to a space at the edge of the camp, close to the path they followed that day. As they dismounted, Aliah was not the only one groaning with relief at having their feet back on the ground.

Boss and Pauley helped her set up one of the tents Baron Rassmussen loaned them, before attending to one for themselves. She would share the middle tent with Amelia, while Daniel and Dominic would sleep in the tent on the other side. One of the guards brought over some stretchers for her and Amelia, saying they did not mind the ground for one night. Grateful for their thoughtfulness, Aliah thanked the man.

With the others having tent erection in hand, Aliah offered to take their mounts to be cared for while the others finished setting up camp. When no one objected, largely because they were all so busy and had likely not heard her, she removed the saddle bags and piled them in a heap. Still no one noticed her, so she gathered the reigns and led the horses round the edge of camp towards the picket line.

'Where would you like these?' she asked the soldier tying up the last of the guards' mounts.

'Just at the end there would be fine.' He pointed down the end of the line, under some trees. 'If you tie them up, I will remove their saddles later, once I have seen to the feed and water.'

Thanking the man, she led the horses to their assigned place, and began tying them up. Halfway through her task, she heard a noise behind and turned, expecting to find the soldier had returned, but she was wrong.

Swinging around to greet him, she came face to face with the one person she had not expected to see. 'What are you doing here?' she asked a little surprised, but more annoyed at finding him here.

Pauley picked up the last of the bags from the pile Aliah left for them when she took the horses. As he did, a package fell out of one of the travel packs. Picking it up to return it to its owner, it partially opened and a note fluttered to the ground.

Although his reading was not the best, the boy could not help himself. Labouring through the words, his eyes widened in astonishment as their importance sunk in.

Checking he understood, he opened the parcel and found something he had been trying to get his hands on for the last couple of days—a tin mirror. Suspicions confirmed, he ripped open the pack the mirror had fallen from. His hands trembled as he placed everything back inside and took the bag and two items to Boss.

'I think you need to see this,' he told the older man.

Taking the letter, the old soldier read it under his breath.

"I have done all you asked, even this last thing, placing the mirror in her pack. I kept up my end of the bargain, I hope you kept up yours and my mother is alive and well, and back in her cottage."

'Where did you find this?'

'It escaped from Aliah's backpack.'

'And where is ...'

Boss did not get to finish as the call to arms was issued. They were being attacked from behind.

The call to arms came as Daniel and Dominic were almost finished erecting their tent. Pauley had tossed their gear just inside, and they fell over each other trying to gather their swords and escape through the tent flap. Leaving their half-collapsed accommodation, they stood side-by-side to assess the situation and identify where they could best help.

The attack had come from the back. It must have been the force who slipped through the pass the day before. Joining the lines on the far edge of the encampment, they fought side-by-side, both boys keeping an eye out for Aliah. Dominic could not believe she would miss the chance for some battle experience, and began to worry.

'You need to go find her,' Daniel shouted over the noise of the battle.

'I cannot leave you to fight alone.'

'I will join the group over there, the one holding the pass ensuring we do not get caught between two forces.'

Daniel started edging towards the soldiers in the midst of the fighting.

'Are you sure that is wise? If anything happens to you, I will never hear the end of it from Aliah.'

'I will be fine. I trained my whole life for this,' Daniel answered confidently as he began inching towards Rasmussen's men.

Dominic was not sure the guard would be fine at all, he still looked a little grey after his stomach upset, and his movements were a little sloppy, not up to Daniel's usual standards of perfection. Preparing to argue, he almost dropped his own defences when Aliah burst into his mind.

Dominic, I need your help. Come find me. I am by the horses with—

Without a further thought for Daniel, Dominic extricated himself from the battle, dodged bodies from both sides, until he arrived at the edge of camp where the horses had once been kept. Cut ropes littered the ground. There were no animals to be found and, more importantly, no Aliah.

He stopped and calmed his breathing, allowing his training to take over. Slowly he let his mind out. Grateful for their time spent practicing mind linking, he searched for the fine thread of consciousness that would guide him to her. There it was. The connection was faint, but still there. He could make her out at the edge of the battle, heading towards tomorrow's meeting place.

Sheathing his sword, he ran back to their tents. Reaching into the middle one, he grabbed the object he came for from beside Aliah's pack, and took off after the princess.

I am coming for you, he sent, but he could no longer find her.

Amelia sat on the fallen tree branch, her back against a boulder. Pauley stood to one side, and Boss to the other. Unbeknown to them, she cast a shield over the group so any stray arrows would fall harmlessly away. More than capable of looking after herself, she took the opportunity to keep them away from the battle by allowing them to believe she needed their protection.

Looking towards the sound of the melee she made out the shapes of the men fighting. She guessed under normal circumstances she would not be able to tell one side from the other. But as she observed without eyes, it seemed to her some of the men fought with real vigour, as if they had something to fight for. Others fought mechanically, as if they fought because they had no choice.

With her newfound insights, Amelia could also identify her close friends from the others. Two figures glowed more brightly, they fought side by side, like brothers. A dark cloud grew inside of one of them, and she knew that to be Daniel. The other figure suddenly broke away from the fighting and headed towards the edge of camp. It was then Amelia realised she had not accounted for Aliah.

'Boss, where is the princess?'

'We are not sure. Pauley and I were going to look for her when the fighting broke out.'

'Why were you looking for her?'

'Pauley found Robin's mirror in her pack, along with a letter. I think he placed the mirror there to lead someone to her.'

Amelia cast her thoughts out, searching for the Warrior. She found Dominic, but no Aliah.

'They have her,' she said.

'I thought as much. There is nothing we can do about that at the moment. If we go after her now, we will be making ourselves targets, and that will not do anyone any good.'

'Agreed,' Amelia said out loud, while thinking to herself that did not mean she had to sit back and do nothing.

Leaving her protection up, she closed her eyes and reached out to search further afield for Aliah. She knew the girl had been practicing mind talking, so would not be surprised if Amelia spoke to her. Unable to find her, she opened her eyes in time to sense Dominic running around the edge of the camp, enter a tent, then run out clutching something. He barely paused before skirting the edge of the battle and disappearing. When he did not come back into her line of sight, she reached out for him.

Dominic?

Amelia?

Yes. Where are you?

I am going after Aliah.

Do you need help?

I am not sure. Let me catch up with her and I will let you know.

Stay in touch.

Once Dominic had broken off contact, Amelia again concentrated on the fight. Enemy soldiers were being rounded up and placed under guard, the main battle was over. Searching, she tried to find Daniel. Panic welled up, she could not sense him anywhere.

No, there he was …

On the ground.

'Boss, I need you to help me. I want to get over there to Daniel.'

A firm hand grasped her elbow and assisted her to her feet. The same hand clasped hers, and tucked it through an arm. Boss Allum led her through the debris of the camp to where she pointed. Dropping to her knees, Amelia searched for Daniel's arm, and found his wrist. Taking his pulse, she found it weak and thready.

'Daniel? Daniel? Can you hear me?'

'Amelia,' his response was almost at the level of a whisper.

BATTLE

'Hold still and I will try to heal you. This is not really my skill, but I might be able to do enough to stabilise you.'

As she sent her awareness into Daniel, his other hand weakly grabbed at her arm.

'Do not waste your energy.' His voice gained a little strength. 'You and I both know you would only be delaying the inevitable.'

Amelia found the cause of Daniel's pain, a wound just under the ribs, a sword had nicked his lung on the way through. The lung had collapsed, causing air to escape, and the wound bled profusely into his chest. Unless she healed the lung and stopped the bleeding, the boy would not survive.

'Daniel, I can help with this, please let me. You might live for another year or so before your disease overtakes you, or we may even find a cure in the meantime. Perhaps even Aliah's sword might be able to help,' Amelia said, attempting to convince him to fight for his life.

'I am a soldier. This is all I ever wanted. Please let me die in battle rather than waste away, being a drain on my friends and family. I do not want to see the pity in their eyes every time they look at me. I am a coward, I know. But if I die fighting for something I believe in, if I die fighting to save Aria, then my death will at least mean something.'

'But ...'

A hand dropped on to her shoulder as Boss crouched down beside her. 'These gents here say Daniel fought off three men who pinned them down. They thought they were done for. They say Daniel fought like a hero of the old tales. He saved those boys, to be sure. Let the lad die a hero if that is his wish.'

Wiping the tears from her cheek, Amelia turned back to the young guard. 'What can I do to help? Can I take away your pain?'

'I feel so light headed, the pain seems so far away.'

'That is because your body is not getting enough air.'

'If it is not too much to ask, could you hold my hand? I am not as brave as I thought.'

The tears flowed freely now as Amelia settled beside Daniel. 'I will stay with you, you are not alone.'

'Tell Aliah I am sorry I could not be there to help her at the end. I would not be much use like this ...'

'You have done so much Daniel, I think she will let you off this once.'

'And tell Dominic ... tell him he is the only one to look after her now ... he best not let me down ...'

'Do not worry, I believe that boy will spend most of his life near Aliah.'

'Seamus ... tell him ... world needs good ... men as well as ... fighters ... take care of him.'

'I will.'

'... and ...'

Amelia leaned close to Daniel to hear these last words.

'... tell father ... died fighting for Aria ... not that ... I was ... sick ... or scared.'

'Oh, my lovely boy, your father loves you and will feel your loss no matter how you die.' A squeeze on her shoulder reminded her. 'Of course I will tell him, and he will be all the more proud of you for it.'

'Thank ... you ...'

BATTLE

The grip on her hand loosened as Daniel passed on his last message.

'Just rest now.' She brushed the hair back from the young boy's forehead. Amelia held the guard's hand as his breathing slowed, then stopped. She held it a while longer, until the hand in hers grew cold and loss tugged at her heart.

Although the soldiers were ferrying away the dead and wounded from around her, Amelia could not let go of Daniel, not wanting the boy to be left alone in this place so far from his home. She wondered how she would break the news of the brave soldier's fate to Aliah, as tears fell freely down her cheeks and soaked into the blood soaked ground beside her. Finally, Boss gently released her grip and helped Amelia to her feet. Leading her back to the tent Pauley had fixed up for her, he led her inside.

'I will let you know when we are ready to bury him. Until then, perhaps you should rest.'

The words jolted her from her grief and she drew a long, shuddering breath then squared her shoulders. 'No, please bring my bag of herbs, there are others here who need my help while we wait for Dominic to return.'

13
INTERVIEW WITH A GOD

Something sharp dug into Aliah's arm. Rolling to ease the pressure, she found herself unable to move. The pain intensified, cutting through the fuzz inside her head. Gaius had knocked her out. Where was she? Why was she unable to move?

Forcing her eyes open, all she saw was green. All right, she was lying on grass. Wriggling her body, she found her arms tied behind her back, and her feet bound together and pulled up behind her. Hog tied? Someone had hog tied her.

'Ah, you are awake. What fragile bodies you people have.'

'Mmm … mmmm.' Aliah struggled to speak through the gag.

'Oh, I forgot. I guess we are far enough away now that no one will hear you scream.' He wrenched the cloth from her mouth, banging her head on the ground and grazing her cheek.

'What was that you were saying?'

Ignoring the sting of the graze, she answered, 'I said your body is breakable too, Gaius, and once I am free, I will show you just how easy it is to break.'

'Yes, yes, this body will break, but by the time you are free I will have no care for this vessel. You can do what you will with it, if you yourself are still alive that is.'

The voice was Gaius', but the words did not sound at all like him. Through the fog in her brain, she tried to remember something important someone said about Gaius. No, it would not come.

'You are a disappointment, Warrior. You are nothing without your sword.'

That tone was familiar. Where had she heard it before? Ah, now it came to her.

'What have you done with Gaius?'

'Mmm, what? You worry about the weak wizard who left this body for my use?'

'He cannot have been that weak, otherwise you would not have desired his body.'

'There are many different kinds of weakness. He was weak of will, he did not even fight me when I decided to use him. Still, he is no more.'

'You killed him for his body? You treat us like we are

worthless.'

'Oh no, little Warrior, you all have value. Your worth is measured by what you are able to do for me.'

'So, if I am still here, you must think I am able to do something for you.' Aliah shivered as she spoke the words. The god could have killed her any time he liked having caught her unawares, but he kept her alive. Why? It would not be for anything good.

'Of course,' the god responded to her question. 'I want you to witness your failure before you die. I want you to witness my coming to this world in my true form, then I want you and the wizard boy to fight me. I want to show you how weak you really are, and what nonsense it was for you to ever dream of taking me on. You are to be an example for others who think to thwart me.'

He kept her alive simply to preen and show off in front of her. To ensure an admiring audience as he took over the world. He would not discard her until he had proven to her how strong he was. For all that he spoke of other's weaknesses, could he really be so blind to his own? Her only thought now was to keep him talking so she could think of a way out of this. She would not let this be the end of her battle.

Dominic? Seamus?

'Do not bother calling for your friends. I wrapped you in a bubble. You cannot send thoughts out, and no one can find you.'

She could not contact Dominic to tell him where she was, and she could not let Seamus know either. A little snake of despair wormed its way into her heart, but she crushed it before it could take hold. There had to be something she could do. The sword had been given to her because of her courage, she did not have strength only because she held it.

'If you are so keen to bring your physical form here, why are you wasting time with me?'

Gaius-god laughed, a hollow sounding laugh with no real mirth, and it grated on her nerves.

'You think I wait here because of you. No, no. You are simply a diversion to fill in time. My servant Millard is bringing me the casket of power so I may make my transformation and be here in all my true glory.'

Now it was Aliah's turn to laugh, and hers came from deep in her belly. 'Perhaps you should not have been so quick to get rid of Gaius. He would have warned you; Millard is no one's servant. The only person he serves is himself. If you wait here for him, you wait in vain.'

'You lie. You would say anything to keep me from the casket. With my help he searched for the vessel, and then offered to go and fetch it for me. He knows I will reward him once we have Aria under our control. Until then, he is my loyal servant.'

'Can you even hear what you are saying? You helped him find something containing great magical power, then he asked you to stay behind while he went to fetch it. What has Millard ever done that would lead you to believe he would give up such an important magical artefact?'

The god glared at her but said nothing. A frown slowly worried its way onto his face. As she thought of something, anything else that might needle the god, an idea flashed into her mind.

'You must have felt the disturbance in the air last

night, and how odd the world is today. Can you be sure that Millard has not already accessed the power of the casket?'

The god paused his pacing. 'I am sure he has, but the little he could hold will not diminish the power by any great amount, there will still be plenty left for me.'

Aliah almost lost her focus. *Millard has the chest, how will we defeat the god now?* Again, she would not let herself sink into despair. They needed to fight until the very end. 'That is if he intends to give the casket to you and not keep it for himself.'

The god's face turned to thunder and Aliah tensed her body for the attack that would inevitably follow. Instead, Gaius-god walked over to her and stuffed the gag back in her mouth. 'We are finished talking.'

Aliah's eyes followed him as he returned to the fire and sat down, then stood, then paced, then sat again.

As she watched the restless figure, her mind conjured an image of Gaius from her childhood. He had been a nasty boy. Always putting everyone down, pointing out their failings and getting them into trouble, making enemies at every turn. As he grew into manhood, he became even more unpleasant.

Once she had tried to befriend him, after her mother admonished her for her uncharitable utterances one day when she wished the boy dead. Her mother's lecture on tolerance made her feel guilty. As did her recount of Gaius' early life.

His own family abandoned him on the Wizard Isle when he was found to have magic. They wanted nothing to do with such an abomination. Compassion rose up inside Aliah, and when she next organised a riding party to escape lessons, she invited Gaius to join them. Instead of his gratitude, she earned his condemnation, and he told her father of the plan.

From that day on, they had been enemies, something she was now grateful for as it made it much easier to hate the god who wore his form. As she glared at her foe, he stood, walked over and began saddling a horse. Leading the animal back over to the fire, the men looked up as he approached.

'I go to meet with Millard and assist him with retrieving the casket. Stay here with the girl until I return. If any harm comes to her, it will be done to you, tenfold.'

With his instructions delivered, he hauled himself into the saddle. Looking down at Aliah he said, 'Do not think this has anything to do with your words. I will return, and you will witness my arrival in your world, and you will be in awe of me as you should be.'

So many responses bounced around Aliah's mind, but all she was able to do was shake her head in frustration, unable to give voice to any of them.

With the god gone, the camp relaxed. Aliah rolled around to find a more comfortable position and her hands touched something cold. Wriggling and stretching her fingers, she grabbed a hold of it. Strength flowed through her.

Her sword? How was it here? She had left it behind with her gear when she went to tether the horses. It was then she realised Dominic was close by; all would be well now.

Fingers still on the sword, Aliah used the artefact's magic to push away the bubble encasing her. Much calmer now, she attempted to sleep until the opportunity came for rescue. She would need all her strength to get away and make it to the rendezvous on time.

The guards glanced over at her, checking to see she was all right. Not wanting any of them to return her to her prison, she wondered how she might hide herself so the wizards amongst them could not sense her. Reversing the process Dominic taught her for casting out her senses, she drew herself back in and imagined herself locked behind a door in her mind. The guards settled back down. She waited for them to sleep, and for Dominic to signal the time for her escape.

An exhausted Amelia paused to take a breath and surveyed the scene around her. Many of the injured guards were sleeping peacefully, having taken a sleeping drought after their wounds had been tended to. Just as many again lay waiting for herself and Baron Rasmussen's surgeon to attend to them.

Sighing, she picked up her bag and moved to the next poor boy, aware she brought this on herself when she insisted they treat the injured soldiers from Carsten as well. As Captain William's objected, the baron himself rode up and she found a surprising supporter when he insisted they treat their enemy as they would wish to be treated should the tables be turned.

Now she paid for her folly, but still, it was good to be busy. It stopped her thinking about poor Daniel, and the other boys who had not survived to be treated by her.

She was so engrossed in her work, Boss had to touch her on the shoulder to alert her to his presence.

'We are ready to bury Daniel now, if you want to join us.'

The ceremony was short, and Amelia struggled to keep her tears inside as she said goodbye to the brave guardsman and friend. Even though his illness may have taken him soon, she mourned his life cut short by senseless fighting.

Once the brief funeral was over, Amelia stayed behind to say a private goodbye.

You are free of the constraints of your body now, Daniel, but we will honour your courage and loyalty by doing all we can to make sure we win this battle. And never fear, we will make sure Aliah is well looked after.

As she spoke to Daniel another voice brushed her mind.

Amelia?

Dominic?

Yes. I have found Aliah.

Good. Are you on your way back here, or will you head directly to the meeting place?

I said I had found her, not that I had rescued her, Dominic corrected Amelia.

I assume you have a plan?

Well, rescuing Aliah is my plan.

I take that as a no then, Amelia was tired and her words were tart.

Amelia, is something wrong?

She though about telling the boy, but then changed her mind. He had enough to worry about.

Nothing that cannot wait until later. Do you need any help?

Thank you, but I think this is a stealth mission and so

BATTLE

I am better off on my own.

All right. Let me know if that changes.

How did we fare in the fight?

We are mostly all right, I am off to tend to the wounded now.

Be well, Amelia, I will be in contact.

Rising from her knees, Pauley and Boss flanked her as she left the graveside. The young boy slipped his hand into hers and gave a small squeeze of understanding.

'What do we do now? Should we go to the meeting place and help Seamus? Or are we to help Dominic search for Aliah?' Boss asked. 'The baron is gathering a party to head out this evening to try and find the princess and chase down any stragglers. He would be more than happy for us to join with him.'

Pausing to see if the future was any clearer, she eventually said, 'Dominic has found Aliah, and I believe our part is done for the moment. We three can do nothing to influence events now. I believe our efforts are best spent staying here and helping with the wounded.

'If things in the coming battle come out in our favour, what we do here will go a long way towards healing the wounds between our two nations.'

Unsure whether or not Boss' grunt signalled his agreement, Amelia had made her decision and turned towards the make-shift hospital. She intended making herself very busy so she had no chance to worry about the fate of her beloved Walter, and Seamus, and Aliah.

With stiff fingers, Aliah grasped her sword and followed Dominic through the surrounding undergrowth. The sun was just beginning to peek above the horizon, and the sleeping guard would no doubt awaken when it fully rose. They wanted to be well away before that happened.

When she realised they were heading towards the rendezvous point rather than back to the pass, she placed a hand on Dominic's arm to stop him.

'Are we not going to pick up the others and get our horses?' she whispered, careful not to use mind speak as she did not want any of the magicians they left behind to be able to trace her.

Dominic shook his head. 'We can make good time on foot, and it is likely the Carstenite guards will assume that is where we have headed, so this might give us a slight advantage.'

Nodding her head in agreement, they continued on, staying within the trees until the sun was high in the sky and no obvious sounds of pursuit disrupted the quiet of the forest. Leading them back to the trail, Dominic explained they needed to move a bit faster if they were going to meet the others as arranged, but it was important they kept an ear out for the sound of horses following.

As they jogged side by side along the path through the forest, Aliah used the sword to revive her energy. Dominic even allowed her to give him a boost, reasoning they both needed to be in their best fighting form should they be found.

Although they were heading towards Seamus, Aliah could not dispel the unease growing in the pit of her stomach. She had not been in touch with her Wizard since the day before yesterday, and she just knew that was not good.

When they stopped by a stream for a breather and to quench their thirst, Aliah voiced her fears to Dominic.

'So you managed to mind speak with Seamus by yourself?' Dominic was amazed.

Hands on hips, Aliah glared at the boy who rescued her, for the moment her gratitude swamped by anger.

'Did you not hear me? I said I could not find him at all yesterday. I think something is wrong, and I do not want to be walking in to a trap.'

With a patience that irritated her even more, Dominic responded, 'These things are not predictable. Sometimes you can contact someone easily, other times it takes a little longer dependent on what they are doing. I would not be too worried just yet. If he is not at the meeting place when we arrive, then perhaps we should risk a little mind linking.'

Aliah humphed, but could not think of anything to counter his argument.

'If you are ready, the meeting point is about a candle mark along here,' he said.

The speed at which they travelled prevented any further speech, but that did not stop Aliah from re-imagining how the last conversation could have gone if she had only thought of her come backs earlier. She was so engrossed in her one-sided re-enactment, she did not notice Dominic coming to an abrupt halt. Slamming into his back, she muttered, 'What ...' Only to be silenced by Dominic placing a hand over her mouth, and pulling her roughly back into the bushes surrounding the clearing in front of them.

Once Aliah had regained her dignity, she surveyed the scene.

'Oh, no, that is not good,' she said under her breath.

On the far side of the clearing, was a group of Carsten soldiers readying themselves for battle. The only good thing about the situation was they were so caught up in their preparations, they had not noticed their two visitors.

'How did they know we were meeting here?' Dominic asked.

'They may not have, this may be a coincidence,' Aliah answered. 'It does not look like an ambush, if it was, they would be hidden. It looks more like they camped here last night and are waiting for orders, which I assume they expect to come soon given their activity.'

Dominic watched a little longer, 'I think you are right, even so, Seamus and the others will be walking right into them any time soon.'

'Not if we can circle round and warn them.'

Dominic nodded his head once, then started moving around the clearing towards the path opposite. They had just made it round the other side, and were creeping through the undergrowth by the track when it happened. Aliah froze at Seamus' call. She took one look at Dominic, broke cover, and ran faster than she had ever run in her life.

14
THE BATTLE LINES ARE DRAWN

'He really is making a habit of fainting.'

'I know, Emer. Do you think we should point it out to him when he wakes?'

'Probably not a good idea. He is glowing after the explosion. There is no telling how that much energy might affect his mind ... I would hate for him to blow up.'

'I can hear you.'

'Oh good, you are awake. Walter, he has come to.'

'No need to shout, Emer, I am right here.'

'Oh, sorry.'

Forcing his eyes open, Seamus found himself back by the fire. Someone had tucked him into a bedroll and he had snuggled down inside. The morning sun was just peeking through the trees, telling him he had been out for a few candle marks.

'How did I get back here? Did someone carry me up the tree?'

'Sometimes I wonder if you have the sense you were born with. After the explosion, there was no need to find a way over the fence. Millard's stupidity blasted a hole straight through it,' Emer responded.

'I feel like I have been run over by a horse,' he groaned as he stretched out. 'It is a good thing we are not due to meet up with the others until tomorrow, I think I need to take it a bit easy today.'

'What are you talking about?' Walter joined them by the fire. 'You slept through a day and a night, we have to get moving soon if we are to be at the meeting place on time.'

Lifting his hand to push the hair back out of his eyes, Seamus stopped and stared. His hand glowed with a golden light. Slowly, his mind grasped onto the fact this must have been what Emer and Liam were joking about.

'Ah, so you found our little problem.'

'Little problem? Walter, I am glowing.' Panic began to worm its way up from the pit of his stomach.

'While you rested, I have been thinking how we might deal with this, and I have a plan.'

'Good, but perhaps you can first explain what this is before we decide what to do about it.'

BATTLE

As Walter settled beside him, Emer and Liam drifted away to get the horses ready to move. As he settled down, Seamus suddenly sat bolt upright.

'Walter, the casket! Did it survive?'

'I am sorry, nothing in the area survived the explosion.'

Abruptly Seamus rose to his feet and started pacing, trailing a fine golden light behind.

'What am I going to do now? The box was the only thing able to hold a god, and it contained the power we needed to send him from this world.'

As suddenly as he stood, Seamus dropped to the ground. 'We are defeated before we even begin.'

'Seamus, if you were not glowing a strange colour I would shake you senseless.' Emer's voice carried from where she tended the horses. 'If all it took to dispel the god was a simple box, any one of us could have done it.'

Turning away from her, Seamus stared sulkily into the fire. 'So what is this then? A minor set back?'

'If you are going to be such a baby about this, I am not going to talk to you anymore. If you want to listen to what I have to say, come and find me when you have grown up.'

'Seamus, although you may not want to hear it, Emer is right. The other night was not a complete loss. Your glow tells me that,' Walter advised.

'My glow? Yes, you were going to tell me about it.'

'I believe your shields were not fully in place when Millard opened the casket, releasing the power inside, and I think you retained some of the stored magic.'

Eyes widening in surprise, Seamus asked, 'How is that a good thing? Correct me if I am wrong, but Millard exploded when he tried to take magic from the casket. Now you are saying that same magic is in me.'

Walter's fingers gripped his arm. 'Stop looking on the bad side of everything. If you were going to experience adverse effects from this magic they would have shown up by now. Quit brooding and think for a moment.'

Tired, scared and worried, the last thing Seamus wanted to do was lift himself from the darkness of his thoughts. Fortunately, he was his father's son and he realised he had a duty to perform, and he could not do that while he was feeling sorry for himself. Keeping his gaze firmly focused on the fire's dancing flames, he shuffled the puzzle pieces in his head until they formed a different pattern.

'If the casket is gone the god no longer has enough energy to bring his body though, so we have that in our favour.'

'And?' Walter prompted him.

'I had to bind the god in some way to force him into the casket, so maybe I can think of some way to strengthen those bindings so we can hold him long enough to send him away.'

Pulling his eyes away from the fire he found Walter nodding his encouragement. The silence from behind told him Emer and Liam also stopped to listen.

'I have lost most of the magic intended to send the god away, but there is still some, quite a bit in fact, within me. Walter, are you able to help me store it until I need it?'

'I can, it is a simple task.'

'Then all I need to do is find more magic to replace

the power Millard squandered. I do not suppose it is still around?'

'Funny you should ask that.' Walter grinned. 'Unused magic is all around us all the time, including the magic that foolish man released. We may be able to add to our store of magic as we travel.'

'Excellent, so we are not completely helpless.'

'Before you get your hopes up, I need to caution you each person can only hold so much magical energy. The amount differs between wizards, but you have already seen the effects of trying to store too much. Between the two of us we will not be able to hold nearly as much as the destroyed artefact did. So we will be limited in what we can do.'

'Still, we are not defeated yet. All I need to do is figure out how to bind a reluctant god, and identify enough energy to push him through to another plane. Oh, and of course we have to meet up with Aliah, then find the god.'

'I am pleased you are in a better frame of mind.' Emer joined them beside the fire, with Liam close on her heels. 'Maybe, though, before we do anything, we should eat something. You have had a day without food, and you need to keep your strength up.'

'We should also store my excess magic then find out how Baron Wexler is.' In response to their perplexed looks he said, 'I will update you all on my time in the cave as we eat, but I need food before anything else, that is if my glow does not need to be dealt with first.'

Walter laughed. 'It has waited a day, it can wait until you have eaten.'

Stomach now full, all Seamus wanted to do was go back to sleep, however he was aware he needed to start building his magical reserves as rapidly as possible. Liam pushed for them to be on their way to the meeting place, but Seamus had other ideas.

'Liam, the fight will be here soon enough, whether we run to it or it comes to us. I need some learning time with Walter. Perhaps you and Emer should go back down to the bay and make sure the baron is all right for me.'

'Come on, Liam, the two of them are best left alone. And I for one would like to make sure none of those Carstenite soldiers are still hanging around. The last thing we need when we are in the midst of confronting a god is for them to spring up from behind.'

'Surely we would have seen them by now if there were any still around.'

Liam was reluctant to move. Emer grabbed the boy's arm and hauled him to his feet anyway.

'You know something,' he said to Seamus as the girl released his arm. 'You know it is going to be today.'

Reluctant to say the words out loud, Seamus did anyway, because his cousin deserved to hear them. 'Yes, it will be today. So we have to prepare as best we can. Emer is right, we need to make sure there are no surprises. This battle will be difficult enough as it is, we need to give ourselves the best possible chance of seeing it through to the end.'

With his fears confirmed, Liam was now happy to be

doing something, anything, rather than sitting around waiting. Although he did throw a concerned look over his shoulder, to check on his cousin one last time, before mounting and heading off through Millard's devastation.

'So, shall we begin?' Seamus asked. 'Walter, I asked if you were ready.'

The older man was silent.

'Walter, what is it?'

'Huh. Oh, sorry. There is something not quite right this morning. I cannot quite place it, but the world feels, um, slightly out of alignment.'

'I know what you mean. It is strange, but now is not the time to be distracted. Today is the day, we need to stay focused.'

'Um, yes, of course. Let us begin. I want you to find your magic.'

Seamus confirmed he had it.

'Good. I know you see it as a glow, now imagine it is in the centre of a container.'

'I think I have,' Seamus told him.

'Good, now can you see the magic gathered around your body?'

Seamus nodded.

'Excellent, now imagine drawing that into your container.'

Seamus concentrated on doing as Walter instructed.

Around the time he could no longer feel any more magic being stored, Walter said, 'Well done.'

Seamus opened his eyes and, to his relief, he found he no longer glowed. 'That was surprisingly easy.' Seamus congratulated himself.

'Well, you sound very pleased with yourself. All we

have to do is expand this process so you can collect magic from the world around you. We have to be a little more careful with this because it can be very dangerous.'

'What, and storing all that magic was not?' Seamus barked out a nervous laugh.

'I guessed you would be able to store the magic clinging to you from the casket because it had not torn you apart already.'

'Oh, all right, and now?'

'Now you are taking on more, and we do not know where your limits are. Do not worry though, I will take you slowly through the process, that should lessen the risk. First, can you tell me about your container?'

'Huh?' Seamus was remembering Millard exploding the night before last, and was now feeling a little more cautious about this whole process. 'I imagined I stored it in a water skin, to allow it to expand as I added more magic.'

'Yes, um, yes I guess that does help. In fact, it is perfect because you already have the idea a water skin can only be filled so far before it bursts. You need to understand you cannot fill your magical water skin beyond its capacity.

'Now, collecting magic is similar to sending out your consciousness to find a person, or maybe even how you can sense the energy of everything living in the forests. I want you to reach out and feel the air around us.'

Seamus closed his eyes, as he always did when concentrating, and allowed his consciousness to flow out of him. He could sense Walter and the living beings of the forest, but nothing else.

'I can only feel living things, Walter.'

'Ah, you are reaching out in a clump. How do I explain

how to do this? When I taught this before, my students were boys who had studied for years to be able to draw in magic, and showed an aptitude for this sort of thing.

'Let me see, imagine you are casting a net, not like a fisherman, one with no holes. No, no, this is better. Imagine you are throwing a sheet over a bed. Cast yourself out like that, only suspend the sheet in midair.'

'Ah, like when I wrapped your essence the other day, I imagined casting a blanket over you.'

'Yes, exactly.'

Seamus tried again, this time imagining himself as very thin and very large, like a blanket. He held himself midair and waited. Tiny pinpricks of something clung to him. Letting himself come back, he explained the sensation to Walter.

'Yes, boy, that is the magical energy of our world.'

'How do I harness it?'

'Yes … mmm, well of course you do that every day. Those with magical abilities absorb magic without even knowing they are doing it, and it settles in their bodies, waiting to be used. When they use their magic, their bodies replace it, like it replaces air in your lungs.

'If you use too much, more than you stored, your body starts to convert your own energy to magic to finish what you are doing. If you do not have sufficient control of your magic and you cannot stop the process, you can steal so much from your body it withers away and shuts down.

'Alternatively, if you take in too much energy, your magical store keeps increasing, much like a pig's bladder when it is blown up to use as a ball for games. If you take in too much …'

'... you explode, like Millard did the other night.'

'Yes, yes. I know you are impatient to get started, but if you interrupt me this will take much longer. I need to be sure you understand the dangers before we begin.'

'Sorry. Continue.'

'There is no way of knowing how much magic is too much until it is almost too late. So, the way to manage harvesting extra is to take a little at a time. Check your body, then check again.

'So what I want you to do is find your magic.'

'I have it.'

'Wait, wait a moment. I missed a step. Do you know what colour your magic is normally?' Walter asked.

'Yes, a deep yellow.'

'All right, check your magic now.'

'That is interesting, it is a bright yellow, almost orange.'

'Good. Now we know the colour, we need to continue to check in between harvests to monitor the changes. As soon as you see any tinge of red, you need to stop,' Walter instructed.

'Does the size I imagined my water skin to be matter? It is only small.'

'I am not sure of the mechanics, perhaps a healing wizard would know more. All I know is your container adjusts to be able to hold your magic, however large a storage container you imagine. It is only when your energy turns red your storage stops growing. If you continue, the container is compromised, spilling out the excess energy.'

'Right, let us do this then.'

'This time I need you to imagine yourself to be as thin as a sheet, but only about the size of a pillow case.

Limiting your size will limit the magic you harvest to a manageable amount. Are you ready?'

Seamus followed Walter's instructions to the letter. He waited until the magical pricks covered him. Holding himself there he said, 'I have some, how do I bring it in?'

'This is when the net analogy worked. You need to imagine closing it and hauling in your catch.'

It sounded simple, but doing it was harder. The first attempt Seamus lost almost all of his haul. With the second, he drew in a little.

Walter then made him stop and check the colour of his internal store. Disappointed, he found it unchanged.

'Interesting. Maybe you are doing it wrong.'

'Or maybe what I am bringing in is such a drop in the ocean, compared to the energy from the casket, I am not noticing any change?'

'That is another possibility. Try again.'

Concentrating, Seamus attempted another harvest, sure he took in much more magic this time. There was still no change in colour. The fourth time, his colour deepened a little and Seamus heaved a sigh of relief. He was doing it right. With his fifth cast he could not sense as much magic, it was more of a tingle than a prick. When he told Walter, the wizard explained,

'Living things generate magic, but it is a slow process. Once it is gone from an area you either cast wider, or move.'

Seamus tried turning his pillow case into a sheet again, and was surprised to find more energy. While Seamus was checking his colour, which was now a dull orange, the sound of hoof beats filled the morning air.

A re-energised Seamus opened his eyes just as a group

of men rode into sight. Reaching for his knives, he relaxed a little when he made out the colours of the baron's men. As they drew closer, he saw Baron Wexler riding with them.

'A fine mess you made of my lands,' the baron said as he dismounted with some difficulty, the stiffness of his movements indicating he was not entirely recovered from his encounter with Millard.

'Not me, I am afraid. It was the thief. He thought the casket's magic was better used to boost his own powers, than passed on to the god.'

'That was a little foolish of him, and not so good for you.'

'No. Now I have to find a way to hold the god until I can figure out how to send him back.'

'So, I may be able to assist you in two ways again today.'

'Two ways? I am sorry, but I do not understand.'

The baron held out his hand. In the palm rested an amber glass vial, which he offered to Seamus.

'This is not the casket, but it may help. In addition to the minor skill of calling, my family's magical ability leans towards protection and wards, which is why we were given the casket to look after.

'However, my mother's family had a different skill. They were healers. In the past, their skills were used in battle. With so many magic users stripping an area clean of energy, they took to storing magic. They became rather good at it, and there is more magical energy in there than you would expect from so small a container.

BATTLE

'When I heard the explosion the night before last, I sent one of my men back to retrieve this. My last one I am afraid as I did not inherit the skill to make more. It may be of some help.'

Seamus was touched by the man's gift. 'Thank you, I am sure this will be most useful.'

'Not as useful as the other gift I have for you: advice.'

'Advice?'

'I am aware the plan was for you to bind the god in the casket. With its loss, I feared you might now fail. As I slept last night I dreamed of my great-grandfather, and of a story he used to tell about the wars.

'When he was on the battlefield and they ran out of cloth bandages, he used to create a magical bandage to bind wounds.'

Seamus had been so busy looking at the vial of magic he had not really been paying attention to the man. Slowly his last sentence penetrated and he immediately realised its importance.

'Really? I do not suppose he told you how he did it?'

'That is the thing, he did. He said he would send out a thread of magical energy and wrap it around the wound. It was more effective in containing that which should remain inside the body than actual bandages, but it took a lot of energy, so it was only used when absolutely necessary.'

Mulling this information over in his head, Seamus realised this was the solution he had been looking for. He was so overwhelmed with gratitude, he hugged the man.

'Well, well, there is no need for that, young man,' the baron said gruffly, but his face told a different story. He beamed with pleasure at having been able to help the young wizard again.

'Remember, when you need some energy, just break the vial. I must return home now. The events of the last couple of days took a little out of me and I really could do with some rest. I have much to do this afternoon.'

'Baron, I think you have done enough. You should take the time to get over the injuries Millard gave you.'

'No, no, my task is not yet finished. The brotherhood and I will spend the afternoon in prayer to our god in support of the coming battle. We also organised the people of the village to attend church and pray to the goddess to lend her support as well.'

Seamus was about to ask what good that would do, then he remembered in the training session when the god explained the power of prayer and how it affected the physical world.

'I will also pray that when I wake up tomorrow you have solved our little problem and our world is safe once again.'

'Once again, baron, I am at a loss at how to thank you for all your support.'

'Am I sensing a but?'

'Yes, I have a question. If your family has been practicing magic for all these years, how is it you do not support the open use of magic on Hand?'

Baron Wexler looked thoughtful, as though he was deciding whether or not to answer. Finally he turned back and placed a hand on Seamus' shoulder.

'Lad, I know after this you will want nothing more than to go home and live out the rest of your life with your family, perhaps even become duke someday as was planned.

BATTLE

'Sadly, although there are some here who would be happy for you to do just that, more than you might even imagine, we are still not the majority. There are many people on Hand who are vehemently opposed to any magic in all its forms.

'You might even be forgiven for thinking some of those people will be so happy you saved them from the god, that they will embrace the use of magic. However, in my experience, people are more likely to take a stronger stance against magical users in these circumstances, claiming if there were no magic at all, none of this would have happened.

'Things are changing, but slowly. I would suggest if you come through this in one piece you think about what else you might do with your life, away from Hand.'

As Seamus watched the baron's party ride away and sensed Walter beside him.

'I fear the baron is right, Hand will not be able to be your home after this. While I know you have been focused on the battle you must face, it is only natural for you to wonder what you will do after.

'Amelia and I have been considering our own futures. After this we will be returning to Sanctuary. She, to take up her training as a seer, and I would like to spend time in their libraries, learning about their use of magic. We also thought of starting our own school to develop the use and understanding of magic. One open to both boys and girls.

'If that interests you, I know Amelia and I would both love to have you return with us. I also suspect there is one other person who may be pleased if you choose to live in Sanctuary.'

With a blush rising from his collar, Seamus chose to ignore the last remark.

'Thank you, Walter, I will think on it should we make it through today.'

'Do that. Sometimes having a future to fight for makes us fight all the harder. Now, we should ready our horses, I see Emer and Liam are nearly here.'

With no sign of the soldiers from Carsten, Emer suggested they head on to the rendezvous point. While they rode, Seamus sunk further and further inside of himself.

He was not worried about the up coming battle. In fact, he felt strangely fatalistic about facing the god. He had worked out what to do, he just did not know whether he and Aliah had the strength to do it.

What he dwelled on was his conversation with Baron Wexler. Although he would not admit it to the others, he always believed he would die fighting the god, because to defeat him would require the ultimate sacrifice. It was only when the baron raised the possibility of him surviving, he considered his life after the battle—a life without needing to save the world.

All his anxiety about his future and what to do if he was not going to be Duke of Hand was back, and he was again mulling over the options. So caught up was he in his own thoughts, he did not notice Emer ride up beside him.

'You are unusually quiet. Anything you want to share?'

'Um, no.'

BATTLE

'Are you worried about today?'

'No … yes, a little of course. I know what I need to do, and I will feel a little better when Aliah is with us again.'

'So you are not thinking about the battle?'

'No.'

Emer was quiet for a while as she continued to ride alongside him. Her company was soothing. With her near, wallowing in his worries seemed impolite and indulgent. After a while Emer broke the silence.

'You know worrying about anything else is a waste of time.'

'Sorry?'

'If you are worrying about what happens after your battle with the god today, it is a waste of your energy. If you do not win, the future will be the least of your worries. If you do win, there will be time enough to consider what happens after.'

'That is an interesting philosophy. Walter says I will fight better if I have something to fight for.'

'Silly, you already do; your friends and family and loved ones. It is them you are fighting for.

'I am talking about the details of what happens after. We can worry about those later.'

Seamus marvelled at how Emer worked out his innermost thoughts and found a way to pull him out of his own head without making him feel stupid. Well, she did make him feel a little stupid. Although he did not totally agree with her, he was now much calmer and began to enjoy the ride, until Liam joined them.

'There is something going on behind us. I caught a glimpse of men through the trees. They saw us ride by and have been keeping pace. I think they are the remnants of the Carsten soldiers from last night.'

'What do you want to do?' Emer asked before Seamus was able to even process the news.

'The way I see it, we have two options; we can try and out run them and meet up with the others, or we can stand and fight.'

'Or we can do both,' the girl said. 'I do not like the idea of fighting here. There are too many trees, and it would be easy enough for them to surround us. We should ride on and find somewhere more defensible.'

'Good idea. Seamus? Walter? Ready to ride?'

Their response was to urge their horses to a canter along the tree lined path in single file, Walter at the front and Liam bringing up the rear. For some time, they fled the enemy soldiers, and it took all Seamus' concentration to keep his mount on the track. Finally, they broke into a clearing and Emer called for them to halt.

Surveying the area, she nodded to Liam, who shrugged in agreement. Unsure just what they were agreeing on, Seamus dismounted and walked around, cooling his horse down and stretching his muscles.

'This will do. It is defensible and close enough to where we were going to meet the others. We will wait here,' Liam declared.

Emer led her horse to the edge of the clearing at the farthest point from where they entered. Tying her mount to a tree, she had a drink of water, then drew her sword. 'Ready, Liam?'

'Yes.'

He handed the reigns of his horse to Seamus, grabbed

his own weapon, and followed Emer back the way they had come.

Seamus overheard him saying, 'We should wait either side of the road about two hundred paces back. That should give us enough room to fight.'

'And what should we do?' Seamus asked, annoyed at being left out of the discussion. He may not be the world's best swordsman, but he was still pretty handy in a fight.

His cousin and his friend turned as one, perplexed at his question.

'I can fight with you, you know.'

'Are you mad?' Liam asked. 'If you die here fighting some poxy soldiers, who will fight the god for us?'

Astounded he had not thought of that himself, Seamus dropped his head in shame.

'Besides, we need you to deal with any who manage to get past us, of course,' Emer told him, a little more sympathetic to his feelings than his cousin. 'And maybe you should cast your mind out and see if you can find the others. Let them know we are here rather than where we said we would be. We could certainly use their help if there are any more stray Carstenite soldiers heading our way.'

Leaving Walter and Seamus standing in the middle of the glade, she joined Liam. Unsure of what to do, Seamus took the two horses over and tied them up. The older wizard joined him and helped him unsaddle the animals.

As they stowed their gear, the horses became restless. Seamus attempted to calm them, but one broke away as something crashed through the undergrowth behind.

Thinking it was one of the stray soldiers, Seamus drew a couple of knives and turned to face him.

'You think you can stop me with puny knives boy?'

Seamus started at the familiar voice.

'Gaius, I did not expect to find you here. Have you come to fight your master's battles for him?'

Caught on the back foot, Seamus needed time, and his first thought was to play dumb, and have the god believe he did not know he inhabited Gaius' body while he thought about his next moves.

'Gaius is no more, and I need no one to fight my battles.'

'You must be Gaius, because I see you in front of me. If you are not Gaius, who are you then?' Seamus looked around and cast his mind out to see if anyone else was close by to help.

'Feel my presence, child. I am a god.'

Seamus laughed, 'So you are stuck as Gaius now. That must be really frustrating.'

'It is temporary, until I am brought through to your world.'

Gaius' face clouded over. Seamus' jibes were clearly hitting the mark, but he still had no idea of how he was going to do what he needed to do to defeat this being. So he kept going, hoping for some divine inspiration.

'Perhaps not so temporary a residence. I assume you thought to use the power of the casket to bring your physical form through the veil?'

'Correct. I sent my faithful servant Millard to fetch it. We were to meet up around here. He should arrive soon, and then you can witness me in my full glory.'

Seamus laughed out loud, surprised he could find

something funny about this whole situation.

'Tell me, when is the last time you could sense Millard?'

The god looked perplexed. 'Not for a day or so. I assumed he had come into contact with you and was masking his trail so you could not find him.'

'Well, that may have been your second mistake, your first being not to realise Millard works for no one's cause but his own. He opened the casket almost as soon as he had hold of it, and let loose the magic it contained. Surely you felt it?'

'Yes, I felt it. But what you do not realise is I knew the fool would not be able to resist opening the it, allowing a little magic to escape into the world. But I knew he would be unable to hold even a fraction of what was contained inside. Now, after I deal with you, I will find him and release the rest of the magic.'

Again, Seamus found this hilarious. 'How could you be so blind? Millard attempted to take all the energy into himself. He managed to blow both himself and the casket up.'

'You lie. There must be something left. Perhaps even the casket itself.'

'I assure you, I never lie.'

Gaius the god stood unmoving, only the twitching of his face betrayed the battle going on inside of him.

'No, not even the casket? I could have at least used that to build up enough magic over time to return my body to me. I will not be trapped in this body. There must be another way. What about a sacrifice of wizards? Might that release enough power? Mmm, how many would I need?'

As the god pondered his dilemma, still not confident

in his eventual success, Seamus heard the sound of metal striking metal nearby.

'Ah, the battle has begun, your end is near,' the god crowed. He turned his face skyward, and literally glowed.

Seamus slowly let his awareness reach out to touch the edge of the god, trying to find out what he was doing. From this slight touch, he could tell the god was talking to someone—the other gods. Seamus pushed a little harder, attempting to find out what they were saying, and found himself faced with a bright light that almost blinded him. In his attempt to eavesdrop, he had entered this god's mind.

His appearance had clearly caused some disruption as the god pulled away from his communication with his siblings, just as Seamus took a deep breath and decided to make his first move in the final battle.

Imagining his power reaching out like an arm, at the same time he called out a name not used in hundreds of years, 'Xanthos'. Unable to resist the pull of his own name, the form was drawn to Seamus, and, as it came close, Seamus grabbed hold of the god's essence with a magical hand. Pulling with all his might, the god attempted to free himself.

Seamus had the god, now he needed his Warrior. Reaching out, he tried to find out how far away she was. As he did, he realised he had not been able to sense her since last night, and in his panic, he almost let go of his enemy.

Perhaps the explosion severed whatever it was that tied them together. No, whatever happened occurred before that, he had not sensed Aliah since before he went into the cave. Something was wrong. How was he to defeat a god without her? She was his arm. He could not go into battle without an essential part of himself.

Trying to damp down the panic, a presence brushed gently against his mind and Walter asked, *She is not here yet, what can I do to help?*

Can you help me hold him so I can bind his light?

With all his attention focused on holding the god in place, Seamus was unable to follow what Walter was doing. However, he knew when the wizard's force joined with his own as the god's tension against his hand lessen. With that small amount of assistance, Seamus was able to release a little of his power and begin the binding process.

Imagining a thread like a bandage, he forced it away from himself and around the god, at the same time he occasionally uttered the god's name, hoping it would cement the hold he had on him. It was a slow process, especially with his enemy fighting him all the way, and he worried this would not be enough.

Aliah, where are you?

15
HOW TO BATTLE A GOD

Bursting into the clearing, Aliah pulled up short as she spotted Seamus on his knees in front of Gaius. Beside Seamus, hand on his shoulder, stood Walter. Her sudden appearance went unnoticed because they were so focused on their enemy.

This was not what she expected their final battle to look like; Seamus locked in a fight with the god, who wore the face of the person she disliked most in the world. She had also expected the sounds of armies fighting to fill the air, but this was eerily quiet, and very intense.

Then again, maybe the real battle had not yet started.

Dominic appeared at her side. 'I did not know you could run so fast, or was that sword assisted speed?'

When she did not reply, he surveyed the scene in front of them to identify the cause of her concern. 'Where are Emer and Liam?'

Aliah had not even noticed their absence until that moment. Now she looked around, searching for the missing members of their team. As she focused, the clash of metal against metal reached her ears and she turned to Dominic.

'I will go and see if they need a hand, that is if you think you will be able to manage here without me,' her companion said.

'Go. I am not sure what you would be able to do if you stayed.'

As Dominic left to find his battle, Aliah turned her attention back to the tableau in front of her. Nothing had changed, no one had moved, and they had yet to acknowledge her presence.

Calming herself the way Dominic taught her, she tentatively let her consciousness flow outwards. Initially it was difficult, but she resisted the urge to grab her sword to boost her link, appreciating subtlety was the best approach here.

Poking around the edges of Walter's mind, he showed her a small opening, and she joined her consciousness with his. As she entered, she felt warm and cocooned, like sinking into a comfy armchair.

Walter?

Now is not a good time. I am lending all my power to Seamus and it is difficult to hold the link. Our friend here is trying to sever it and isolate him.

As she stood patiently by, Walter shared information in small pieces.

… casket … exploded … killed Millard …

Walter's thoughts drifted away.

All right, just say yes if I am correct. Millard had the casket, it blew up in some way, killing him. The god cannot use the power, but nor can we. And we have nothing to contain his essence in.

Yes.

Walter's relief at her understanding his message was clear. He and Seamus obviously needed her help, but Aliah had to find out more before she did anything. If she did the wrong thing, she was more likely to hinder them than help. How could she get more information?

Allowing her consciousness to expand into the space Walter created for her, she could almost feel the link he held with Seamus. Closing her eyes, she attempted to visualise the connection.

There it was. With a calming breath, she stretched out along it until she met resistance. Then, with a gentle push, she left the welcoming comfort of Walter into, well it could only be described as chaos.

She lost her hold on Walter, but quickly regained it. Expecting the man to have created a full link with Seamus, she was surprised to find herself inside the battle field of Gaius' mind.

Now she had her bearings, she let go of Walter and looked around. What she saw worried her. In the centre of complete darkness was a fiery ball of light so bright it hurt to look at it. Attached to the light were two pure silver strands, thick and strong.

Nothing moved. It was as though the two silver ropes were in a tug of war with the orange-yellow light. Both sides were evenly matched. This could go either way.

Unsure what to do, but knowing she had to do something to tip the balance in their favour, Aliah placed her hand on her sword. Immediately the battle became clearer.

Walter's silver light had a hook on the end, and it was sunk deeply into the ball, as if anchoring it in place. Yellow fingers of fire were trying to prise the hook out as it attempted to sink deeper inside.

Seamus' strand of light was split in two. One part held onto the fire like a hand holding a ball, the other part was snaking around again and again, reminding Aliah of winding wool into a ball. Orange fire pushed against the hand, attempting to loosen the grip, while squirming to free itself from the wrapping.

She watched for a moment more to ensure she understood what was happening. It looked as though Seamus was trying to bind the god. Understanding the situation did not immediately give her any ideas on how to help.

He is weakening them. Unless you do something, he will win.

What ... who?

Aliah looked around. She must have been imagining things.

Why are you just standing there? You are the Warrior. Do something.

The sneer in that voice was familiar.

Gaius?

Yes, you dolt. We need to help them.

BATTLE

Why should I trust you?

Because I want out of this prison and you are the only people who can help me.

I thought you were working with the god, Aliah said.

I was, until he took over my body and tried to obliterate my soul. I have hidden in a small corner of my own mind for endless days, shielded, waiting for my revenge. Now quit talking and start acting, or neither of us will ever be free from this nightmare.

I would love to help, but I do not know what to do.

Perhaps if you had spent more time on your studies and less time trying to get out of them, you would be able to think this through rationally. The sneer in Gaius' voice was back.

Hello, Gaius, I missed you.

Concentrate. Seamus is trying to bind the god's essence into as small a ball as possible.

Ah, that is what the thread is.

Yes, of course. You need to help with that.

How? Aliah asked.

He cannot let go of the god to take the power thread around fast enough to contain and weaken him.

Mmm, if I can grab the thread and somehow run it round would it help?

Yes. Gaius' answer was as swift as it was short.

I do not suppose you have any tips on how to do that?

Honestly, I cannot believe you were chosen to save us all. Have you not learnt anything about your powers that might help?

There is no need to be snippy about it. You have trained all your life to use your gifts, we have had less than a moon turn to prepare for this.

Watching Seamus laboriously wind his luminous silver thread around the god fireball, Aliah thought about all she and Seamus had done together, all the training sessions, and all the conversations. Surely she could use something from there.

Then she remembered back to their trials. Although they were the Wizard and Warrior, and they shared a single prophecy, they were tested separately. Seamus was tested on his ability to control magic, and her test had been around her physical abilities and endurance.

If you are going to help, you need to do it soon, Gaius interrupted her thoughts.

All right, do not rush me. I may only get one chance at this.

She did not need Gaius to remind her time was running out and she needed to hurry. *Ah, hurry.* The sword lent her speed when she needed to get here quickly. It could lend her speed now.

Imagining herself in her physical form, her body instantaneously appeared. She walked over to Walter's now pewter-grey light. It was taking all his energy to simply hold the god in position. She placed her hand on him. Drawing energy from the sword, she passed it on until his light once again shone a pure silver.

As she pushed energy through Walter, the god pushed some of it back. Unlike the pure clean feel of Walter's energy flow, the power she fought was swirling and chaotic, and when she broke off, she nearly stumbled from dizziness.

Ignoring the nausea, she walked over to Seamus. His

light had dulled so much she was surprised he still held onto the god. As she stepped closer, she thought she heard him whispering something, perhaps a prayer. No, it was the same word over and over again, like a mantra.

Blocking everything else out, she repeated the process to brighten his light, feeding him energy. This took a little longer as the god was concentrating more of his attacks on Seamus, seeing him as the major threat. When Seamus was sufficiently bright again, she reached out her hand and took the end of his silver thread. Then, she ran like she had never run before, round and round the massive ball of power.

Of course it was not quite that easy. As she wound the thread, the god presence pushed back, wriggling so the thread slipped and she would have to backtrack and tighten it up. Every time she touched him, she became dizzy and had to force herself to push through the sensation and keep going.

Exhausted, she paused when she estimated the god was two-thirds covered in the magical binding. As she drew some energy from her sword, she was dismayed to find binding him did nothing to diminish his strength. Inside he still glowed as brilliantly as when she arrived. On the other hand, Walter and Seamus had used so much magic they were now storm-cloud grey.

Holding the magical thread, she fed energy via her sword through to the wizards so they could hold the god in place while she finished wrapping him.

One last push. If she had run fast before, it was nothing to how she ran now. Knowing if she did not finish this soon the god would break the hold they had on him, and all their good work would be for nothing, lent her extra speed. Everything became a blur, and all that remained was running and binding.

You can stop now, it is done.

Absolutely spent, Aliah stopped running in time to see Walter's light wink out. Without thinking, she followed him out of Gaius' mind only to find herself in the middle of total chaos.

While they had been intent on binding the god, a battle had found them. They were in the centre of a group of Hand guards who seemed intent on defending them from a greater number of Carsten soldiers. Seeing they were safe for the moment, she knelt to check on Walter.

The older wizard looked pale and drawn, and there was a sheen of sweat on his brow. She let out a sigh of relief as she saw his chest rise and fall. Placing one hand on him and the other on her sword, she channeled a little healing energy, and was relieved when Walter opened his eyes. He managed a weak smile before falling back into unconsciousness.

Knowing it would take all she had to fully heal the man, she gave him energy until she saw his chest rise and fall with a good rhythm, then stood. Finding Baron Rasmussen in the ring of defenders, she made ready to join him.

The defensive circle was two men deep, the men fighting in pairs. When one man tired, he dropped back and his partner took his place. Likewise, if a man was injured, he was soon replaced.

BATTLE

Aliah took position in the inner-circle, and when a man took a strike to the arm, she quickly replaced him on the Baron's right. The fighting was fierce, and Aliah had never faced anything this intense.

The knot of fear in her stomach soon disappeared as her training took over and she cut and thrust with her sword. Never tiring as her weapon fed her energy, she was pulled back for a break by the panting baron. He slipped between two men, dragging her behind him. The look of anger on his face drawing her to a stop.

'What do you think you are doing?' he yelled at her over the sound of fighting around them.

'I am doing what I am meant to do, fighting to win this battle.' Aliah was perplexed. Surely as the Warrior this was what she had trained for, keeping Seamus safe while he dealt with the god.

The baron removed his helmet and ran a weary hand through hair that was darkened with sweat. 'Princess, I may only be a soldier raised to rule by a benevolent duke, but even I know the gods did not give you that sword to fight men. Your job is to stand beside the Wizard and fight whatever is behind this invasion.'

Aliah blinked, and shook her head. All this time she had seen the sword as a sign her role was to fight their physical enemies while Seamus took care of anything magical. Was the sword symbolic? Were its magical abilities more important than its physical ones?

'Princess? Aliah? You need to go and fight your own battle. We have this covered.'

The baron replaced his helmet and joined his men holding the circle. Left alone in the middle of the chaos,

Aliah remembered Seamus' words about her acting rather than thinking being the thing that might actually help them win against the god. Without wasting another moment, she returned to her Wizard.

Gaius?

Concentrating on making his link with the god smaller and smaller until it melted away, Seamus opened his eyes. Well, mentally opened his eyes inside Gaius' body.

Gaius, Amelia thought you were still alive but I thought the god of chaos killed you when he took your body.

So did he.

Walter? Seamus asked.

His light faded out moments ago.

Aliah?

She went after Walter, I guess to make sure he is all right. She will be … ah here she is.

How is Walter? Seamus queried her.

He is weak but breathing easily, Aliah answered. *What do we do now?*

Well, the plan was to make the god smaller, then push him through to the next realm, Seamus informed her.

I am sensing a but.

Mm, it took more energy than we planned to bind him. I knew he would be strong, but I never imagined … Seamus simply ran out of words, unable to describe what he experienced when he touched the god's essence.

I can feed you through the sword.

I am not sure that will be enough. I believe the sword

channels magical energy from the natural environment. It will take a huge burst of power to make him smaller, then another much larger one to push him through the veil. Wexler gave me a magical boost in case I needed it. Perhaps it will be enough to make him smaller.

And we cannot use that to push him through as he is now?

Not from what we know, no. It would be too difficult, even with the veil as thin as it is at the moment.

All right, one step at a time. Use your boost and we will make him small, Aliah took control.

Unsure whether or not this was the best approach, Seamus knew they had to do something because he could sense inside his bindings the god was already working his way free.

His physical hand grasped the glass vial Wexler had given him, and crushed it. Pain lanced through his hand as the glass cut his palm, but it was minor compared to the pain his body experienced as the great store of magic pushed its way through his very being.

Just when he thought he might explode from excess power, it stopped. Before he could think too much about it, he began the process of reducing the god. He imagined his hands growing until the bound god was like a ball held between them. Then he pushed and pushed and made his hands smaller, until the god was a tiny ball inside tiny baby hands.

Dropping to his knees, he was spent.

Aliah stood by as Seamus grew to an enormous silver light, encompassing the god. The light became so blinding, she closed her eyes. When she dared to open them again, Seamus' body had turned a dull grey, and in his hand was a bright silver pea.

Seamus, you did it.

I … I made him small, but I do not think there is much time. He is fighting back.

As Seamus spoke the pea rolled out of his hand to the ground.

I can fix him.

The two of them had been so engrossed in their work they had forgotten Gaius was there. Aliah swung around to find him in his human form, even if only in his mind. Walking over to them, he raised his foot to stamp on the pea sized god.

Seamus moved to create a protective barrier as he shouted, *NO.*

Gaius reluctantly returned his foot to the ground. *Why not? He has tortured me for long enough. I deserve to be the one who kills him.*

You would not be killing him. You will only break the shell, releasing him again, Seamus explained.

Oh. We cannot do that. What do we need to do with him then? I am not having him live in my body forever. You mentioned something about pushing him through a veil.

Yes, there are different planes of existence, and they are separated by protective layers. I need to push him back through the way he came. Baron Wexler and his people are praying in an attempt to thin the barrier around here, but I will still need a great boost of power to push him through, and I am out.

So let me summarise; he is fighting his way out of his wrappings, and the only way to be rid of him is to send him back where he came from, and to do that you need a great deal of magical power. If we do not do this soon, he will be back in my body and very angry, Gaius paced as he outlined their situation.

Yes.

The wizard stopped and looked directly at Seamus. *I think I may be able to help.*

How? Aliah and Seamus asked together.

I have been stealing bits and pieces of the god's magic and storing it in my prison. Millard breaking the casket gave my stockpile an unexpected boost. I held it against the day I found an opportunity to free myself. I guess this is that day.

Aliah watched as Seamus brightened a little in colour, and it gave her an idea. Walking over to him, she placed her hand on his back and fed him energy through the sword until his body brightened. As she did so, she found she was having to reach further and further away to find energy. The area around them was stripped bare. This was the last time she would be able to help boost their power, which was all right, as this really was their one and only chance to rid themselves of the god who plagued her home.

Standing tall, Seamus picked up the god-pea, placed him in the palm of his hand, and looked at Gaius.

I have not done this before, so before we waste your energy store let me find out if I can find the veil between the realms. If I can sense it, I will say now, and you give me all the energy you can.

I understand.

Gaius had a sly smile on his face as he answered, causing Aliah's stomach to knot. Was he up to something?

Seamus picked up the god between two fingers, raised his arm, then seemed to push upwards.

I can feel it, it is like trying to push a pea through cloth. I need your magic now.

Not trusting her former enemy, Aliah began searching as far as she could for additional magic. The countryside around them had been bled dry. There was nothing.

Wait a minute …

There were two bright lights. Sending her senses closer she found Emer and Dominic. Their stores of magic were a beacon in a magical wasteland. With no time for niceties, she reached in, tapped into their energy, then sent the boost to Seamus.

Sorry, it was necessary, she sent before she broke off.

The veil is stretching, but the more I push the more it expands. This is not enough. Seamus' voice was laced with effort and worry.

It is time, Gaius said, and he pointed to the sword. *You know what you have to do.*

What? Aliah started. *Are you joking? Just share your power with Seamus.*

You and I both know that will not be enough. However, when a wizard dies, all the power in his body is released in a massive surge. That should work.

Before she had a chance to object, Gaius pushed her from his mind.

BATTLE

Aliah grasped the sword in her hand, aware it was the only thing preventing her collapse. As she regained her balance, she found herself staring into Gaius' eyes.

Panic momentarily clouded her vision. Calming her breathing, she settled her nerves, and looked around. Still safe in the defensive circle, she was worried by the number of Baron Rasmussen's men who were now contained inside, injured and unable to re-join the battle.

There was only one layer of men desperately fighting to keep them safe while they dealt with the real threat to Aria. They needed to finish this soon or all would be lost. She turned back to Gaius.

'Gaius, no, there must be another way.'

'There is not, it is too late for me. I had hoped, but now I realise I was dead as soon as that monster took over my body. Maybe this is the true reason why I managed to stay alive? You have to do this. Either you do it and we win, or he wins and will kill me when he gets the chance to leave my body.'

Many times in the past Aliah had wanted to kill Gaius. But now, faced with the very real possibility, she could not do it. All she could think of was the poor child abandoned by his parents because of his magic.

'Before you do this, I just wanted to say I have had time to think over the last few days. I gave my life to Millard, trusting in him completely. I see now how he used me, and how desperate I was for his approval that I did everything he asked of me regardless of who it hurt.

In that desperation, there are many things I did that I perhaps should have done differently.'

'Why, Gaius, do not go all soft on me now. You will have plenty of time to make amends.'

'No, Aliah, you have to do this. My stored power combined with the extra energy when I die, along with the boost from your magic sword will end this. You must do it, do it now! Or I will haunt you forever for leaving me to his mercy.' Gaius beseeched her as he stared into her eyes. 'Do it, quickly, please, before I lose my nerve.'

As he pleaded with her, Aliah knew in her heart what he was saying was true, she had no option if they were to win. Slowly raising her sword, a tear escaped and made its way down her cheek. 'You die a hero, and I will see to it you are remembered that way.'

One swift swing of the sword and it was over. Tears flowed unhindered now as she stared at the body on the ground in front of her. Although part of her registered Seamus also collapsing beside her, she fell to her knees and emptied her stomach in the grass.

Sometime later she stood on unsteady legs and turned slowly, realising the fighting around her had simply stopped. The baron was busy rounding up the Carstenites, who seemed to have surrendered just when they were on the verge of winning.

Dazed, she searched for Seamus and Walter. Walter had dragged Seamus over to the shade of a tree and was busy making the boy comfortable. Standing beside them was Liam, supported between Emer and Dominic, his face grey and pinched with pain.

Stumbling over to them, she did not know where to

start. The shame she felt at stealing magic from her friends, combined with her grief at having to kill Gaius, warred inside.

'I am sorry …'

She did not get a chance to finish. Dominic bundled her into his arms and whispered into her hair, 'You did what you had to do in the heat of battle. It will be all right. I promise.'

Sinking into his embrace she could almost believe it would be.

Every ounce of his energy and concentration was taken over by the need to push the tiny god form through the veil. As he pushed, the veil stretched and stretched. Every fibre of his being ached as he exhausted his store of energy.

Despair overwhelmed him, and at the very moment he thought I can do no more, a massive surge of power infused him.

All through this journey, he believed he and Aliah would finish the final battle together, but he could not sense her presence. Never had he imagined the final act of banishing the god would be done alone.

Seamus coiled for one last, massive push. The veil expanded some more, and then a little more. Then, with the smallest of pops that was altogether unsatisfying after so much effort, he broke through. Letting go of the pea, the god essence drifted from his hand.

Just as he was about to withdraw his fingers, something grabbed hold of them, and pulled him through into another realm.

The sensation of moving between worlds was somewhat like being dragged through mud, and was most uncomfortable. That discomfort was nothing compared to the churning in his stomach.

Surveying his new surroundings, he found to his surprise, the landscape was similar to where his body was on Hand. There were minor differences; flowers he had never seen before bloomed, the grass was an unusual shade of green and the sky had a purple hue. As he looked around, he realised he could no longer see the god, and he had no idea who so clumsily requested his presence.

Unsure of his next move, he collapsed on the ground, suddenly aware of how weary he was. Reaching out, he searched for magical energy. It was there, but it felt very different. He attempted to produce a small flame, but either his magical reserves were depleted beyond his expectations, or the magic behaved in a different manner here. Either way, it meant he was not going anywhere anytime soon.

Closing his eyes, he rested his back against a tree and tried to rest. He had plenty of time to worry about getting home when he regained his energy.

He could not say what made him open his eyes when he did, maybe it was a slight change in the air around him, but whatever the reason, he found himself watching six gods appear on the other side of the clearing.

As he wondered why only six of them had journeyed here, the seventh god walked from behind Seamus to join his siblings, answering the unasked question of how he had arrived.

BATTLE

One of the gods bent and picked up the now very dull looking god-pea between two fingers. Squeezing the tiny ball, there was an audible 'snap' and the gods were joined by their errant brother.

At first, the god faced his siblings defiantly. Then, as they surrounded him in a group hug, he almost seemed to crumple. The group joined together and pushed upwards, returning home.

No matter how many times Seamus imagined the end to the invasion of his homeland, it was not this. The god forgiven by his siblings and he, the supposed hero, left alone on another plane of existence; one with no sounds of life.

Oh well, at least he was comfortable, and he could congratulate himself as being part of the team who saved the world.

'Seamus.'

He had not sensed the gods appear this time, but six of the seven who named him Wizard stood in front of him.

'We brought you here so you might see you were successful, and remove any doubt about whether or not you banished our brother. Aria is now free from his meddling.

'Unfortunately, your victory came at a cost, but not so great a cost as there would have been if our brother succeeded.

'Thank you for returning him to us. It is now time for you to return home.'

Before he could open his mouth to ask some of the many questions he still had, Seamus was squished back through the barrier.

16
ENDS

For a moment Seamus thought about disobeying orders and getting up, that was until his sister poked her head around the door.

'Mother said to make sure you are still in bed. Are you still in bed?'

Slipping his feet back under the covers, he lay against the pillows.

'Yes, I am still here.'

'Good, because she said if I found you up and about, I was not allowed to let your visitor in.'

'Visitor? What visitor? Is it Amelia?'

Since awaking the day before in his old bed, in his old room in the palace, Seamus' mother had been a strict nurse. Having rushed back from Port Marden to take care of him, she was allowing no visitors, and no talking about anything that happened until Amelia could check him over and pass him as fit.

At first Amelia had been on her way back from the plateau. She stayed a day or two with Baron Rasmussen, caring for the injured soldiers, arriving back a few candle marks after Seamus and Aliah. Then she had been visiting and caring for Walter, who had been more seriously affected by fighting the god than Seamus. Now, hopefully, it was his turn.

'Of course, silly, and she has brought someone with her.'

'Off you go now, Cara, I want to spend some time with your brother. Perhaps you could go to the kitchen and fetch him some soup.'

'Soup? I am sick of soup. I want some real food.'

Seamus' wishes were ignored as Cara said, 'Yes, Aunt Amelia.'

Before he could argue, Cara launched herself out the door and ran off on her mission.

'I would ask how you are, but I can see for myself,' his aunt said as she led Walter to the chair beside his bed.

Once the older man settled in, she herself sat on the edge of the bed and took Seamus' hand in her own.

'There is a lot to talk about, and I want to make sure you are strong enough for this conversation.'

Seamus groaned. 'Please do not tell me the god is back.'

'What? No? Is there reason to suspect he might be?'

Amelia gripped his hand tightly and Walter sat forward in his chair.

'No. Sorry. I just thought from the tone of your voice you had bad news, and that was the first thing that popped into my head.'

'We do have news, and it is not the best.' Walter sat back again. 'Before we go into that, I am interested to find out why you worried about the god returning. Are you certain he is gone?'

'Yes, I saw the other gods take him home. They expended a lot of energy to show me where he had gone, I think so I would be certain and we could all move forward.'

'Good.' Walter relaxed back into his chair. 'I do have another question for you. Before I joined you in battle, I heard you call a name. It was a name I had not heard spoken aloud in my lifetime. You then repeated that name over and over as we held the god in place. How did you find out his name?'

Seamus laughed. 'I guessed. There were eight gods, I met seven. Of those seven four were women, so I knew our god was male. He also seemed to cause massive upheavals wherever he went, so I took a leap and called out the name of the god of chaos.'

Walter seemed impressed. 'Seamus, there is hope for you to become a scholar yet.'

Amelia had not moved a muscle during their conversation, and Seamus remembered they had come to give him bad news.

'Amelia, if you did not come to talk to me about the god, then what did you come about?'

He looked at his aunt. She appeared the same as

before, in fact she was more confident than she had been when he saw her last. She had entered the room leading Walter, not the other way around. He turned his gaze to the wizard. The older man's skin appeared waxy and grey, his face wore a few more wrinkles, and some of his hair had turned white in the few days since the battle.

'Walter, are you all right?'

'This stupid, brave man is fine, but lucky to be alive. He gave more of himself than he should to rid this world of a great evil.'

Seamus reached out for Walter and found his magical energy barely there.

'Oh, Walter, please tell me you did not burn your magic away when you helped me?' The worry was a crushing weight on Seamus' chest.

The wizard took both Amelia and Seamus' hands in his own. 'There is still a little magic left, but I will never be able to weave great workings again.'

'I am so sorry, I ...'

'Please, Seamus, it was my choice to do what I did. Do not take that away from me. My life will be no less rich for the loss. I will still be able to teach and study as I planned, and I will always be proud of the contribution I made during the battle. Perhaps the history books might even make slight mention of me.'

Biting back his sorrow at his friend's loss, Seamus said, 'I will make sure they do. We could not have done any of this without you. And if that is all we lost in this battle then we came off lightly.'

He looked from Amelia to Walter.

'All right, I see there is more. I am well enough for you

to tell me it all.'

Amelia took a deep breath before responding, as if stealing herself to his reactions. 'I am unsure if you realise, Gaius also gave more than he should when helping you. He sacrificed his life to send the god away.'

'I was surprised when he offered to helped me. I am even more surprised to hear this, but it does explain where that last lot of energy came from, the one allowing me to push through the barrier. I will not sully his memory with a lie and say I will miss him, but I appreciate his sacrifice and I am saddened by his loss. Is there anything else?'

'Emer and Liam were pretty beaten up by the Carstenite soldiers. Emer is healing well, but the wound in Liam's leg is very deep. If he gets to keep his leg, he will carry a limp for the rest of his life. I am afraid his fighting days are over.'

Pausing to let the information settle, she took another breath before rushing on. 'And Daniel died bravely fighting for Aria.'

'I must go and see them. Hold on. What did you say? Daniel? No? No!' Seamus clutched at his chest as the loss of his friend nearly broke his heart.

'How is Aliah taking it? Are you certain? Goddess, I must go to her.'

Before anyone could stop him, he leapt from his bed, rushed out of the family rooms and down the corridor to the guest quarters. Bursting through the door, he found Aliah staring forlornly into a raging fire. Dominic sat in a chair across from her. He rose when Seamus entered.

'It is good you are finally here, I think she needs to talk with you. But, um, wait a minute.' Dominic ducked into the bedroom beside them, returning with a blanket. 'You might need this.'

Looking down, Seamus realised he had fled through the palace in only his underclothes. Grateful, he took the offered blanket and wrapped it around himself.

'I shall leave you two alone. Call me when you are done, I do not want her left by herself at the moment.'

Seamus hesitantly walked over to the chair beside Aliah, and placed a comforting hand on her arm. The girl looked up, her eyes red rimmed and her face pale, and one cheek marred by an angry red graze.

'I thought we would all make it, or none of us would,' she said. 'I was not prepared for this loss.'

Unable to put into words his own sorrow at the death of someone who had become his friend, he sat down beside her and held her hand.

'He was ill, did you know?' she asked.

'No, I had no idea,' Seamus admitted, wondering how he had missed the signs.

'I suspected, but Amelia confirmed it this morning. Something was growing in his stomach and Amelia did not know how to deal with it. He would not wait until we returned home to see if the wizard physicians could help. No, he went out and sacrificed himself saving a group of fellow guards.'

'So it was serious? His illness, I mean. Was it life-threatening?'

Aliah nodded, still too angry at her childhood friend

to speak.

'He chose to die on his own terms. You cannot be upset at a person for that.'

Turning towards him, her face a picture of fury, something about his own sadness took the wind from her sails. 'I want to agree with you, I do. But I am so annoyed with him for not coming back, I cannot see past it.'

'We shall all miss him, but I cannot help thinking he died as he would have wished, in battle. No doubt a hero as well. For me, that makes my grief a little easier to bear.'

They were silent for a time, lost in their own thoughts. Sighing heavily, it was Aliah who broke it by taking his hand.

'I killed him, Seamus.'

'Killed who? Daniel?'

There was another deep sigh before Aliah answered. 'No, Gaius. He knew it was the only way to get enough energy to send the god away, and he asked me to do it.'

'Oh, Aliah,' Seamus wrapped her in an awkward hug. 'I thought my task was hard, but in the end, it was you who had to do the most difficult thing of all. I have no words.'

She allowed him to hold her for a little longer, before pulling herself together. She shrugged off his embrace and stood.

'I bet you have not even been to see Emer and Liam yet. Come on, we can mourn the dead later, it is the living who need us now.'

Before he joined her, Seamus stared thoughtfully into the fire, then asked, 'Do you think we should talk about it some more, what happened, I mean? I thought I would come here, see you, mourn Daniel, then say some miraculous words that would put all of this behind us.'

'Oh, Seamus, this will never be behind us. It is too much a part of who we are now. No doubt there will be celebrations once the Carsten fleet return home, then we will be relegated to the annals of history as having helped defeat a foreign invasion.

'Only we will know the truth of it, and how it changed us all. And maybe, someday, we will want to talk about it—but not now.'

Smiling at how her words reflected his own feelings, he stood and followed her to find their friends. Pausing at the door, Aliah turned and raised an eyebrow.

'Are you forgetting something?'

Following her gaze, he realised he was still dressed only in a blanket. 'I suppose there must be some of my clothes left in the bedroom here,' he said as he ducked inside, only to return moments later, dressed and ready to face the world.

'Do you know what this is all about?' Aliah asked as she and Dominic joined the group assembled in the main reception room.

Seamus shook his head. 'No, no one does. All we know is that Amelia asked for us all to gather here, dressed for a celebration. We think she is throwing a farewell party.'

'Where are your father, and Amelia and Walter then?'

'What, are you surprised someone is later than you?'

Dominic asked, and earned a glare from the princess.

Ignoring the dig, Aliah turned her back on him, focusing her attention on Seamus.

'I do not know about Walter and Amelia, but my father is in his office talking to Robin, who showed up earlier today.' Seamus braced himself for an outburst from Aliah, but he was more than surprised with her answer.

'I hope your father goes easy on him. I know he betrayed us, but it was for a good reason. They were holding his mother captive, after all.'

'Father and I talked about it before they met, he asked my opinion on whether or not the punishment he planned was suitable.'

'Oh, no, he cannot punish Robin for protecting his family.' Aliah had tears in her eyes as she spoke. 'That poor man must have been under so much pressure.'

'I am afraid there must be some consequence to his actions, after all he did set up your kidnapping. From what father said, I think he is going to release Robin from his duties, but he will be given a small holding in recognition for his years of service.'

Aliah was prevented from commenting by the clattering of a chair falling to the ground. Tired of waiting, Cara and Pauley had commenced a game of tag, much to Jonas' obvious dismay. Seamus' brother was at the age, no longer a child he was not yet an adult, although he was trying hard to be.

Before Duchess Elise had a chance to sort them out, the library door opened, admitting Duke Damon, Walter, Amelia and a cloaked figure. The duke took his place on the dais and called them to attention.

'I would like to welcome you to a very special event, not as special as I would like to make it, but it is what Walter and Amelia wanted, and I guess that is all that matters.'

'Damon,' Duchess Elise's tone threatened censure, and the duke sighed.

'Anyway, without further ado I would like you to welcome Father Christopher, who has agreed to perform a marriage ceremony for my sister and her chosen husband, Walter.'

There were audible gasps of surprise as the father led the happy couple up to the dais, to be joined there by the duchess.

It was a short, but moving ceremony, and throughout Seamus could not help but notice the glances between Dominic and Aliah. He thought to himself they would not be long in following his aunt's example.

After the formalities and congratulations were over, they all retired to the banquet hall, where the cook had managed to put on a grand feast, even given the short notice. As they sat, Seamus felt happy and relaxed for the first time in ages. All the people he cared about were here. They were safe, and he just wanted to enjoy the moment.

Dominic spent most of the meal trying to convince Pauley to take up a position at court with the king's spy-master. He had already turned the job down once, when King Terion himself had asked before departing the previous day, and he was unlikely to change his mind now. It seemed he had found his niche as Amelia's apprentice and was not interested in anything else.

Relieved of his role as heir to the duchy, Seamus smiled to see Jonas taking his new duties so seriously as he sat next to their father.

'Any regrets?' Emer leaned over to ask.

He smiled at her. 'None. I have just fought the battle of my life, I do not want to spend the next few years battling to have magic accepted on Hand. I want to go where I will be welcomed.'

Emer blushed. 'You will certainly be welcomed in Sanctuary.'

A warm glow spread through him as he thought how pretty Emer looked in the finery she had borrowed from Aliah, but if he was honest, he thought she was far more beautiful in her travelling clothes.

'What is that stupid grin about?' Aliah interrupted.

'What?'

'Never mind. I just asked your father what happened with Robin. He said he was so ashamed of his behaviour he would not accept the holding. But Duke Damon is going to put it aside for him anyway.'

'Aliah, this is a celebration. Leave Seamus alone and let him enjoy the, um, company,' Dominic interrupted, nodding his head towards Emer. 'There is plenty of time for business tomorrow.'

Seamus felt a blush rising, but none-the-less was grateful when Aliah sat back down and he could return his attention to Emer.

Standing by the ship leaving for Port Marden, Aliah waited for Seamus to say goodbye to his parents and brother. Cara had been so upset at Seamus' leaving again, she refused to come out of her room. Understanding how much her rejection hurt Seamus, Aliah had persuaded the young girl to at least say goodbye to her brother, but Cara drew the line at coming to the docks.

The new heir to the Duchy of Hand wandered over to stand beside Emer, who appeared very uncomfortable at being included in the family farewells. Jonas gave her a rough hug goodbye, and she seemed to relax a little.

Maybe Seamus and Emer were not quite there yet, but everyone else knew these two were much better together than they were apart. Perhaps once Seamus was settled in his new home, he would feel confident enough to start courting the girl from Sanctuary.

'Matchmaking, I see.' Dominic's voice came from close by her ear.

'I really wish you would make some sort of noise when you approach.'

Laughing, he answered. 'Sorry, occupational hazard.'

'Have you forgotten already? You are now Ambassador to Hand. You need no longer skulk in the shadows. And I do not think those two will need any assistance finding they are made for each other.'

She leaned back into the arms Dominic wrapped around her. 'Besides, is it wrong to want everyone to be as happy as I am?'

'I guess not, I was merely stating my surprise at your not having managed Seamus and Emer's lives as well as you organised our own.'

The lightness in his tone told Aliah he was teasing. In fact, Dominic knew just how abysmal she had been at sorting out their future. She had consulted with Dominic before meeting with her father after his arrival on Hand a few days ago. They had discussed what they both wanted, but she feared she did not have the skills to enable her to persuade King Terion.

Flushed with the success of their campaign, and relieved Aliah survived unhurt, King Terion wanted nothing more than to wrap his daughter up and return her home to Bannock. Part of Aliah wanted that too, but mostly, she knew she could not return to her old life. She had proven to herself she was more than an adornment, and she wanted a real role governing Aria.

She also wanted Dominic, and there in lay the problem. The second son of a duke was not going to be accepted as the next King of Aria, which meant they would not be able to marry, something Aliah planned for their future together. Aliah even had a solution to that problem. When her father was ready to step down from the throne, they would become joint rulers of Aria.

Now all she needed to do was convince her father. Arming herself with as many arguments as she was able to cram into her head, she met with the king in private. After their reunion, he sensed she was anxious about something.

'Father, we need to discuss my future.' She raised the subject in a non-threatening way, just as Dominic schooled her.

'We do indeed. I asked Duke Damon if you can stay here with him a while longer. Although most of the Carsten Army decided to return home and rebuild their country, there are some who lost everything and wish to remain here in Aria. I would like you to work to find them all suitable homes and employment. Of course, you will also have to help overcome some resentment from many Arian's who do not wish to have the enemy stay on. Are you up to that?'

Taken by surprise, Aliah was unsure of what to say. 'I can only try,' was the best she could come up with.

'That is all I can ask for in such a difficult role. I instructed the leaders of each town and village to come up with a list of skills they lost with the deaths of our soldiers during the war. I would like you to work with the people left here. Make sure they are housed, clothed and fed, and start matching them to the gaps. Then there will be plenty of work helping the two communities accept each other.'

This was more than she hoped for; a real position helping real people. Her delight in her new role was tempered as she remembered the other side of her problem.

'I would be happy to do that father, but it is too big a job for one person. Perhaps Dominic could aid me.'

Her heart sank at her father's answer. 'I am afraid that will not be possible. I arranged a very important job for him, if he will take it.'

'And that would be?'

'Between him and me, my love. Are you interested in helping the refugees, or shall I find someone else for the job?'

'No, I am interested, it is just I wanted to talk to you about Dominic too.'

'I felt certain you would, but I need to talk with him first, and there are a number of other people I have to meet with. Maybe we can talk again later.' Kissing her on top of the head, he practically bundled her out of the room.

Unable to speak to Dominic until later that evening, she spent a very fruitful day with Martha sorting out long term living arrangements. Since Robin's disappearance, the housekeeper had taken on more of the household management, and was thriving with her new duties.

Before dinner that evening, Dominic slipped into her room, excited to tell her what he had agreed with her father.

'You agreed to something without talking with me first?' she demanded, hands on hips.

'So are you telling me you did not accept your father's offer already?' Dominic did not back down. 'I at least got your father to reassure me we would be together, or close by, over the next few moon turns. Did you even do that?'

Scrunching her face in annoyance, Aliah admitted she had not thought to check where Dominic would be before saying yes. 'All right, I am sorry. Clearly I am not as good at this as you are.'

Dominic drew her into his arms. 'You are forgiven. Now, do you want to hear my news?'

'Yes, I do. Please tell me you are not to be sent off spying somewhere. Or that my father has appointed you Chief Spymaster.'

'No, I am not going anywhere. I am to stay in Hand as Ambassador from the Court of Aria. There has been no posting here, ever, but the duke has agreed to my staying. In return, I am to assist with moving Hand towards accepting more of the laws of Aria, including the use of magic.'

'Wow, Dominic, that is fantastic news. If you can bring

Hand into the Arian fold, well …'

'… people will begin to look to me as someone who might be able to rule at your side someday?'

'Exactly, and as I am …'

'… staying here on Hand, we can still be together. Although the duke has provided a house for me, and you will be residing here, in the palace.'

'You found out about what father asked me to do? That is so annoying.'

'No, what is really annoying is your father planned this all before he even arrived. I am not sure whether to be upset he organised us in this way, or grateful for his forethought.'

Dominic moved into his residence, and Aliah moved into Seamus' old room in the family quarters. As the Heir Apparent, Jonas had been given his own suite in the palace, and Cara had been moved into his old room. Duchess Elise thought Aliah would be more comfortable living with the family, adding Cara would benefit from having the older girl for company. Aliah also thought Duke Damon was more relaxed with her being close by until she and Dominic were formally betrothed.

'What are you thinking now?' Dominic's words brought her back to the present.

'I am thinking how lucky we all are.'

She pointed to Liam making his way up the gangplank on crutches. It seemed he would get to keep his leg, but he would never become the Guard Captain he had hoped to be. Still, his future looked bright.

'Liam has a new position as Ambassador to Sanctuary on behalf of Aria and Hand. Also, from what Emer tells me, there is a certain young lady waiting for his return.'

Gesturing to Walter, who was overseeing the correct storage of some special trunks, she added, 'Walter has raided the library here and cannot wait to ensconce himself in Sanctuary, comparing histories and starting a magic school. I have no doubt he and Amelia will settle in well together.'

Dominic and Aliah laughed as Amelia headed towards her new husband. Although unable to see as such, she could now confidently move around using her "new sight" as she called it.

'I am going to help Walter with those trunks. He will not be happy until they are stored to his satisfaction.' Dominic kissed the top of her head before leaving her to her thoughts.

Although pleased to have survived their recent ordeal, and she was happy she and her friends were embarking on new phases of their lives, she was somewhat reluctant to say goodbye to Seamus.

They met only a few moon turns ago, yet their experiences together had drawn them closer than most brothers and sisters, and for him to be heading away felt like losing an arm.

Oh, no, he was coming over. What was she going to say? What could she say as a suitable farewell to someone who had become such an important part of her life; to the boy who helped her grow from a disenchanted princess to a potential queen?

As he walked towards her, Aliah looked like an animal caught in a trap. If he had not known better, he would have thought she did not want to say goodbye to him at all. Pausing for a moment, he thought, I do not really want to part from her either.

'Stay here with us,' Aliah said as he stopped in front of her. 'Well, at least in Port Marden, until your father fixes things here.'

'You know that would not work. Jonas needs to be seen as the heir now, and that will never happen while I am still around. Also, I cannot spend my life waiting for something that might never be.'

She sighed as he hugged her. 'I know.' Her voice was muffled by his chest. 'You might still take father up on his offer of a position as one of his advisors. We could see each other more often if you did.'

'I could, that is true. And believe me I gave it deep consideration. But I think it is time for me to figure out what I want to do with my life on my own. I have put it off for too long now.'

Seamus stopped, trying to put into words the turmoil he experienced the last few days as he attempted to plan his future.

'When I rescued you and left home, I knew I was never going to be Duke of Hand, but I did not know who I was other than Heir to the Duchy. Nor did I know what to do with my life. I thought my only option was going to train on the Wizard Isles, but even then, it was just to be doing something.

'I guess back then neither of us were happy with our futures, but you know you want to rule Aria. You always have. Now you are openly working towards that goal, and it obviously makes you happy. Well, that and Dominic.

'I am a work in progress. I am not a duke, nor will I ever be. I am a wizard with unusual skills. Not good at one thing in particular, except fighting gods, and I hope there will not be much call for that sort of thing in the future.

'I need more. I need to know what I can contribute. So, I am escorting everyone back to Sanctuary and I agreed to stay on and help Amelia and Walter set up their school. I will also work with Walter, showing him how my magic is different.

'While I am in Sanctuary, perhaps I can find out who I am and what I am meant to do with my life.'

Aliah pushed herself out of his embrace. 'Seamus, that is plain self-indulgent. Not everyone in life needs a grand plan, nor will they play a pivotal role in history and have ballads sung in their honour.

'Most people are happy to have enough food in their bellies, a roof over their heads and to be around people they love. While you have family and friends, you are someone—someone special, to them.

'We have been lucky—is that the right word? We were involved in some of the greatest events in our lifetime. Nothing else will be able to compare to that. All we can do now is what is right for us. Why did you decide to go to Sanctuary, given all the other options on the table?'

Seamus thought for a moment before answering. 'The people. If I cannot be with my parents and siblings on Hand, I want to be with the rest of my family; my family, and Emer. And I will be doing more with my gifts than fighting, I will be adding to our understanding of magic and the gods' influences on the world.'

In the whole time he had known Aliah, he had never really felt comfortable in his own skin, but at that moment, she had given him something greater than any other gift he had received; she had given him his identity. He finally realised he was no longer running without direction, but was headed right where he needed to be.

Hugging her to him again, he whispered, 'Thank you,' into her hair.

EPILOGUE

Xanthos glared belligerently at his brothers and sisters. 'You think you have won, but deep down you know the real threat is still out there. Only one of us had the guts to go and attempt to stop it from destroying all the lands of the furthest world.

'It has been waiting a long time, and you know once it is finished there, it will turn inwards, to us.'

'We know. We also know you still believe you might have stopped it, but at what cost? Would any life have been left on that world once you were done? Or on any of the others it must travel through to reach us? Would there have been balance in the universe?'

Oh how it made his blood boil when they spoke to him in one voice.

'What is your solution? Another prophecy? More human heroes? The darkness will not be obliterated that way.'

'Our role is not to destroy, but to maintain the balance.'

'Do you believe keeping things in balance will be enough? I think not. But what can I do now I am trapped back here with you all? You won, and now we are forced to do things your way.

'When the great evil stirs, as it inevitably will, we will find out whether or not your way is enough.'

Xanthos turned his back on the gathering, and waited for them to leave his home. Suddenly weary, he sank into a chair and closed his eyes.

As the God of Chaos, he had drawn power from the turmoil he created in his time on the far world. He had not done it for his own glory, but to fight their greatest foe. If he had managed to send the whole world into chaos, he may still not have generated enough power to defeat the evil presence lurking in the darkness below.

However, his brothers and sisters had ensured he would never know.

ABOUT THE AUTHOR

Vivienne has been writing books since she was fifteen years old, but only friends and family were allowed to read them. Forced to give up work because of family commitments she was encouraged by friends and family to finally put some of her writing out there for others to read.

In the real world after leaving university with a BA in History and Politics she worked as a Personnel Officer, an Office Manager, a Project Manager, a DBA and IT Manager then as a Business and Data Analyst, adding an MSC in Information Systems along the way. In her world she continued to write.

Born in Invercargill (New Zealand), she has lived in; Dunedin (New Zealand), London (England), Petersfield (England) and currently lives with her husband and son and their dog Trouble and kitten Lola in Sydney (Australia).

For future releases and current news you can find Vivienne at **www.viviennelfraser.com.au** or on Facebook at **www.facebook.com/vivienneleefraser**

ACKNOWLEDGEMENTS

As the last book in my first series, Battle has been especially hard to let go. While Seamus and Aliah went on a journey to find themselves, so did I. While writing and publishing these books I leant the difference between writing a story and producing a book, and I could not have done this without help.

Firstly to Heather. You challenged me to write better and to improve my story and characters, and I shall miss your little comments as you edited. I wish you only luck with your own writing, I for one certainly enjoyed reading your books and I am sure others will too.

Also, thank you Kim. Without you I would not have known I needed Heather. Without your guidance and support I would not have had the confidence to publish anything, ever. You also provide covers to bring my stories to life, and make my books look pretty enough to eat. Then, to top it off, you write tales I enjoy reading when I am not writing.

Anna and Jim have provided some great artworks for

this series. It is the strangest thing to see a world that was only in your head come to life. Thank you for working with me to do that.

A special thanks to Jim and Sam, who have allowed to me hide away in my office and loose myself in other worlds while they kept things running. Thank you also for reading my books and being kind enough to offer some interesting suggestions and improvement.

Thank you also to any of you who have taken time out to join me in Aria. Two special readers, Marj and Sandy have worked hard to help me perfect my grammar, something I will always be grateful for. Really, though, I am grateful to anyone who has taken the time to read my books. If I have taken you away from the world a while I have done what I set out to do.

Finally, thank you Seamus and Aliah for allowing me to write your story, although I fear your job is not yet done. Sam has asked what you did next, and a story has already started to form in the recesses of my mind.

You can keep up with Wizard and Warrior news
on Facebook @wizardandwarrior

www.ingramcontent.com/pod-product-compliance
Lightning Source LLC
Chambersburg PA
CBHW070052120726
47909CB00002B/369